LION
EYES

LION
EYES

a novel

CLAIRE
BERLINSKI

BALLANTINE BOOKS / NEW YORK

Lion Eyes is a work of fiction. Names, characters, places, and incidents are the products of the author's imagination or are used fictitiously. Any resemblance to actual events, locales, or persons, living or dead, is entirely coincidental.

Published in the United States by Ballantine Books, an imprint of The Random House Publishing Group, a division of Random House, Inc., New York.

BALLANTINE and colophon are registered trademarks of Random House, Inc.

ISBN 978-1-4000-6295-9

Library of Congress Cataloging-in-Publication Data
Berlinski, Claire.
Lion eyes / Claire Berlinski.
p.   cm.
ISBN 978-1-4000-6295-9
1. Women spies—Fiction.   2. Blogs—Fiction.   3. Iranians—Fiction.   I. Title.
PS3602.E758L55 2007
813'.6—dc22   2006047815

Printed in the United States of America

www.ballantinebooks.com

2   4   6   8   9   7   5   3   1

First Edition

Book design by Susan Turner

For my mother and my father

And to the memory of Peter,
my little Fu Manchu

ہمیشہ گمان مبر کہ خالی است   شاید کہ پلنگ خفتہ باشد (سعدی)

Although the sun shines bright,
Though nothing stirs in sight,
When traversing the desert
Do not forget your gun.
Although the plain stretched wide,
Good men before have died,
Who failed to see a lion
Curled sleeping in the sun.

—SA'DI

PREFACE

Shortly after writing my first novel, Loose Lips, *I began corresponding with the Lion. Within days of our first exchange of e-mails, I was fascinated. Within months, I was obsessed.*

I then discovered that the Lion was not who I imagined him to be.

The story that follows is my attempt to reconstruct, to my own satisfaction, how I—an intelligent, well-educated, professional woman in my thirties—fell so powerfully in the thrall of a man I knew only through an epistolary exchange.

ONE

PARIS

*Or don't you like to write letters. I do because it's such a swell way
to keep from working and yet feel you've done something.*

—ERNEST HEMINGWAY

CHAPTER ONE

. . . It's more than a little obvious that Selena Keller is Claire Berlinski,
or maybe it's her sister. The title page has "A Roman à Claire" written under the
title, which leads me to believe the fetching drink of water that's described by
Ms. Berlinski in the book is actually the author herself, even though I've been assured
it's not. Did Berlinski dip her toe into the Central Intelligence Agency? Go to the Farm?
Get trained for work in the CST unit of the CIA? . . .

—FRANK BASCOMBE,
book critic, writing about *Loose Lips*

I don't drink," said Jimmy, when on our first date I suggested we order a bottle of wine; and I wasn't *so* blind that I didn't immediately appreciate, particularly given the tattoos on his arms and his ethnic background, that the words meant *I'm working the steps.* But he was handsome, in a rough, ruined way, and he had swagger. There was something disarming about his smile, too—so disarming, in fact, that when my cranky and suspicious ninety-two-year-old grandmother visited my family in Paris, she fell for Jimmy as well. He gently helped her up and down the stairs and conversed intently with her about James Joyce and Edna O'Brien. He brought her his beaten-up copy of *Angela's Ashes*. She read it in one sitting and said the descriptions of hunger and poverty reminded her of her own upbringing in wartime Germany.

Angela's Ashes has a lot to answer for, actually. When our affair began, shortly after I arrived in Paris, he read the book to me out loud. *Och, aye!* He had a superb gift for mimicry and a working-class Belfast accent, so it was hard not to confuse him with the characters in the book and easy to ascribe to him all the book's wit and sensitivity—a confusion he did nothing to dispel by noting, repeatedly, the analogies between his own life and Frank McCourt's.

He was a former boxer. He had grown up during the Troubles and had seen awful things. He was tough and streetwise. He had a tender Irish sentimentality, and he loved books. If he did not seem particularly ambitious or driven, I reckoned that an appealing quality: I had dated many men who were, and would not have been sorry never again to feign interest in my date's aggressive business plan for the penetration of the competitive Finnish telecom sector. It was fine with me if Jimmy taught English lessons and did odd jobs for a living. I figured there was only room for one big ego in a couple. I was right about that, I think; I just didn't realize that there were, in fact, two in ours.

I would have been well advised to pay more attention to *Angela's Ashes*.

A few weeks after we broke up, I ran into him by accident up by Montmartre. I was satisfied by the way he looked at me. He had just purchased a motorcycle from a bass player who was going back to Manchester. The attraction was still there, unfortunately, and when he offered to give me a lift back to my apartment, judgment failed me once again, and I accepted, even though generally I never ride motorcycles, for all the obvious reasons. Before he even pulled out into the street, he miscalculated the distance between my hip and the car parked beside us. It made an awful sound, like tongs being fed into a Cuisinart.

When I returned from the emergency room to my empty

apartment, on crutches, even the narcotics I'd been prescribed for the pain did nothing to relieve my sense of desolation.

That was the way I was living when the first letter from the Lion arrived, and that, I think, explains a lot.

· · ·

I wrote *Loose Lips* in Paris, where I live now. My apartment is on the top floor of a brick building overlooking the Place Dauphine. It is physically impossible to live closer to the heart of Paris. I can't say that I'm close to my neighbors, however. The elderly Hungarian woman who lives below me once sent an official registered letter to my landlord, informing him that I had placed my garbage bags on the landing instead of taking them down to the basement Dumpster. She is sensitive to noise. She has complained that I run my bathtub too loudly. Below her lives the man with an incontinent Irish setter. No amount of lavender air freshener will ever make the elevator right again.

The concierge and his wife live on the ground floor. Monsieur Tubert has an incomprehensible Provençal accent and the sly face of a village grocer who puts his finger on the scale. I speak to him only when my hot water stops working. Whenever I ring his bell to tell him this, Madame Tubert, wearing a stained housecoat, opens the door just a crack. A cloud of ancient dust billows from the apartment. After appraising me suspiciously for a good long time, she relays the bad news to her husband, who slowly levers himself erect and wheezes upstairs with his tool belt. He inevitably spends four hours in my apartment, taking apart the plumbing, leaving parts all over the floor, sighing, and muttering incomprehensibly to himself before declaring that it's *bien foutu* and calling the plumber.

The linden trees on the Place Dauphine are elegant in the winter; in the spring they explode into exuberant buds. This summons the local workmen in their blue coveralls, who come to the plaza to shake each other's hands for a good half hour and play *pétanque* all afternoon. Young lovers sit on the benches, kissing each other on the eyelids and earlobes and cooing tenderly.

The restaurants on the Place Dauphine look so inviting, with their belle époque painted storefronts and their outdoor tables. The waiters write the day's menus on chalkboard easels in that careful round cursive they teach in French schools, and at lunchtime the tables fill up with plump, well-appointed attorneys and their mistresses. The women wear leather pants and carry unhappy small dogs; everyone smokes furiously. The food comes stacked in artful little pyramids: galettes of this and confits of that, all drizzled with a coulis of something-or-other and served in the summer with a cold Sancerre.

My L-shaped studio is not spacious. The stumpy little half bathtub has a hose in place of a shower, and the alley to the minifridge between the cupboard and the sink is almost impassable. But from my windows I see all of Paris, from the Eiffel Tower to the Pantheon. I see the Palais de Justice, the spires of Sainte-Chapelle, and the banks of the Seine. The cobblestones on the plaza glow when it rains, reflecting honey-colored light from the wrought-iron street lamps. At night, I watch the sun set over the rooftops of Paris as the glittering *Bateaux Mouches* churn serenely down the river, leaving phosphorescent ripples in their wake.

It's quite a glamorous life, except for one thing. Sometimes I go for days hearing only one human voice. It emerges from my laser printer, solemnly informing me in a mechanical British accent that the printing has started and the printing has finished.

· · ·

Before moving to Paris, I worked as a democracy officer in the Elections and Political Processes sector of the Department of Agriculture's Foreign Agricultural Service. I had originally moved to Washington in the hope of finding work with a think tank, or perhaps as a staffer on the Hill. I took the job with the USDA because I wanted to be posted overseas. "Do you have a yen for travel, a passion for agriculture, and enthusiasm for international trade?" asked the department's website. I had a yen for travel. What more could they want? But after accepting the job, I found myself sitting in a windowless office in Washington, preparing a series of briefing papers on electoral systems in the developing world.

My father had moved to Paris several years before. A year after taking the job in Washington, I came to visit him over the winter holidays. He had just finished writing another book, and on the last day of my visit, I said wistfully, "I wish I could quit my job and move to Paris and be a writer, too."

"Why can't you?" he asked.

Why couldn't I?

Begin with a voice, everyone says; finding one was hardly my problem. The voice that I heard never shut up. The first time I heard it was the day I moved into my apartment complex in Washington. I was in the lobby, fumbling with the key to my new mailbox, when a door slammed several flights above me and a voice, rapid-fire and insistent, began to echo down the stairwell. I couldn't make out what the woman was saying, but she was surely saying a *lot* of it. The voice began descending from the top to the ground floor, accompanied by the chattering click of high heels. The babbling and clicking grew louder. There was a sudden pause in both the heel clicking and the babble as for a moment she stopped to listen to someone; then a resumption of clacking and jabbering, then a crescendo of clacking and jabbering, and then at last a leggy, slender black woman burst into the lobby, a bright yellow scarf tied elegantly around her head and fixed above her forehead with a glittering brooch. "Hold on one sec," she said to the cell phone cradled between her cheek and shoulder. "Well *hiya*, new neighbor," she said to me as if she'd known me for years. "Welcome to the building. I mean, you must be my new neighbor; I saw all your boxes. You need a hand with those? I'll drop by when I get back." Without waiting for me to answer, she returned her attention to the cell phone and began babbling again. Still talking, she gave the mailbox next to mine a vigorous karate chop with the side of her hand. It flew open. She pulled from it a stack of letters, flyers, brochures, and postcards; leafed through them quickly; and shoved them back in her mailbox. She opened the last letter and—still talking—quickly skimmed the contents. She squinted and frowned. "Dang it, he didn't even proofread it." She balled up the paper and tossed it over her shoulder. "Gotta run, honey," she said to me, "but I'll drop by later and say hello to you proper." And with that, she pranced off, leaving a cloud of babble in her wake.

I had not said one word.

Some prurient instinct prompted me to pick up the piece of paper she had just tossed to the ground. I smoothed it, checking furtively to make sure no one saw me snooping. "Charlene, FYI" was written by hand at the top of the page.

FOR IMMEDIATE RELEASE

LAWSUIT SEEKS TO CHALLENGE CIA'S
CENSORSHIP OF FORMER BLACK OFFICER'S MEMOIRS

Washington D.C.—Charlene Pierce, an African-American who is suing the Central Intelligence Agency (CIA) for racial discrimination, today filed a new lawsuit in the United States District Court for the District of Columbia challenging the CIA's decision to censor her memoirs. Formerly employed as a CIA Clandestine Service Trainee (CST), Ms. Pierce asserts the CIA is abusing the classification system to defeat her discrimination lawsuit.

I looked at the label on the mailbox she had just opened. It read C. PIERCE.

I looked behind me again, puzzled.

Later that evening, my mysterious new neighbor dropped by with an apple cake. "Hey there! I'm Charlene, and I just wanted to be neighborly; I'm from North Carolina and that's what we do. You need any help with all those boxes?" I opened my mouth to thank her but didn't get past the first syllable. "Hey, you have a better living room than mine! Can I step in for a sec?"

I thought I had happened earlier upon a secret, or at least something private, but I was quite mistaken. It took her no more than fifteen minutes to tell me that she was suing the CIA and that they had fired her, ostensibly for her indiscretion but really, she claimed, "because they're a big bag of shitbag racist jerks." She had been relieved of her position when the agency's security officers, tipped off by an anonymous informant, caught her sending e-mail to her sister describing the skills she was acquiring in spy school where she had been training to become a CIA case officer. "You know, like how to do land navigation? With a compass? Which is *nasty*, by the way. Out there in the woods with ten billion mosquitoes, and chiggers, and gnats, and bats, and poison ivy, and poison oak, poison you name it, and these ticks that have what's-that-disease? That gives you a rash? And these things in the woods made *noises*; oh, man, it was *nasty*. So I told my sister, you know? But talking about chiggers—that's no big deal. That stuff's all on the Internet anyway. Lots of white folks at the CIA do things just as bad as talking to their sisters about chiggers. Happens every day. They don't get fired. They get some damned administrative warning."

I supposed.

Charlene and I palled around a lot that year, and I don't believe she was ever once silent. Much as I was charmed by her and wanted to take her side, I could see exactly why they had fired her. "Hey, do you want to read my memoirs?" she asked me one evening as we shared a bottle of wine on her balcony. "They're technically still classified, but I know I can trust you." She had known me for three weeks.

Of course I accepted—who wouldn't? The manuscript was not particularly well written, but it described the CIA's secret training program in great detail. What intrigued me most was her account of her downfall. She suspected that her jealous boyfriend, another CIA trainee, had turned her in after snooping through her mail, looking for evidence of her infidelity.

The CIA never let Charlene publish her memoirs, but they didn't go to waste.

· · ·

So there I was in Paris with a voice in my head put to rest. *Loose Lips* had just been published. I was still moping about Jimmy. And then the thermometer began to rise. The *canicule*, the great European heat wave of 2003, had begun, and by the time it was over it had claimed 35,000 lives.

The proximate cause of the *canicule* was an anti-cyclone that had anchored itself stubbornly over the European landmass, holding back rain from the Atlantic Ocean and permitting hot, dry air to be conveyed over the Mediterranean from the North African desert. Indeed, Paris felt like a desert, not only because the heat was blistering and dry but because the light, refracted through the haze of dust and pollution, made the landscape shimmer and turned the skyline reddish brown.

At the flower stall, the blossoms hung limply; the long-stemmed roses drooped over the sides of their buckets. Nearby, the ordinarily voluble merchants stood quiet and motionless by their vegetable displays, their clothes damp and their hair lank against their skulls. No one was making pleasantries, particularly not the waiters in the outdoor cafés. They refused defiantly to wear lightweight clothes, filling buckets of ice and pouring gallon upon gallon of Coke and Ricard, all the while wearing long-sleeved starched white shirts, black trousers, formal black leather shoes, and fully lined waistcoats. Rivers of sweat poured from their temples. They smelled rank and sour, even from a distance. The fish and the fruit stalls stank to high heaven. Even the produce in supermarkets was rotten and mushy.

The neighborhood winos stripped to their underwear and sprawled half naked on the streets, too exhausted even to beg for spare change. Two blocks from my apartment, businessmen swam in the Seine and children splashed in the Châtelet fountain among the sphinxes and the statues. This was, generally speaking, not done, and ordinarily, nothing so troubles the Parisian soul as the sight of children doing something that's not done, particularly if they look as if they're enjoying it. But no one was stopping them or admonishing them. Even the old ladies were too hot to get exercised.

My apartment was directly below a corrugated metal roof. I had no fan; in another triumph of French capitalism, every fan in Paris had been sold out. I spent the *canicule* moving slowly between my bathtub, where I lay in cool water reading for hours—my leg, still not quite right after the accident, poking out and braced against the wall—and my computer, where I sat in my underwear, a wet towel around my back like a cape. I did no work; I gave in to abject laziness. I surfed the Internet and listened to broadcasts of *This American Life* while desultorily playing a devilishly addictive computer game called Snood. I have to admit that at first there was something pleasant about it, something dreamy and languid. It was a moment outside of time, as if Paris had been merged with some dusty, one-horse Mexican border town.

By the eighth day of the *canicule*, the heat—the highest recorded in the northern hemisphere since 1757—was drying rivers, shriveling crops, warping railway tracks, decimating livestock, melting the glaciers of the Alps, and setting forests throughout Europe ablaze. The elderly and infirm were dying at a prodigious rate. Mortuaries in Paris were unable to cope with the overflow, and the authorities were forced to commandeer a disused farmer's market on the outskirts of the city to store the mounting pile of bodies. The tone of the headlines had changed from amused to concerned to frantic. (Zoo Bears Snack on Mackerel Ice

Cream. Europe Broils. No Relief in Sight. Killer Heat Wave Continues. Catastrophe Exposes French Health Care Crisis. Heat Wave Threatens French Nuclear Reactors. Pope Leads Prayers for Rain.) The temperature in my apartment reached 110 degrees, then 112, then 116. At night I slept on the cool tiled floor of my kitchenette. No one in Paris had air-conditioning—summers here are not usually particularly warm—and tempers were frayed. Everyone's windows were open, and we could all hear one another's voices, televisions, arguments: Couples screamed at each other through the night. Of course I was dying for the heat to break, but some small part of me, relishing the extremity of it all, perversely urged the mercury upwards: Could it go higher? Higher still?

I awoke early during those days, drenched in sweat, unable to keep sleeping in the heat. After sitting idly in the tub for a while, I slowly made my way to my computer to check my e-mail and track the sales of *Loose Lips* on Amazon. On the tenth day of the heat wave, seventy-eight messages were waiting for me. Of these, seventy-six were concerned with my mortgage rate, the health and velocity of my spermatozoa, and the estate of the late Dr. Jumil Abacha, director of the Nigerian National Petroleum Corporation. One was from Jimmy: I still had his coat; it was in my storage room, and would I please leave it outside my door for him to pick up? The message upset me, first because it was there at all; second because it was not the apology I had yet to receive for his role in nearly crippling me; and third because it was preposterous: Why did he need his coat, of all things, right now, in the middle of the worst heat wave in European history?

I was struggling to reclaim my equipoise when I opened the next message. It was from an address I didn't recognize.

From: arsalan@hotmail.com
Date: August 15, 2003 07:40 AM
To: Claire Berlinski claire@berlinski.com
Subject: (No subject)

Dear Claire Berlinski,

Please allow me to assure you that I am writing to you with the greatest of respect. I encountered the first, and, alas, the only chapter of your novel on the Internet. I live in Isfahan, and Isfahan, as perhaps you do not know, is in the ancient seat and sword of the Persian empire.

But Amazon does not allow itself the luxury of delivering books to my country. Is it possible to order a copy directly from the publisher, and if this is so would you have the kindness to tell me as to how? There is something in what you have written that intrigues me.

With all my very grateful sincerity,

Arsalan

ارسلان صفوی
دانشکده باستان شناسی
دانشگاه اصفهان

How nice, I thought. I sent him a copy of the whole manuscript as a PDF file, with my compliments. It didn't occur to me to wonder how, exactly, this person had found my book on Amazon, or what he had been looking for when he found it. A fan is a fan.

• • •

Through the Internet, I kept in touch not only with my oldest friends but with quite a few people I had never met. I considered Samantha Allen one of my closest friends, even though I had never once seen her or spoken to her. My agent—who was also her agent—had the year before suggested she introduce herself to me.

From: Samantha Allen allens@aol.com
Date: August 18, 2002 04:22 PM
To: Claire Berlinski claire@berlinski.com
Subject: Please read, this is not spam!

Dear Claire,

Rita Steinberg suggested I get in touch with you since I'll be in Paris next week and you and I are both writing books about people with secret lives. (Except my book isn't fiction.) Would you like to get together for a drink while I'm there?

Best,

Samantha Allen

From: Claire Berlinski claire@berlinski.com
Date: August 18, 2002 06:27 PM
To: Samantha Allen allens@aol.com
Subject: Re: Please read, this is not spam!

Samantha,

I'd be happy to. What kind of book are you writing?

Claire

From: Samantha Allen allens@aol.com
Date: August 18, 2002 06:43 PM
To: Claire Berlinski claire@berlinski.com
Subject: Re: Re: Please read, this is not spam!

It's the gender equivalent of *Black Like Me*.

From: Claire Berlinski claire@berlinski.com
Date: August 18, 2002 06:50 PM
To: Samantha Allen allens@aol.com
Subject: Re: Re: Re: Please read, this is not spam!

It's *what?*

From: Samantha Allen allens@aol.com
Date: August 18, 2002 07:01 PM
To: Claire Berlinski claire@berlinski.com
Subject: Re: Re: Re: Re: Please read, this is not spam!
Attach: Sam.jpg (36.5 KB) Samantha.jpg (41.5 KB)

I'm disguising myself as a man for a year and hanging out with men. Then I'm going to write a book about it.

Below her message was a photograph of a tall, handsome woman in a skirt and heels; she had broad shoulders, intelligent eyes, and a strong, jutting nose. Below that was a photograph of some nebbish in chinos and a button-down men's shirt, wearing a baseball cap and glasses. He had a distinct five-o'clock shadow— and precisely the same nose as the woman above him.

From: Claire Berlinski claire@berlinski.com
Date: August 18, 2002 07:22 PM
To: Samantha Allen allens@aol.com
Subject: Re: Re: Re: Re: Re: Please read, this is not spam!

Holy shit, that's amazing! How do you get the stubble?

From: Samantha Allen allens@aol.com
Date: August 18, 2002 07:28 PM
To: Claire Berlinski claire@berlinski.com
Subject: Re: Re: Re: Re: Re: Re: Please read, this is not spam!

It's from my head; I put it on with spirit gum. It takes for-ever. Good, isn't it?

From: Claire Berlinski claire@berlinski.com
Date: August 18, 2002 07:32 PM
To: Samantha Allen allens@aol.com
Subject: Re: Re: Re: Re: Re: Re: Re: Please read, this is
     not spam!

It's *really* good. I wouldn't have known at all. But isn't your voice a giveaway?

From: Samantha Allen allens@aol.com
Date: August 18, 2002 07:50 PM
To: Claire Berlinski claire@berlinski.com
Subject: Re: Re: Re: Re: Re: Re: Re: Re: Please read, this
     is not spam!

No, it's naturally really deep, that's the beauty of it. I got the idea for the book the five billionth time some receptionist asked if I'd mind holding, *Sir.* Must ask before I get too attached, though: You wouldn't happen to be of the Sapphic persuasion, would you?

She didn't seem to hold it against me that I wasn't. Several days later, however, she wrote to tell me that she was canceling her trip; she had decided to go to Antigua, instead. Nonetheless, we kept in touch. Our friendship was confined to lighthearted exchanges about the books we were writing until, late one night, I had received a message from her asking, "Isn't it four in the morning over there? What are you doing awake?" For some reason I had told her the truth: I was miserable. I couldn't sleep. Jimmy and I were still dating then, and he had disappeared several days before. When, at last, I had gone to his apartment and let myself in with my key, I had found him sprawled on his fold-out sofa, snoring and impervious, surrounded by empty wine bottles. "*Your* kind of love," he'd said to me after I shook him awake, "doesn't *nurture.* It *destroys.*"

Samantha proved a patient interlocutor. Never before had I encountered someone with first-hand insight into male behavior *and* an eagerness to discuss my relationships at great length. I didn't feel that our relationship lacked anything because we had never met. In fact, in some ways I enjoyed my epistolary friendships more than ordinary ones; they seemed to me to function more smoothly. An e-mail relationship is, after all, undemanding. When you want it to go away, you just shut down your computer: Three clicks of the mouse and voilà—it's gone.

. . .

On the twelfth day of the *canicule*, I was reading a message from Samantha when I received another message from Iran.

From: arsalan@hotmail.com
Date: August 17, 2003 04:22 PM
To: Claire Berlinski claire@berlinski.com
Subject: Re: Re: (No subject)

Dear Claire Berlinski,

I am touched by your generous nature and I shall greatly enjoy your gift. I send my very sincere regards and kindest wishes.

Yours respectfully,

Arsalan

ارسلان صفوی
دانشکده باستان شناسی
دانشگاه اصفهان

Out of curiosity, I clicked on the hyperlink embedded in the words below his name. It took me to a page of photographs without a single word of English, only row upon row of incomprehensible, curvaceous Persian script. The photographs were the kind you find on someone's personal web page: *this is my neighborhood, this is my family.* One showed the exterior of a small mosque, speckled with a glittering cream-and-peach mosaic. Perhaps it served as a bathhouse, because towels hung to dry at the entrance. An elderly man with a hawkish nose and graying stubble on his cheeks stood beside the billowing towels in the intense light, balanced on a cane, staring past the camera but not smiling, an inscrutable expression on his face. His face was traversed by deep lines, and his cheeks draped inward. I wondered if he was the man who had written to me.

I scrolled down the page, studying the snapshots of a lazy Middle Eastern city: straw-roofed shops, a child riding his bicycle along an alley shaded with plane trees, a street vendor selling pomegranates from crates. Bright sunlight splashed over the plastered mud walls and the old Persian roofs, creating a spectrum of beautiful colors. The scenes in the photos would have been timeless had it not been for the television antennas on the roofs and the surprisingly artistic graffiti spray-painted on the walls.

One photograph showed a group of women of various ages, all in black chadors, picnicking by a still, turquoise pool. They were smiling. They looked as if they were enjoying themselves. Were those my correspondent's relatives? His mother and sisters? If so, how had a family like that produced an enthusiast of American spy novels? The face of a girl of about sixteen stood out; she was the only one looking directly at the camera. She was not particularly pretty, but her eyes were clever and amused, as if she and the photographer were sharing a sly joke. Could Arsalan be a woman's name? Was *she* the one who had written to me? I entered the name Arsalan in Google. There were thousands of them, and it was definitely a man's name. It meant "the Lion."

Two larger photographs at the bottom of the page were extraordinarily clear and detailed, as if they had been taken with a much better camera. One showed the interior of a room framed by a

large, wide-open window overlooking a skyline of turquoise
minarets. Thin muslin curtains billowed in from the window,
through which poured an intense, almost white light, illuminating
every detail of the shimmering carpet below. The carpet was intri-
cately woven with ivory palmettes, crimson rosettes, and floral
shapes in shades of dusky rose and alabaster. Creeping vines and
arabesque tendrils framed the centerpiece—a golden bird with
wild plumage and flashing ruby eyes.

The other photograph showed the same room from a different
angle. A bowl of crystallized sugar filled with pomegranates sat
atop a low rosewood coffee table. Beside the bowl stood a tea set
and a tarnished copper samovar. Strewn haphazardly around the
table were half a dozen luxuriant silken cushions, and on the
plumpest cushion lay a small gray cat, sprawled on its back, batting
at a mote of dust caught in the sunbeam.

The air in my own apartment was absolutely still.

• • •

My relationship with my friend Imran was outstanding now that
we communicated almost exclusively by e-mail. We had met years
ago when we were both graduate students; he was now a clinical
psychotherapist with a busy practice in London. We had seen each
other in person only rarely since we graduated; Imran led an *extremely* scheduled life. There was no "I'll meet you outside the museum and we'll see how we feel" with Imran; it had to be "My
11:30 patient leaves at 12:20, and it will take me four minutes to
get there, or six if I take the stairs, which I'm committed to doing
these days. I have the tennis court booked for 2:15, so we can
spend fifteen, no more than twenty minutes on the Braque exhibit,
and the rest of the hour with the Giacometti mobiles—not the
sculptures, though; I've already seen those twice. Lunch at the
sushi place on the northwest side of the gallery would work for me.
I have four phone calls booked between my 9:30 and my 10:30,
and I shave between 11:20 and my 11:30, so you'll need to make

the reservations. Tell them we'll take the table at the window, because the music isn't as loud there—*not* one of the ones by the counter." Imran had an immense gift of insight into the behavior of others, which of course made him both an interesting interlocutor and tremendously good at his job, but about the prominent role of timekeeping in his life he was, if not precisely blind, then not unusually perceptive.

The *canicule* had entered its thirteenth day, and, stuck in my studio, I found myself checking my e-mail repeatedly, then returning to the photographs of what I had decided must be arsalan@hotmail.com's apartment. It looked peaceful and pleasantly breezy. I had been roused early by the heat and was looking at the photographs again, in fact, when I received an e-mail from Imran. (These arrived at precisely 6:45 in the morning, except on Sundays, when they arrived at 9:15.)

From: Imran Begum imranbegum@gmail.com
Date: August 18, 2003 06:45 AM
To: Claire Berlinski claire@berlinski.com
Subject: Booked!

Dear Old Friend,

I have signed up for speed dating! Once per week I shall present myself at an upmarket venue in Mayfair, where over the course of an hour I shall go on twenty dates of three minutes each.

How *perfect* for him, I thought.

. . . in other news, I've been experimenting with prefacing my remarks to patients with the phrase, "It is entirely possible that I am mistaken . . ." This preamble seems to disarm the rebel in those patients who are rebellious, which is about 40% of my usual caseload. Something to do with me questioning my own phallus so they don't have to. I need to look more carefully at who the problem parent was in the patients for whom this seems to be a pivotal issue in the transference.

I'm delighted to say that I've reduced hours worked, income (and tax bill) bang on schedule, 20% down, 30% better life!

Anyway, must run; 25 minutes remaining.

Much love,

Immie

After replying I found myself at loose ends. I felt guilty that I wasn't working, but it was already so hot in my apartment that there was no hope of being visited with concentration or industry. I returned yet again to Persia and contemplated the photographs in the middle of the screen. They had been taken at a bazaar, where light fell in patterned shafts from the skylights onto the ornate arcades. Under loose awnings, samovar-makers and tradesmen sold housewares and artwork; a coppersmith hammered a cauldron held by a young man with bare, muscular arms. I wondered who they were—acquaintances of the photographer, relatives, just people on the street? Light shone upon the old Persian scales outside a general store, its copper color contrasting with the huge ripe melons on display. An old man—the shopkeeper? The man who had written to me? Or maybe his father?—sat in the shadow next to the Persian clothing and bolts of Persian fabric, the awning above him anchored to an ice-cream stand. I imagined that the shade from the tree beside him, a mulberry tree perhaps, must provide a cool respite from the blistering sunshine, pouring from turquoise skies over the ancient mud walls.

And that was that; there was no more to see. Over the past

few days I had spent hours looking at those photographs. Impulsively, I went back to the first e-mail Arsalan had sent me, and hit Reply.

"Who are you?" I wrote.

. . .

The heat wave was baking all of northern Europe, and it was having an unsettling effect on Imran, in London. He wrote anxious messages to me all through the week.

> **From:** Imran Begum imranbegum@gmail.com
> **Date:** August 19, 2003 06:45 AM
> **To:** Claire Berlinski claire@berlinski.com
> **Subject:** Re: Re: Re: Re: Re: Re: Booked!
>
> Old Dear Friend,
>
> I'm 39 and $7/12$ today. My mind makes me sad about this. Something to do with still being single and not yet having found a woman, age 33–37, to marry within 10–12 months. (Children 6–8 months after that.)
>
> But as I may have told you, I designed two pairs of shoes to celebrate my birthday! Both will be made to the shape of my feet. The first pair will arrive this week, a heavy walking brogue in grained cordovan, an American wingtip style. I hope you see them one day!
>
> One of my birthday resolutions is to give up talking about money and expensive purchases. I find it alienates me from people with less material ease. Or rather, they alienate themselves. So. No more talk of weekly averages, workshop revenue, or the latest Triangle Magellan concerto amplifier and bass driver (equipped with a perforated shield fitted over the motor's cylinder head in order to provide thermal dissipation!). Suffice it to say that I'm enjoy-

ing my burgeoning jazz collection more than ever and that treble definition and bass clarity are adequate!

News from you, I hope, prontissimo!

Distant as ever, devoted as usual,

Immie

From: Claire Berlinski claire@berlinski.com
Date: August 19, 2003 06:50 AM
To: Imran Begum imranbegum@gmail.com
Subject: Re: Re: Re: Re: Re: Re: Re: Booked!

Why ten to twelve months? And why age 33–37? Christ it's hot. Too hot to write more, sorry.

xxxC.

His reply, as usual, came at the end of the fifty-minute analytic hour.

From: Imran Begum imranbegum@gmail.com
Date: August 19, 2003 07:58 AM
To: Claire Berlinski claire@berlinski.com
Subject: Re: Re: Re: Re: Re: Re: Re: Re: Booked!

Dear Distant Friend,

In my experience, for at least ten months my judgment of any woman to whom I'm attracted is thoroughly queered by fantasy and idealization. I would prefer someone my own age, since partnerships between men and women separated by more than five years in age are inherently neurotic, but considerations of fertility are paramount, so I'll have to make do with a compromise. Younger women are rather attractive to me and I still dip my toe in periodically, but I'm very clear about the context. It's like dining out at a special restaurant. A yearly treat but not like the daily eggs, bacon, bread, and beans that we must live on. Conceptual caviar, we might call it. The wise person knows where the edge of the ledge is and doesn't fall off the mountains. Next patient is Anna, 55, judgmental and abusive. Like doing therapy with Goebbels. Must run.

As ever,

Immie

On the following scorching hot day, Imran had an anxiety attack.

From: Imran Begum imranbegum@gmail.com
Date: August 20, 2003 06:45 AM
To: Claire Berlinski claire@berlinski.com
Subject: Re: Re: Re: Re: Re: Re: Re: Re: Re: Re: Booked!

C. Quite frightened about my upcoming foray into speed dating. Thinking about it brings on hollowness in stomach, tightness in chest, sensitivity to noise and light, breathlessness, loss of appetite (70%) and loss of sexual desire (45%). I have an unpleasant fantasy of facing twenty painful romantic rejections in less than an hour. Must run to buy new shirts, braces, socks, bowties, colognes, and cuff links. Love, ~I.

I was not particularly worried on his behalf, however, and responded right away to tell him so. Imran was unusually attractive to women, partly because he was a fine-looking man, but in larger part because after years of practicing psychotherapy, he would by habit immediately ask any woman he met about her emotional life, then, also by habit, arrange his body and features to suggest he was listening compassionately, actively, and without judgment. This caused approximately forty to forty-five percent of the women he dated (according to his statistics) to unburden themselves to him with unusual candor and then to fall in love with him, although when he wrote about this, he placed "fall in love" in quotation marks, for he found the sudden intensity of their emotions suspect.

That said, Imran *was* lovable. A more curious student of human nature you could not hope to meet, nor a man more touchingly devoted to the ideal of curing pain and easing suffering. I was certain that for the right woman—an *extremely* punctual one—he would make a wonderful husband.

. . .

The *canicule* entered its third unrelenting week. I was irritated with the elderly Hungarian woman below me, who complained again that I was running the tub too often. I was irritated with the shopkeeper at the appliance store down the street, who had a fan sitting right in his window but refused to sell it to me because it was the *display* fan, not the *selling* fan. I was irritated with the old ladies in the grocery stores who never thought to get their wallets out while the clerk was ringing up their purchases. And when several days later I had still received no reply from arsalan@hotmail.com, I found myself irritated with him, too.

That evening, the smell of ozone entered through the open window, and I heard a portentous rumbling. Perhaps, I thought hopefully, it might be about to rain? It *had* to be, I decided, and determined to go for a run by the Seine—something I had not done since the accident.

The whole sky turned dark purple as I stepped outdoors. I set out at a trot through the Paris Plage. Bertrand Delanoë, the first openly gay mayor of Paris, had transformed the banks of the Seine for the summer into a faux beach. Two thousand tons of sand, potted palm trees, little café tables, and parasols had been set up along the river. The press kept talking about what a terrific, openly gay idea this was. I usually liked to run down the banks of the Seine to avoid traffic, but with the beach there, I had to dodge and weave through crowds of men in little leopard-print bikinis. There was nowhere to swim; everyone just sat there, sweating, in the pollution. The rain I was hoping for had not begun, and everyone looked hot and miserable, except the giggling all-girl trombone ensemble at the end of the *plage*. They were playing their trombones and smoking at the same time, all barefoot and gamine despite the heat.

I passed through the dreaded Tunnel of Piss, which in the *canicule* reeked even more than usual. Still no rain. I wondered why French men, like dogs, felt it appropriate to urinate anywhere, any time, the moment the urge struck them. I ran under the bridge where the homeless people lived. Paris still has great winos, real 1950s-style winos, not the horrible ghoul-eyed crackheads you see in American cities. They look so *happy* to be drunkards, as if nothing could be finer than to spend a great day lying in the gutter, surrounded by empty wine bottles, reeking to high heaven and singing old French songs about *la bicyclette* and *les femmes*. In the winter, the winos under that bridge make elaborate, wonderful-smelling meals on their camp stoves, like *boeuf bourguignon* and coq au vin; they dine at tables made from overturned crates covered with checkered tablecloths, decorated with candles and single red roses stuck in empty wine bottles. But in the *canicule* it was way too hot to cook. They sprawled on the ground in their underwear, slowly scratching their fleas.

I reached the houseboats. Still no rain. A houseboat dweller was placing an elaborate houseboat picnic on his wooden table, with candelabra, champagne in fluted glasses, and at least six kinds of pâté. His picnic looked better than his geraniums; although it was high summer, the *canicule* had twisted and shriveled the plants on all of the houseboat decks. The heat had even turned the trees prematurely autumnal, and as I ran I kicked up piles of dead brown leaves.

Still no rain.

At the Eiffel Tower, the Japanese tourists were standing on the bridge with their video cameras, making homemade movies of Japanese tourists standing in front of the Eiffel Tower. People with video cameras always forget that they're in a real city, where other people need to use the street, and not a movie set. When they see a runner coming their way, they move right into the *center* of the sidewalk rather than stepping to the side. If you shout at them, they look confused and they giggle, but they still don't get out of the way. Somewhere out there, there's a Japanese businessman whose home movie of Paris during the *canicule* stars Claire Berlinski, in her sweaty running clothes, yelling at him to *move*.

The heat still had not broken. Above me the clouds had dissipated, and the crepuscular sky turned brown again. Now it looked as if it weren't going to rain after all. It had become intensely humid as well as hot. I was dehydrated—I had thought it unnecessary to bring change with me to buy water because I had been *sure* it was about to rain. I turned back, running at first, then walking, then limping. The city was a hot mirage of lavish lampposts, gilded statues, golden ornaments, winking gargoyles, nymphs and cherubs, crabby Parisians and more crabby Parisians—all of us hating one another in that God-awful heat. The Seine was churning and turbid. A *Bateaux Mouches* filled with tourists struggled to stay on course; for a moment I thought hopefully that it might crash into a bridge.

When I returned, I checked my e-mail. There was a message from arsalan@hotmail.com.

From: arsalan@hotmail.com
Date: August 23, 2003 08:22 PM
To: Claire Berlinski claire@berlinski.com
Subject: Re: Re: (No subject)

Dear Claire Berlinski,

I apologize for my delay in response. I am writing to you with a heart overflowing with grief. My mother has died, and like any orphan I must now undertake the journey to come in solitude.

Strange, is it not? that of the myriads who
Before us pass'd the door of Darkness through,
Not one returns to tell us of the Road,
Which to discover we must travel too.

With all my respect,

Arsalan

ارسلان صفوی
دانشکده باستان شناسی
دانشگاه اصفهان

• • •

As I lay in the tub my irritation dissipated, replaced by an uneasy melancholia. I wasn't sure why—after all, I didn't know his mother. When I returned to my desk, however, an e-mail from Samantha distracted me. She was in Los Angeles and woke up roughly as I was winding down the day. Samantha—or Sam, as her masculine avatar called himself—had placed Sam's profile on Nerve.com.

From: Samantha Allen allens@aol.com
Date: August 23, 2003 09:02 PM
To: Claire Berlinski claire@berlinski.com
Subject: Nerve

So far, so good! I seem to be a hit with the Nerve ladies. Hubba-hubba! They really appreciate my flair for the romantic. You know, the effect of a tender letter—or better still a poem—on the straight woman's psyche is astonishingly powerful. Hilariously so. Why is that?

To: Samantha Allen allens@aol.com
Date: August 23, 2003 09:08 PM
From: Claire Berlinski claire@berlinski.com
Subject: Re: Nerve

Gosh, Sam, that's probably because they're getting about a hundred misspelled illiterate letters a day from men whose first question is whether they can see more photographs. Real men, you see, suffer from a terrible fear that they might be writing to a woman who's secretly a wide load.

From: Samantha Allen allens@aol.com
Date: August 23, 2003 09:12 PM
To: Claire Berlinski claire@berlinski.com
Subject: Re: Re: Nerve

Well, Sam's got real dates with three lucky Nerve ladies this weekend! How should I act? What do you straight women like in a man?

To: Samantha Allen allens@aol.com
Date: August 23, 2003 09:18 PM
From: Claire Berlinski claire@berlinski.com
Subject: Re: Re: Re: Nerve

Ask her about her emotional life, then arrange your body and features to suggest you're listening compassionately, actively, and without judgment. Oh, and ask her about her father. Most women have screwed-up relationships with their fathers. The more screwed-up her relationship with her father, the more drawn to you she'll be. It's a transference thing.

That was Imran's special trick. I'd seen it in action. My brother had tried the Imran Method. He reported that the results were astonishing, but the method had one terrible drawback: you had to spend hours listening to women talk about their fathers.

After I sent off my reply I began reading the latest posts on my favorite long-distance running forum, where an argument about shin splints had broken out. Just after the moderator posted to remind members of the forum's regulations on obscenity, Samantha wrote back to me.

From: Samantha Allen allens@aol.com
Date: August 23, 2003 09:23 PM
To: Claire Berlinski claire@berlinski.com
Subject: Re: Re: Re: Re: Nerve

I should talk about their feelings? *That's* what women want? So what you're saying, right, is that straight women want men who are really just women in men's bodies?

To: Samantha Allen allens@aol.com
Date: August 23, 2003 09:24 PM
From: Claire Berlinski claire@berlinski.com
Subject: Re: Re: Re: Re: Re: Nerve

Oh, no. Do *not* propose splitting the check.

From: Samantha Allen allens@aol.com
Date: August 23, 2003 09:26 PM
To: Claire Berlinski claire@berlinski.com
Subject: Re: Re: Re: Re: Re: Re: Nerve

Huh. No wonder men hate women.

Samantha didn't write again that evening. Perhaps she had gone out. I began reading the Drudge Report. When I came across an article about Iran, I remembered that I should reply to the sad message I'd received from arsalan@hotmail.com. I composed a note using more or less the words that I had used the night before when a member of my runners' forum reported that his wife had died of skin cancer.

From: Claire Berlinski claire@berlinski.com
Date: August 23, 2003 10:22 PM
To: arsalan@hotmail.com
Subject: Re: Re: Re: (No subject)

Dear Arsalan,

I'm sorry for your loss. Please accept my sincere condolences.

Yours truly,

Claire Berlinski

I looked at what I'd just written and thought it sounded cold. It was tricky, though; I truly had no idea who he was, and I knew nothing of his mother, so I could hardly write a touching elegy to her memory. I erased the message and started again.

From: Claire Berlinski claire@berlinski.com
Date: August 23, 2003 10:30 PM
To: arsalan@hotmail.com
Subject: Re: Re: Re: (No subject)

Dear Arsalan,

All I know of you is that you live in Iran, and you enjoy spy novels, as I do. We are perfect strangers. But even a stranger knows what it means to lose a mother, and I can imagine acutely the loss you must feel. Please accept my sincere condolences.

With my sympathy,

Claire

Before going to sleep, I made a point of sending an especially nice e-mail to my mother.

• • •

It was windy and overcast when I woke up, and I was surprised to realize, when I looked at the clock, that it was nearly noon. It was the first time in weeks I'd been able to sleep past dawn. I had come to think of the heat as an intractable, unconquerable enemy, and as I stood up and put my head outside my window, breathing in the cool air, my relief was tempered by suspicion. Was this a bluff?

I went to my computer to check the weather forecast, and before doing that checked my e-mail. A letter from Iran was waiting for me.

From: Arsalan arsalan@hotmail.com
Date: August 24, 2003 09:45 AM
To: Claire Berlinski claire@berlinski.com
Subject: (No subject)

Dear Claire Berlinski,

Thank you for your kind and gracious words.

I have taken the last of my mother's books, her tattered divans of poetry, from her apartment and brought them to mine. I have swept up the things that fall from books. I have found this way an indistinct photograph of my mother, in her wedding gown. I have found a list, in her hand, of things to buy for the Norooz celebrations.

I have sorted, alone, through her possessions . . . her rosewood coffee table . . . her tea set . . . her copper samovar. But what will become of her cat? They were inseparable. She read and he slept on her lap. She slept and he lay on her pillow. He looks at me now reproachfully, and the words of Sa'di come to my mouth.

No shield of parental protection his head
Now shelters; be thou his protector instead.

So the orphan Wollef is my responsibility now, it is clear. It is what my mother would want.

Poor creature! He knows she is gone forever; I believe this to be so. He wanders from one corner of my unfamiliar apartment to the other and cries. He growls when I try to stroke him. He paces, he searches, he smells the place she sat when last she visited, he waits by the door, listens for her footsteps, wonders when she will come for him.

She has escaped from the cage now, I tell him, *her wings spread in the air.*

He looks at me; he does not comprehend. There are no words to comfort a cat.

With my sincere respect,

Arsalan

ارسلان صفوی
دانشکده باستان شناسی
دانشگاه اصفهان

I read the note several times.

I was surprised, of course, to receive such a personal letter. Yet I understood. He had just lost his mother, and I had just asked who he was. Perhaps the event prompted him to ask that question of himself, as it might any of us, and if his letter seemed raw and vulnerable, that seemed to me only natural. Who wouldn't be at a moment like that?

Where had he learned to write such excellent English, I wondered? Perhaps he had been educated in the West—had he left during the Revolution?—but then why had he returned to Iran? What did he do for a living? How old was he?

My mind wandered. The apartment I had seen in the photo-graph—perhaps it was his mother's? And the cat I had seen was *her* cat? Any woman, I thought, so tender with a small animal must surely have been even more tender with a small child.

I imagined my correspondent as a boy, returning from school to that sunny apartment. There was his plump mother standing in the doorway. She had spent the afternoon preparing sweets made of almonds and cardamom, honey and rosewater. The warm smell of baking in the apartment was inseparable from the scent of her skin. They sat together on those plump silk cushions; she poured tea from the samovar into tiny, gold-rimmed glasses. He helped himself to sweets and told her what he had learned that day in school.

My heart went out to him, whoever he was.

CHAPTER TWO

As to people waxing ecstatic about the attention to spy detail . . . umm . . .
Google much? You can find all this information online.

—Customer review
of *Loose Lips* on Amazon.com

There was no washing machine in my building, so I had to haul
my laundry to the Laundromat several blocks away. I always put off
the chore, especially since the Laundromat was cramped, moldy-
smelling, overpriced, and always full of cranky old ladies who
couldn't figure out how to use the machines, or loud, rude, Spanish summer exchange students.

I had just put one load into the wash and was sorting another
into lights and darks when the last person in the world I wanted to
see walked in. Jimmy was wearing a sleeveless ribbed T-shirt that
showed off his extremely well-developed biceps, his triceps, his

deltoids, his trapezius muscles. Somehow, no matter how he abused himself, he still looked like the agile middleweight boxer he used to be. He *should* have looked like fifty miles of bad road, all things considered, but even the lines on his face only made him look rugged. I then realized that he was, in fact, the *second*-to-last person I wanted to see. Right behind him, and clearly with him, was a pair of five-inch stiletto-heeled *sandals*—gold-lamé sandals with gold-flecked clear platform soles, delicate gold ankle chains, and thin gold toe straps fringed with turquoise medallions and crystal beads, encasing ten perfectly painted, Rioja-red nails on the tips of the slender toes of a tall girl of about twenty in Argentine air-hostess sunglasses.

I was wearing sweatpants and a Morrisville State College T-shirt. Everything else I owned was in the wash.

I looked at Jimmy. He looked at me. "Hi," he said at last, looking at me a bit as if I were someone whose face he couldn't quite place.

"Hi, Jimmy. How are you."

He looked at a loss for words. He attempted to smile; it came off as an unsuccessful smirk. Finally, he said, "Need to do me laundry."

"Yeah." My hands were full of dirty running clothes. I couldn't leave; half my clothes were already in the machine. I took a good long look at the Sandals. She had the same coloring as he did—black hair and olive skin, which on Jimmy, I suppose, was the legacy of the Spanish Armada. His Mediterranean ancestors had evidently had a swell time in Ireland. Together, Jimmy and the girl looked as if they'd walked out of an advertisement for coconut suntan oil. She was a Spanish summer exchange student, from the looks of it. I expect he'd found her on the rue Saint André des Arts, adjacent to the Laundromat. The street was nicknamed Bacterium Alley by the Anglophones because of its many crowded bars, where at night it was easy to pick up not only a summer exchange student but an embarrassing itch.

Jimmy shrugged and went to put change in the soap dispenser. She hopped up on the counter behind him and began swinging her sandals back and forth. "*Jee-mee*," she asked, "deed you bring dee theeg-a-rettes? I tink you leeve dem in my bedroom?" *Jee-mee* reached into the pocket of his jeans and pulled out a packet of to-bacco and some rolling papers. She obviously didn't know him that well, I thought, if she imagined some wild Spanish monkey sex would make *Jee-mee*, the most committed smoker I've ever known, forget his tobacco. He handed the pouch to her. She began rolling a cigarette, delicately licking the rolling paper with the tip of her adorable pink tongue, and he began unpacking her laundry from her little wheeled hamper. That's when I saw her underwear, which made her sandals look practical by comparison, and that's when I decided to leave my laundry in the washer to rot. No one needs clean towels that badly.

When I returned to my apartment, I sat down and stared mor-bidly at the walls for a while. Then I began writing a letter to Samantha. "That must be some *nurturing* kind of love," I wrote. "Those sandals. *Those fucking sandals.* How much more, God, how much more? I want to strangle her with the straps of her sandals and smash his nose with their platform heels." He had a perfectly straight Roman nose. He was proud of it. Somehow, in all his years as a boxer, it had never been broken. I thought it was high time. "Well at least he's someone else's problem now. Just wait until she gets tired of paying for dinner."

I sent the message off, brooding miserably and contemplating my own unpedicured toes while I waited for Samantha to write back. After an hour, I still hadn't heard from her. Another message from the Iranian man arrived, however.

"That wasn't *precisely* the response I would have expected to a letter about my bereavement," he wrote, "but I'm certainly glad for the distraction."

· · ·

I've sent e-mail before to people for whom it wasn't intended, and so has everyone else I know. Once, I sent a message to my father complaining about my "bozo editor" to that very bozo editor. Their names were right next to each other in my address book. Needless to say, I never worked for *that* bozo magazine again. So perhaps it was just an act of carelessness.

Imran, however, thought not.

From: Imran Begum imranbegum@gmail.com
Date: August 26, 2003 06:45 AM
To: Claire Berlinski claire@berlinski.com
Subject: Re: Ack!

Dear Old Claire,

It is entirely possible that I am mistaken, but that was of course a *textbook* Freudian slip. By sending an inappropriate, seductive message to this Persian fellow you symbolically betrayed Jimmy as he betrayed you, and drew to yourself the masculine attention you crave to compensate for your feelings of invisibility as a woman. Sending the message "accidentally" spared you the burden of taking conscious responsibility for your inappropriate impulses. Well done!

I would have liked to discuss this with him at greater length, but he was off to Mayfair to go speed dating.

. . . The lady places are sold out so it will be full of them. I'm quite apprehensive. I'm putting myself in the firing line for twenty consecutive rejections, as are they, brave one and all! Have just spent fifty minutes on shaving and shoe shining. Now wearing green cords with turn-ups, green cord waistcoat with lapels, red knotted silk tie, a brushed-cotton tattersall check country shirt with double-button barrel cuffs, and one of my favorite pocket watches, a very rare, late-eighteenth-century continental in a gilt consular case, with two escape wheels of thirty teeth, geared together to act directly on the staff of the balance. My hands are freezing cold. I feel as if I'm facing twenty consecutive medical school interviews. I even dreamt last night that I might puncture one of the tires of my car *en route*!

Wish me luck,

Immie

• • •

I wished him luck, then went back to Arsalan's message and read it again.

... I would love nothing more than to give your heartbreak the full attention it merits, but I am obliged this evening to entertain twenty Saudis. Would you perhaps know how one prepares a lamb stew *without* rice or potatoes? I beg your indulgence for such a ridiculous inquiry, but I am rather at my wits' end.

Yours sincerely and with utmost respect,

Arsalan

ارسلان صفوی
دانشکده باستان شناسی
دانشگاه اصفهان

Was he making fun of me? I wasn't sure. I decided to take the question at face value. "Yes, I do know. Why?" I replied.

He didn't write back immediately, but when I checked my mail the next morning—having been woken up early by a round of hearty salutations among the *pétanque*-playing workmen on the Place Dauphine—he had replied.

From: Arsalan arsalan@hotmail.com
Date: August 27, 2003 08:15 AM
To: Claire Berlinski claire@berlinski.com
Subject: Re: Re: (No subject)

Dear Claire, if I may take the liberty of addressing you in this familiar fashion, I am obliged to host a banquet for a team of visiting Saudi donors. The event was planned long ago. My mother, in addition to her many other gifts, was an accomplished hostess. She was to have supervised the cooking. Despite her passing, it cannot be canceled. The donors will fly in from Riyadh specially for the ceremony. I have delegated the preparations to the maid and her daughter, but they have not prepared so grand a banquet before, and the Saudis have made a most bizarre request: they wish to be served a meal without bread, potatoes, sweets, or starches. I have no idea why. Do you? With warmest regards, Arsalan

ارسلان صفوی
دانشکده باستان شناسی
دانشگاه اصفهان

I had no idea why he was asking *me* this, but I did happen to know the answer to his question. Evidently Isfahan was the only place on earth where no one had been apprised of the New Atkins Diet Revolution. I entertained myself for a moment by imagining twenty plump turbaned Saudi sheiks in white robes, hungrily eyeing the basket of warm Persian breads, then patting their waistlines and shaking their heads regretfully.

From: Claire Berlinski claire@berlinski.com
Date: August 27, 2003 08:18 AM
To: Arsalan arsalan@hotmail.com
Subject: Re: Re: Re: (No subject)

Please do call me Claire. Are your guests fat? Because I believe they're on a popular weight-loss diet. Try going to this site: www.lowcarbcooking.org, then do a search under "Persian Cuisine" to see if there are any suitable recipes your maid could prepare. Hope that helps, Claire

Within minutes, he replied.

From: Arsalan arsalan@hotmail.com
Date: August 27, 2003 08:22 AM
To: Claire Berlinski claire@berlinski.com
Subject: Re: Re: Re: Re: (No subject)

Yes, they're very fat, Claire, like mountains. I took a look at the site you kindly suggested. There are a few Persian recipes, I thank you very much. I think I will discover something suitable there. Do you perhaps know secrets about cats, as well? It is such a small, foolish thing, but at the moment it is the central problem of my life. Wollef behaves in a disturbing way. He follows me everywhere, even to my bath. He cries all night, keeping me awake. I am concerned for him, and for my own sanity if I cannot sleep. What am I to do, I wonder? I hope you do not think less of me for this query. Respectfully Yours, Arsalan.

ارسلان صفوی
دانشکده باستان شناسی
دانشگاه اصفهان

Think less of him? I knew nothing about him in the first place. But I did know about cats; in fact, I knew more about cats than I did about carbs. My brother and I had rescued three of them once, as orphaned kittens, and raised them with milk from an eyedropper.

From: Claire Berlinski claire@berlinski.com
Date: August 27, 2003 08:30 AM
To: Arsalan arsalan@hotmail.com
Subject: Re: Re: Re: Re: Re: (No subject)

He's probably very confused and frightened. Cats don't at all like changes in their environment. You could try feeding him a bit more. You can't do it all the time or he'll get fat, but right now he's stressed, and if you give him a bit more to eat it will reassure him—and tranquilize him, too. Try giving him canned food, if he's used to dry. He'll probably gorge himself on it, then sleep for hours. Best, Claire.

PS: Who *are* you?

His response arrived no more than thirty seconds later.

From: Arsalan arsalan@hotmail.com
Date: August 27, 2003 08:31 AM
To: Claire Berlinski claire@berlinski.com
Subject: Re: Re: Re: Re: Re: Re: (No subject)

Canned cat food? You mean special food for cats? This is Iran, not Los Angeles. They shot the dogs during the Revolution. Cats here eat mice.

ارسلان صفوی
دانشکده باستان شناسی
دانشگاه اصفهان

He hadn't *fed* the poor cat? I pressed Reply:

From: Claire Berlinski claire@berlinski.com
Date: August 27, 2003 08:38 AM
To: Arsalan arsalan@hotmail.com
Subject: Re: Re: Re: Re: Re: Re: Re: (No subject)

Well then! I suspect your new cat is *hungry*, very hungry.
I'm sure your mother fed him. He probably has no idea
what to do with a mouse. Tell your maid to mix some fish
with a bit of warm milk and cooked rice. Give him as much
as he wants. He'll go right to sleep.

An hour later, he wrote back.

From: Arsalan arsalan@hotmail.com
Date: August 27, 2003 09:40 AM
To: Claire Berlinski claire@berlinski.com
Subject: Re: Re: Re: Re: Re: Re: Re: Re: (No subject)

You were absolutely right, Claire. He is sleeping now very
peacefully. Thank you. I feel sadly for the poor creature; it
had not occurred to me that he might, like me, not know
how to feed himself. So we are both too used to my
mother's cooking, it seems.

I have chosen recipes to prepare, but I am not familiar
at all with cooking terms—what is it to julienne? I am not
sure how to translate this for the maid?

ارسلان صفوی
دانشکده باستان شناسی
دانشگاه اصفهان

I offered to help, of course. Would the maid be able to purchase all
those low-carbohydrate ingredients? I asked. He replied indignantly:

From: Arsalan arsalan@hotmail.com
Date: August 27, 2003 09:42 AM
To: Claire Berlinski claire@berlinski.com
Subject: Re: Re: Re: Re: Re: Re: Re: Re: Re: (No subject)

Of course! She can get anything at our magnificent market! Cattle, calves, sheep, lambs, ducks, geese, doves, stags, gazelles, everything! Just not pet food.

ارسلان صفوی
دانشکده باستان شناسی
دانشگاه اصفهان

I took a look at the recipes he'd found, and sent him a grocery list. He translated it, gave it to the maid, and sent her out. Then, hungry myself, I went out for a slice of apple pie and a Coke.

Hours later, Arsalan wrote to say that the maid had acquired the necessary ingredients. Throughout the afternoon, as I sat at my desk trying to work, we exchanged messages. Arsalan translated my instructions, then replied with his maid's questions; I offered my best culinary hints and a few more veterinary ones as well. After a while I stopped trying to work.

If it seems odd that I spent my day writing to some stranger in Iran, or that he spent his day writing to me, consider this: I was trying to write another novel, and finding it hard going. Arsalan was an archaeologist, I later learned; he was working on a short history of medicine in Mesopotamia. His book was now a year overdue. He had resolved not to return to the field before finishing it, but, as he later wrote to me, he had never much liked the part of his profession that involved sitting indoors day after day in front of a computer. It was the digging he loved, the outdoors, the adventure, the discoveries; writing up the results of his research bored him. When it came to writing he was a terrible procrastinator, he admitted, and I certainly sympathized.

We were not the only ones. Samantha wrote that same day to say that she had just wandered into a Barnes & Noble and surveyed all the books. So *many* books. So many writers who, unlike her, had *finished* their books. She'd had to sit down in one of the big comfortable chairs and put her head between her knees for a minute or two. So if we all found ourselves checking our e-mail a bit compulsively, and answering it with *especial* enthusiasm and diligence, chalk it up to the profession.

Arsalan wrote that the maid had slapped her thighs, crying *"Bah! Bah!"* in amazement when informed that an American stranger had come to be involved in the preparations for the banquet. I found this just as remarkable as she did. It was a miracle, really, that by means of the Internet I could sit at my desk in Paris and coach an illiterate sixty-five-year-old maid in some batshit-crazy country in the Middle East through the preparation of an eggplant appetizer with yogurt sauce and a lamb-vegetable *khoresh*—all in real time. I would have loved to know why the Saudis were on the Atkins Diet (or perhaps it was South Beach), but Arsalan was as mystified as I was. One of them, he said, was a diplomat who had spent time in Washington, D.C.; perhaps he had learned about it there.

I asked him again who these Saudis were, exactly, and why he was hosting this dinner, and where had he learned to write such lovely English, but he neglected to answer, though he did tell me that he had fed the cat again, several times.

From: Arsalan arsalan@hotmail.com
Date: August 27, 2003 04:22 PM
To: Claire Berlinski claire@berlinski.com
Subject: Thank you

Wollef is contented. He eats everything he is served, licks his paws elaborately, cleans his whiskers, thanks me politely,

then goes to sleep. I have now to fetch the Saudis at the airport. I thank you deeply for your help; you were my angel
today.

ارسلان صفوی
دانشکده باستان شناسی
دانشگاه اصفهان

   After Arsalan left for the airport, I found myself at loose ends.
I had no plans for the evening, and so out of idle curiosity began
searching through some websites with news from Iran. I was surprised to learn what had been going on in his neighborhood while
he and his maid were devoting themselves to the banquet. Students, armed with assault rifles, had clashed that day with the military in the city of Semiram, near Isfahan. The regime's militiamen
had opened fire on the crowd. A photograph showed a street thick
with protesters, their faces covered by bandannas, forming a sea of
electrified—and totally insane—black eyes. They were running
and choking on tear gas. A police car had been set ablaze. Several people had been killed. My correspondent hadn't mentioned
that, and I wondered if he even knew. Again, I thought how
strange the Internet was. It was possible, I supposed, that I was
better informed of the happenings near his home that day than he
was.

· · ·

Unusually, Imran wrote to me from London at one in the morning
that night. I was still awake; I had been catching up on Iranian
politics.

From: Imran Begum imranbegum@gmail.com
Date: August 28, 2003 01:05 AM
To: Claire Berlinski claire@berlinski.com
Subject: A success!

Dear Old Friend,

It was all much easier than I thought! Lots of pretty girls. Mainly executives, twenty-two in all, open and good at conversing. My first date was named Caitlin. She was quite nervous. I suggested she focus on deep, steady, good breath and be very wary of all teas and coffees. Got to get the basics right before worrying about the unconscious. I knew immediately that I couldn't feel romantic about her, and thought at first I couldn't feel sexual toward her, either, but after two minutes I began to feel erotic stirrings. I didn't want to mislead her; she seemed a very decent person, so I was completely honest with her about feeling nothing romantic but having erotic stirrings. We discussed where we might go with that until the buzzer rang.

Next was Tara, a difficult woman. Loads of unresolved anger, very political, the sort of person who thinks that calling my patients "patients" instead of "clients" really "changes the power dynamic." She said she was a vegetarian, and when I told her I was quite interested in the role of vegetarianism in female depression and anxiety, she went right into a neurotic reaction. Three minutes seemed a frightfully long time.

But then I met Rebecca, an excellent conversationalist who shares my interest in Ralph Ellison, the new Roth, jazz scholarship, and the Fischer-Spassky chess match. Incompatible life plans, alas! Then Eleanor, who was lovely and intelligent and maternal. My concern about her was that after eighty seconds she started talking palmistry and homeopathy. I didn't react, just focused on listening. I didn't want to argue and create another separating experience.

Caroline was my next date. She and I had an excellent exchange about mind, body, soul, and self-concept. Her parents sounded fine, father highly anxious and keen to please, mother well medicated now, no more psychotic episodes or bipolar disorder. We even had our first row and came through admirably, listening well and compromising nicely. I may well be sufficiently different from her dad that we could make a go of it. I was impressed enough with her as a person that I truly wished I found her more attractive facially. I'm ambivalent about her; I checked her name, but now find myself 55–44 against another date.

(I wasn't sure *what* the remaining one percent was angling for.)

I wanted Jessica, a lively and emotionally adult actress, but sadly I was not wanted in the same way. She wants to be friends, though. She was gracious and prompt in her clarification, and I accepted with pleasure. I enjoyed our three minutes together so much that I was quite sorry to have to move on to Winkie, a rather hysterical girl who said she was looking for her soul mate. Relationships, I offered her, are hard enough without getting into advanced unrealism.

Finally there was Marianne, who needed to slay her father to become a full person—I told her not to feel guilty, just *get it done*. There's little more important in life. I take it very seriously and I hope one day she'll feel empowered to do the same. I had to do it with mum, of course. Painful, but the lesser of two evils. I was very impressed by her self-awareness, humility, reasonableness, and availability. She's also highly orgasmic, unlike Kirsten, whom I didn't tick off, even though she was posh, intelligent, and five-foot-eight—with *Déjeuner sur l'Herbe* tattooed on her lower back! But she didn't have the warmth I need.

All in all, *much* better than I expected. I ticked seven of them off. I would have been content to receive three friendship ticks and one romance tick, but with half the results now in, I've received three romance ticks already, including one from the überbabe of the evening, Helen the ice-swan sculptress! So I shall have three dates this week: Marianne, 33, for Tuesday supper; Helen, 31, on Wednesday, same time; and Caroline, 41, on Friday afternoon at 3:45. I feel proud to have taken the bull by the horns! I'm reading lots of Thackeray as well as a history of geology. And the cool weather is so lovely; I had all four car windows down today en route to my own therapy. Gerry Mulligan on the stereo, clear as freshly rinsed Baccarat champagne flutes drying in the sun next to a window with spring dawning outside!

Much love to you,

Immie

When I try to describe Imran to other people, they never believe me, but really, I'm not exaggerating. Once I had asked Imran why, precisely, he devoted such attention to his attire. "It's a narcissistic compensation," he explained, thoughtfully rubbing his lapel. "I've always hoped that if I dress carefully enough, women won't notice that in reality I'm a dark, hairy, Pakistani weirdo." The odd thing is that they rarely *did* notice; I guess that's what a green corduroy waistcoat will do for a man.

I checked my e-mail one last time before going to bed and was pleased to see that Arsalan had written.

From: Arsalan arsalan@hotmail.com
Date: August 28, 2003 02:20 AM
To: Claire Berlinski claire@berlinski.com
Subject: Once more, thank you

The banquet went well, all thanks to your advice. The fat Arabs ate every last scrap of the lamb and the eggplant. Alas, they did not touch the lentils, but I am certain this has nothing to do with your culinary suggestions. I mean no offense, but I must say this carbohydrate business is absurd. They are fat because they eat so much. One of my colleagues pulled me aside to praise me for the meal and for my "dignity under the circumstances." So a success, thank you. But I must inquire: Is it normal for a cat to eat so very much? Wollef is beginning to look a bit like a Gulf potentate himself. Though, unlike them, he is very quiet and polite now. He shows a sweet nature now that he is at ease. I begin to see why my mother was so attached to him. I wonder if he would enjoy the remaining lentil *pollo*? Do you think so? You were extremely kind to help, my gratitude is great, and perhaps tomorrow I will have time to discuss your romantic difficulties. Until then, sleep well, Claire.

ارسلان صفوی
دانشکده باستان شناسی
دانشگاه اصفهان

And that I did.

• • •

Arsalan wrote to me the next day about Jimmy. His letter was sympathetic. There had been a romance like that in his past too.

. . . I saw her last, the torment of my dreams, several years ago. It was a party in Teheran, and she arrived on the arm of some rotten pimp. I heard her say to all the fawning men what she had said to me so many times before—she was a poetess, she lived for poetry, without poetry for her life would have no meaning. Someone persuaded her to sing— "Sing, Layla, sing a song for our pleasure!" She required little coaxing. It was a song, she told us, that she herself had written. She began singing and did not stop. At last came the crescendo—*"My heart! My pain! My heart! My pain!"* When she finished, red and breathless from her exertion and entirely too moved by her own display, all the men applauded, much too loudly. "Another one," cried the pimp. A mean, clever girl standing beside me said, in a low voice but a voice loud enough for me to hear, "No, please. My heart can't take it anymore."

The candle flame went out; the wine spilt.

It seemed natural after this exchange of intimacies to begin writing to each other about anything and everything. We began exchanging letters, long ones and short, throughout the day as we worked. We discussed his mother's cat at great length. With each passing day, he grew more fascinated by Wollef.

. . . I have never had a pet before. You see, Claire, I have never known an animal well; my father was a very traditional man and did not allow us to keep animals in the home. But my mother was so tender hearted, a house of love with no limits. She found poor Wollef in a flowerpot, a damp small creature all alone in the world. She said that he cried for his mother with the very cry of a human baby. When she picked him up and comforted him he began to suckle on her finger, and this so aroused her fierce maternal instincts that she took him into her home and adopted him as her own. She could not help but nurture him; it was her nature, gentle and giving. She said always that Wollef had a complicated soul with many deep emotions, and I see now that she was right. He can smell my mother on the chair that was her favorite. He will sleep on it for hours until he wakes, looks about, and realizes she is not there, upon which his disappointment and grief are clear beyond all dispute. . . .

His letters were for the most part mournful. He too missed his mother. But he appreciated the distraction of our correspondence, or at least he often said he did. Imran later suggested to me that my display of culinary expertise might have persuaded him at some level to view me as a replacement for his mother; this, Imran imagined, may have been why he wrote to me so often. Perhaps. I couldn't really say. I wrote to *him* so often because it was a distraction from my work and because I found his letters charming; at least, that's the way I looked at it at the time.

Over the course of the next few days, I came to understand more about my correspondent's life. He was a member of Isfahan University's archaeology faculty, he told me; the fat Saudi donors were funding a dig that he was to supervise come wintertime, at Persepolis. And he wrote English well because it was his first language.

. . . I was born in Persia, but my childhood was passed in London, the grey city of exiles, and we also were such exiles. My mother's uncle, Claire, had been a parliamentarian, loyal to the Shah. But on my father's side I had a cousin, a misguided young man, a reckless dreamer who joined the MKO, which as you may not know was the People's Mujahedin, much feared and loathed by the Shah. On one day my young cousin was arrested by SAVAK. He was tortured brutally; I do not even wish even to tell you what they did to him for fear of troubling your sleep. My father's heart was broken into daggers, and his anger made him incautious. "The Shah is nothing but a sword pulled from a dog's ass!" he said to his colleague, forgetting for a moment the danger we all knew too well. Forgive me, Claire, for repeating those vulgar words; I mean no disrespect, but this is so you know how little was required to tear our lives apart.

That bald, jealous little imbecile before whom he spoke was a man with no honor, an informant. My father received word one morning from a friend that he was to be arrested that night. With no time to prepare we fled, hiding first in the house of friends and then, with their help in securing documents and a vehicle, escaping the country by motor. I was too young to understand. I was only sixteen months old. My mother carried me in her arms as my father drove from Iran to Turkey, Turkey to Yugoslavia, Yugoslavia to Venice, Venice to Calais, Calais to London. They brought nothing with them. *Don't cry, Maryam, don't cry*, my father said to my mother; *Our wind whereby we are moved and our being are of thy gift/our whole existence is from thy bringing into being.* But she cried nonetheless, my poor mother, my poor mother who was not made for a life of adventure, my poor mother who would have been content all her days to tend her rose garden in Isfahan. . . .

His family had not been rich. Although he had been a physician in Iran, his father could not practice medicine in England and so took a poorly paid job as a medical transcriber. The elegant Persian with the noble bearing had been demoralized by his loss of professional authority; he had been the last of a long line of distinguished physicians and was accustomed to deference. Arsalan did not say so explicitly, but I surmised from his description that theirs had been an aristocratic family. It had been difficult for them to adapt to life in a small flat in East London amid the bus drivers and the bricklayers. He had never felt at home in England.

. . . School for me there was beatings, fighting. Children hate someone who is different and I was different with my strange skin and my strange family and my home that smelled of spices. I became an inward child, contenting myself with books from my father's library. My father bought for me one day a book about archaeology. It was called *The Treasures of Ancient Mesopotamia*. The Lady of Warka was on the cover. Do you know the Lady of Warka, Claire? She is the Sumerian Mona Lisa. I read the book with enchantment, and it was then I began to dream of the life of adventure I would have as an archaeologist! It is silly now and embarrassing to tell you, but as a lonely child I pretended that I had discovered her, this mysterious Lady of Warka; I imagined cradling her in my arms as I rose from the site I had excavated. In my lonely child's mind I imagined telling the other children in school of my magnificent achievement. What envy and admiration they would feel!

He had met the news cheerfully, he wrote, when the Shah was deposed and his father announced that the family would return to Iran, a place, he imagined, where all the children would look like him. Our birthdays, we discovered, were two days apart, so like me, he was eleven years old when the Revolution came. When I read this, I remembered hearing about the Revolution on television; I remembered the hostage crisis and the yellow ribbons. But of course it had seemed to me then as distant as the moon.

His parents were ecstatic when at last his father came home with their airline tickets to Teheran.

. . . My mother was so unhappy in England. English women with faces like hungry dogs assumed she had no education, was a backward woman, because she covered her head. What they did not know is that even so their

English husbands stared and stared at her, calling out to her in the street. She was too beautiful to be given peace. This is why she covered herself—so that "no tainted eye shall gaze upon her face, no glass but that of an unsullied heart." She was not backward. She was highly educated, a sensitive woman. She knew poetry and music. She spoke French and English and Arabic and the most musical Persian. No one understood this. She was so lonely. She missed the markets and bazaars of her Isfahan, the groves of Seville oranges in blossom, the gardens of perfume and roses and babbling fountains, the sight of old persimmon trees in autumn. England was cold and wet and dark. For ten years, she had been lonely.

And my father—my father, Claire, had the fortune unlike me to be a devout man. Europe to him was a machine without a soul. He could not understand how men in England could wake each morning, day after day after day, to a universe without the mystery and grandeur of Islam. "What do they believe in here?" he asked us at night at the dinner table. "They kick a football about and they go to the pub, then they go to the doctor and complain that it hurts everywhere and nowhere, and they have no idea why."

I had no memories of Iran. I was too young when we left, but my parents had spoken of it in such a way that I believed it would be a paradise. I remember the dazzling sunlight at the airport, a white, brilliant light such as I had never imagined. But on the night we arrived we stayed in my cousin's home in Teheran, and I heard *"Allaho Akbar"* in the streets, and "Death to America!" I did not understand at all. For me America was Starsky and Hutch—brave heroes!—why did people here want them to die? I saw piles of sandbags in the streets, everywhere, and logos sprayed on the walls—a fist, a gun, a star, all in paint red like blood. I saw smoke. It was not how I had imagined it for so long. And soon, Claire, I learned that here too I was an exile. I did not speak Persian like the other children, and I did not understand the strange words that they used. Here, as in England, school was beating, taunting, fights.

Two years after we returned, my brother, who is older than me, was conscripted into the army. During the terrible bloody battle for Susangerd, which is in Khuzestan, he was gassed by the monster Saddam Hussein. He spent more than a year in hospital. Overnight my mother became an old woman. My brother suffered disfigurement in his face, and to this day he labors in his breathing. Most of the schoolboys of my age were sent to the front. I escaped this fate. My father, by then a disillusioned and heartbroken man, paid certain people to keep me out of the war. But these are sad things to talk about, Claire. . . .

Arsalan and I, we discovered, both had memories of celebrating our birthdays in May. But while his parents were fleeing for their lives, mine were pushing my stroller through the leafy suburbs of San Francisco. While teenaged boys in Iran were dying in the trenches I was living with my family in Seattle, where we had recently moved. I was preoccupied with my first love, Jude Kremer, a freshman at the University of Washington four years my senior, who grew huge *Cannabis indica* plants in a special greenhouse he'd kitted out with halide lights in his basement. While Saddam Hussein bombed Iranian cities and Arsalan's family lurched from hysteria to despair, Jude and I were stretched out on the lawn chairs on his porch at night, overlooking Lake Washington, smoking a fat one and listening to Grateful Dead bootlegs. We were both dimly aware of the Iran–Iraq War. But it certainly wasn't weighing heavily on our minds.

Our letters tread delicately around the American invasion of Iraq.

. . . You must understand what we suffered when Saddam Hussein, curse him, rained missiles on Iraq . . . there was such a fear, a panic that never abated. The missiles could land anywhere—on women, on children, on your neighbor's house—or maybe on yours. The sky would crackle— you could see the missile coming and hear it! But where would it come down? Who would it kill this time, who would be left without a mother or a son? One of my classmates, Claire, a little boy named Hossein with whom I played games in the street, was crippled forever—his leg neatly sliced off—and his brother and mother were crushed to death by falling concrete. I remember seeing his house and the broken glass, the cracked walls, the front door blown to the middle of the kitchen—the blood everywhere, barely dry. His father died a madman. To this day, I confess to you, I cannot bear the sound of fireworks.

Saddam Hussein was a demon. To the donkeys and fools who say he had no weapons of mass destruction, I say: Do not say this to my brother's face! But now the Iraqis too know what it is like to feel the hail of missiles, and has their suffering lessened his?

Your military, Claire, is careless. I do not wish to insult you, but I must say this. They are careless with the present and careless with the past. When the museum in Baghdad was destroyed, I wept. . . .

He wrote of the museum more than once. He was appalled by the American military's failure to protect the priceless archaeological treasures at the Iraqi National Museum. Of course he was: he was an archaeologist. He took artifacts seriously.

In one letter, he told me of his awe as he stood above the Burnt City at dawn:

. . . I looked down to the oblong rooms I had excavated. I saw the graves, the bones, the stone dishes, the pottery that had shattered. I reached down and picked up a fragment of a woman's comb. Everything about these people, their beliefs and their thoughts, their feelings—all had disappeared. No one even knew they existed until I came.

Oh, Claire! It was magnificent. This was the largest city in the world at the dawn of the urban era. This was an advanced culture, so advanced. It was the meeting point of the great civilizations of Mesopotamia, India, and China.

Did you know, Claire, that on my last dig there, I uncovered the earliest evidence of brain surgery?

When I expressed my surprise—I had never even heard of the Burnt City, to my embarrassment—he sent me the link to the paper he had published about it in the *Athena Review*. Reading his byline, I realized that he had been modest about his career: he was the leading Iranian authority on the third millennium BC and the author of a three-volume history of Mesopotamia.

It's not unusual to encounter someone who has lived through events like those of his childhood, but it *is* unusual to encounter someone who can recount them in one's own language. I'm sure the Vietnamese woman who sold spring rolls at the dingy Asian cafeteria down the street from me in Paris had stories every bit as dramatic to tell, but when I asked her about them, the linguistic barriers between us had proved insuperable. After trying and failing to make herself understood in broken French, she had resorted to sign language, making a slicing motion across her throat.

I grew more bold in my questions. What, I asked, did he think of the Iranian Revolution now? I wasn't sure whether he would reply, but his answer was frank:

. . . I am of many emotions, mostly sad and angry ones, but I am not like the Iranians who believe life was very beautiful under the Shah. When people learn that I was once in London, sometimes they make a little speech. "Oh, I've

been to London, it was in 1351! I went there with my wife
and my children for Norooz! I even remember Hyde Park!
One pound was twelve Tomans at that time; you could
spend money so easily, and now? It's 1600 Tomans! What a
pity, you see this beautiful city, center of art and culture of
the East, what's happened here? They've ruined things!
Before, people were happy, they had good lives, easy lives,
then the Revolution, the war . . . now everyone's nervous, people don't even smile . . . Before, an Iranian was an
important person, when we went to London, everybody
spread red carpets before us when we told them we were
Iranians, but now, when you say you're Iranian, what
comes to their minds are mullahs and terrorism. They've
taken away all our credit in the world." They say this and
I nod politely, but I remember that not long after we arrived in London we received word that my cousin had been
tortured to death. My mother wept for weeks when we
learned the news. . . .

I asked him next what he thought of the protesters on the
streets of Iran demanding democracy, but to this question he
didn't respond. I did not ask again. Perhaps, I thought, he felt it
unwise to commit those thoughts to paper. That certainly would
have been understandable. Instead, I asked him if he'd ever
thought of returning to the West.

. . . Yes, Claire, I was offered a fellowship at the School of
Oriental and African Studies once in London. But I did not
take it. The Soviet empire had collapsed, and students
were demonstrating in China. I dreamed the whole world
would change. My country would change with it.
    Perhaps I missed that chance. But I am not a political
man; I am a man who sifts through time. There is no better place in the world to be an archaeologist than Iran. It is

my home, and it is my ancestors' home. I would not want to sit in the coffeehouses in London mourning the Peacock Throne with the exiled ghouls who introduce themselves with their old titles: "Sohrab Kadivar, Minister of the Navy!"

I am not English. I will never be English. So, what to say. I am an outsider everywhere. In Iran, at least, there is black tea, and the smell of frankincense, and flat bread with feta cheese and fresh herbs. Everyone here knows Hafez and Rumi and Sa'di. From my window I see the minarets of Isfahan.

It is not the best of all possible worlds. Nor is it the worst.

It seems hard to believe now, but not once did it cross my mind in those early days—not consciously, at any rate—to think of our correspondence as a romance. It was an odd friendship, one made entertaining and pleasurable for me by his combination of obvious intelligence and his exoticism, but I thought of him as a confessor and a curiosity, not as a lover, and it did not seem to me urgently important to know exactly what he looked like, or even to imagine what it would be like to meet him in the flesh.

It was just a way to pass the time, and it beat working.

CHAPTER THREE

This looks like an insider's account.

—ROBERT BAER,
former CIA case officer, about *Loose Lips*

If you live in Paris, sooner or later all of your friends show up. Charlene showed up the next weekend, prancing through the towering mahogany-and-bronze doors of the Hotel Meurice, laden with shopping bags and babbling into her cell phone. "I gotta go; my friend's already here," she said to the phone, then snapped it shut. "Claire! I can't believe you *live* in this gorgeous city!"

To judge from the hotel she was staying in, Coca-Cola was treating my friend well. The lobby had recently been remodeled in the style of the Napoleonic Empress Eugénie's ballroom. Overlooking the Tuileries, the Meurice had been the headquarters of

the Gestapo during the Occupation. Doors were opened and ciga-
rettes lit for guests as if General von Choltitz still ran the show.

Charlene was in Paris for a bottling conference. She had joined
Coca-Cola's international marketing division soon after losing her
job at the CIA; eventually Coke had posted her to Eastern Europe,
where she thrived. Soon she was running the marketing operations
of Coca-Cola Bottlers in Slovenia, and recently she had been promoted to a senior position in the Czech Republic. She had called
me that morning to tell me that she was in town. Was I free for
lunch? Of *course* I was.

Usually, people who visit Paris want to see the Louvre and the
Champs Elysées, but Charlene had other plans: she wanted to go
to the African fish market in the Eighteenth Arrondissement. "It's
the world capital of hair weaves." She left her bags with one of the
cowed employees at the front desk and took me by the arm, babbling excitedly in her scattershot, distracted fashion about the fabric samples she'd bought for her curtains, the men she was dating,
and the way there was *nothing* wrong with the bottling plant in
Belgium, the toxicology reports had come back *totally* negative, it
was all *completely* psychosomatic, but you just try convincing these
hysterical Europeans of that. I barely said a word.

I'd never been to the fish market and was amazed when we
stepped out of the Métro and found ourselves in a neighborhood
that looked the way I imagined Senegal would, only noisier and
more crowded. Even the drug dealers were dressed in dashikis and
headdresses. In the back-alley shops the fortune tellers and the
Sangomas were throwing bones. Charlene was delighted to discover she could buy bootleg cassettes of Papa Wemba and
M'Pongo Love—as well as an authentic sanza hand piano—from
the old African men who materialized on the street corners the
second the police van was out of eyeshot and dematerialized just as
quickly when it came back. A fishmonger named Mama Osibisa
answered Charlene's questions about how to prepare the foufou
from Cameroon, and she told us we could sample the second-best

in Paris if we went to the restaurant without a name down the street. It had a secret door; she told us to look for the leopard curtains.

The restaurant was just where Mama Osibisa said it would be. Canvas sacks of plantains, okra, and weird root vegetables that I'd never seen before were stacked up in huge piles on the stairs leading to the dining room in the cellar; its tiny tables were lit with kerosene lanterns. The cook was shouting at a monkey scampering among the rum bottles over the counter: "*Fou le camp*, Dr. Nkrumah!" The room was tiny but packed with drunken customers singing along to the Zouk music from the jukebox. A stout woman dressed in a *grande boubou* brought a plastic bucket of silver baby sharks into the kitchen, carrying them on her head.

After we ordered, I gave Charlene a brief sitrep on Jimmy. When I got to the part about Jimmy telling me that my love didn't nurture, she said, "Well, don't *you* have a talent for finding men who're dumber than a sack of hair." The foufou arrived at the table. "Never mind him," she said. "Who are you seeing now?" When I told her I wasn't seeing anyone, she was horrified. "Do you mean to tell me you just sit in front of your computer *all day long*?"

We took the Métro back to the Tuileries, then walked through the garden and over the Seine. As we walked she told me about a Slovenian gymnastics medalist with whom she'd just spent a particularly acrobatic weekend, "and, honey, would you just *look* at this beautiful view!" She stood at the edge of the Pont des Arts, throwing her arms wide with delight. "It looks just like the movies!"

It did, too.

Since we weren't far away, I suggested we take tea at Mariage Frères. "Sure, my treat," she said. "I'll put it on the card and tell Coca-Cola we were discussing the size of your refrigerator. Did you know we had to withdraw our two-liter bottles from Spain because their fridges are too small? *Can you imagine?*" I wondered if

I could fit a two-liter bottle in my own refrigerator; I doubted it. "But we're still beating Pepsi like a rented mule," she added re-assuringly, misinterpreting my expression. "Oh, would you *look* at this!"

We'd arrived at the tea shop. Most of the tables were filled by Japanese tourists dressed in the latest absurd Issey Miyake collection. In the corner sat a deathly pale man in a silk smoking jacket and slippers, with a stuffed parrot on his shoulder, slowly waving a silk-screened fan. We both tried not to stare.

There were more than five hundred varieties of tea according to the menu, which was printed in a turn-of-the-century typeface and designed to look like an expensive private wine list. Each tea had an exotic name—Cloud Temple, Himalayan Pavilion—and an exotic story: Full Moon tea, for example, was inspired by the heavenly bodies and the realm of dreams, and it was—I quote—a *moon-beam* of a tea, a poetic blend combining fragrances evoking the feast of the full moon, an enrapturing bouquet of bergamot oil, rare Laotian spices, and a touch of Mirabelle plum from the north of France.

The waiters wafted by with steaming pots and silver trays of golden madeleines. One of them presented himself at our table with a slight bow. *"Mesdames?"* I ordered the first tea on the menu, the Darjeeling Nouveau (an exceptional limited edition pressing, apparently, from the first harvest of the garden of Ambootia), and a crème brûlée infused with the Solitary Poet's Tea of Tibet. The waiter nodded gravely and turned to Charlene. *"Et vous, Madame?"*

"I'll have a Coke," she said. The waiter fixed Charlene with a dismal gaze, but when she met his eyes and stared him down he lost his nerve and shuffled off with a dejected *"Oui, Madame."*

As we waited for our refreshments we chatted about both members of the Slovenian jet set, fabric samples for her curtains, and the latest gossip from the CIA. "Now, how do we get you back into circulation?" Charlene asked. "You could take out an ad on the Internet, you know. My sister met a really sweet fella that way."

I wasn't sure about that—Samantha's accounts of Internet dating certainly weren't the best advertisement for it. I told her about my friendship with Samantha and her forays onto Nerve.com. Charlene was fascinated when I recounted Samantha's adventures, but she couldn't figure out why I trusted her. "If she lies to all these people, how do you know she's not lying to you, too?" she asked. "Maybe she's really a man pretending to be a woman pretending to be a man? The Internet is full of lying freaks."

I thought this was a bit rich, coming from someone who used to live under cover and lie for a living herself. I shrugged. "How can I be sure you're not still in the CIA? Maybe you just said they fired you so you could go under *really* deep cover."

"Yeah, right. Seriously, I don't get it. Don't you at least want to meet this Samantha person before you tell her all this intimate stuff?"

"What difference would it make? I write to lots of people without having met them."

"You *do*?"

"Sure. Why not?" I told her about Arsalan, and his lovely descriptions of Isfahan and the Burnt City.

"An *Iranian* guy? You live in the City of Lights, the most romantic city in the world, and you're playing footsie with some *Iranian* guy over the Internet?"

"I'm not playing footsie; I just write to him."

"How often?"

"Now and again."

"*Now and again?* You just described every street, bridge, and mousehole in Isfahan. You need to go on a date. A real one." For a moment, she was distracted by the man with the stuffed parrot on his shoulder, who for no obvious reason began flapping his fan wildly around his head. "Honey, what did you say that place was again? Bird City?"

"The *Burnt* City." To change the subject, I asked her if she'd ever heard what happened to her old boyfriend, the one she thought had reported her to security.

"I really like to think," she said, licking a bit of tea-scented crème brûlée from her varnished fingernail, then sipping the last drops from the cup of tea I had convinced her to try—a blend called Opium Hill, a rose and ginger "meditation," according to the menu, cultivated in a Tibetan monastery and transported to Paris via caravan—"that he's freezing his constipated ass off in some cave in Afghanistan, worrying about his promotion panel and eating a yak bladder."

• • •

Samantha had sent me links to the profiles of the women with whom she was corresponding: There was Vertigo, who thought strong, soft, wet lips were sexy, but feeling them on her own strong, soft, wet lips was sexier, and Missbehave, who wrote that the five items she couldn't live without were trust, love, and kindness. (She lived fine without the ability to count beyond three, apparently.) Vertigo hadn't answered the question about the last good book she'd read, and Samantha suspected this was because she had never read one. Missbehave had written that it was *Five Simple Steps to Emotional Healing*.

Over the past few weeks, however, Samantha had also been writing to a woman on Nerve.com named Lynne, and her interest in Lynne, she confessed to me, was more than anthropological. Lynne, according to her profile, had just finished John Blofeld's *City of Lingering Splendour: A Frank Account of Old Peking's Exotic Pleasures*. Her photograph showed a woman of an almost consumptive pallor with a high, curved forehead and a slightly weak chin. But it was her eyes that had captured Samantha's imagination. Samantha kept above her computer a reproduction of a 1765 pen-and-ink sketch of Voltaire at his writing desk. Lynne's eyes, Samantha thought, looked remarkably like Voltaire's. I had looked at them myself: they were pitch-black and small, like nuggets of coal.

. . . and, Claire, Lynne's letters are even cleverer than her eyes. Do you know what she told me this morning? She told me that deaf people with Tourette's syndrome tic in sign language! Isn't that fascinating? . . .

The two women had been corresponding for several weeks, although only one of them realized that they were both women; the other thought she was writing to a man. Lynne lived in a cabin near Big Sur, so they had not yet met. Although it was the logical next step, Samantha found herself hesitant to propose a meeting. She feared that in person, Lynne would either be what she seemed to be, or she wouldn't—and in the first case, she would meet an enormously desirable woman who desired *her*, but only as the man she was not; in the latter, she would meet yet another woman who disappointed her.

A message from Samantha was waiting for me when I returned from my day with Charlene. She was wondering if perhaps the connection between her and Lynne might be strong enough for Lynne to overcome her heterosexuality.

. . . lots of women surprise themselves by falling in love with other women. I didn't realize I was a lesbian at all until I was in college. It only became clear to me when one night I had a dream that I was sitting at the breakfast table in my bathrobe, drinking tea with Martha Nussbaum.

Arsalan was writing to me when he should have been working. I was writing to Samantha when I should have been working. Samantha was writing to Lynne when she should have been working. "What would a *real* love letter from her be like?" Samantha wondered. She had not written a word of her book that day, she complained: "I'm still in my pajamas. I'm a loser and I hate myself."

Of course, it's not as if busy people with more active jobs are immune to rogue fantasies and vagrant infatuations. Imran, the busiest man I'd ever known, had also met a woman who seemed to him exceptional. He had known Larissa for only three minutes and one dinner date—he had met her on his second speed-dating session—but according to the e-mail he had sent me while I was out with Charlene, she was

> . . . a dream come true, and we're going forward. I'm so ex-
> cited and lovestruck. I can imagine her pregnant and wad-
> dling around the kitchen. No problem parents, they're
> both dead.

I was glad to hear him sound so happy, but astounded—and slightly worried—by his tone. I'd never heard him say anything quite like that; this was *Imran*, after all, who generally discussed the categories of love with the taxonomic precision of an Eskimo discussing snow. "The word *love*," he had written to me not so very long ago,

> . . . should not even be applied to the emotions experienced
> by people in the honeymoon stage of a relationship, which
> can last up to eighteen months and tends to last six to nine.
> The correct terms are sexual attraction, projection, fantasy,
> fixation, idealization, and infatuation.

I suppose knowing the weaknesses of the human psyche is no proof against succumbing to them, which is why analysts are themselves obliged to undergo analysis. I hoped his therapist was on top of this situation; I certainly didn't want to be the one to rain on his projected, fixated parade.

Everyone I knew, in fact—Charlene excepted—seemed to be experiencing a degree of detachment from the Reality Principle. Arsalan was increasingly convinced that he was communicating intimately with his mother's cat: "It's a pity I don't know more about

Mesopotamian cat iconography. Wollef and I would have such interesting things to talk about." He had come to think of Wollef as somewhat mentally retarded, as cats go. The cat reliably tripped over his own paws whenever he attempted to jump up to the counter, and he took no interest in grooming himself properly, wandering about blithely with milk-matted fur and crumbs in his whiskers.

. . . But we have had an exciting morning, Wollef and I! A small bird flew in through the open window! Wollef is no athlete and succeeded only in frightening the thing half to death. I spoke to Wollef sharply—"Wollef, *let it go*!" Then I caught the poor little bird myself and released it. Wollef has since been sulking. He is on my lap now, remonstrating with me for ruining his fun.

As for your question, Wollef is not a Persian name and moreover could not be a Persian name; we do not have a "w" in Persian. The name was my mother's confused corruption of the word "wally." Perhaps you know what this rude word means, and for using it I am sorry. Once I had returned from school as a child, calling one of my classmates this word which I had just learned. My mother enquired what the word meant. I feared I would be reprimanded for my coarse word, so cunningly I replied that it meant "a very sweet and well-behaved child." My mother was never the wiser and from that day called anything small and dear to her a "wollef."

I did, in fact, know what that rude word meant. But I gathered that if the cat objected to being called a wanker, he never let on.

* * *

A few days after my lunch with Charlene, Arsalan asked me if I knew how to clip a cat's toenails.

. . . I believe my mother did this, but he refuses to submit himself to the procedure. Still, I am sure it must be done. He resembles now a Chinese dowager empress. This morning I discovered him honing his claws still further on my mother's carpet, a Mashad of great artistry with a rare peacock motif.

I wondered if he was referring to the carpet I'd admired in the photograph on his website. I remembered that I had thought the carpet unusually beautiful. I went back to the site to look at it again. A new link had been added at the top of the page. The text was in Persian. I clicked on it. It took me to the most recent issue of an obscure online archaeology journal. One of the articles, in English, concerned a dig at the Burnt City. It was illustrated with a photograph. The photograph, according to the caption, had been taken six months ago.

The snapshot was overexposed, and the details weren't entirely clear. Shovels, brushes, sieves, and buckets surrounded a square pit in the desert, cordoned off with tape. In the background, white sunlight poured down upon a dusty landscape dotted with scrubby bushes. A tall man in his late thirties, lean but powerfully built, dressed in faded jeans and a white cotton shirt rolled up at the sleeves, was standing with one foot in the excavation site. He was cradling a goblet in one hand and holding a measuring tape against it with the other. He was covered in dust. Everything was covered in dust.

According to the caption, this man was Arsalan.

But the face in the photograph wasn't at all the mournful face I had imagined. It was the face of a diamond smuggler, or an insubordinate but supremely courageous World War II flying ace—a vibrant, swashbuckling face.

He had deep lines around his eyes, as if he had spent years in the sun, and the kind of lean musculature that men develop when they work outdoors all day. His features were Persian, no doubt:

his long nose and his expressive, hooded eyes reminded me of certain Moghul paintings I'd seen in books—paintings of emperors and palace guards, scenes of royal intrigue. Clearly he had the blood of Darius and Xerxes in his veins. But there was something European in his manner: he had wild, long curly hair, but no beard or mustache. His posture and expression were assured and confident.

I stared at his eyes for a very long time.

He was aptly named, I thought. There was something leonine in his broad shoulders, and in that thick wild mane of hair, and in the powerful way he carried himself.

When I saw his photograph, I began to think of him as I think of him to this day.

As the Lion.

T W O

ISTANBUL

In every psychoanalytic treatment of a neurotic patient, the strange phenomenon that is known as "transference" makes its appearance. The patient, that is to say, directs towards the physician a degree of affectionate feeling (mingled, often enough, with hostility) which is based on no real relation between them and which—as is shown by every detail of its emergence—can only be traced back to old wishful fantasies of the patient's which have become unconscious.

—SIGMUND FREUD

CHAPTER FOUR

As others have pointed out, it is fairly evident that Ms. Berlinski
had some "inside" information on the training of CIA agents . . .

—Customer review
of *Loose Lips* on Amazon.com

I was in Istanbul—and sleepless—because I no longer loved Paris.

"There is nothing wrong with you," the Lion had written. "You have been there for years. Even the most exciting place grows old with time, and Paris has grown old without remaining exciting. I suggest a new adventure."

Several hours later, he wrote to me again.

From: Arsalan arsalan@hotmail.com
Date: September 20, 2003 05:11 PM
To: Claire Berlinski claire@berlinski.com
Subject: Fw: Housing Exchange, Istanbul–Paris

Here is an idea to cure your restlessness. This gentleman was my dissertation supervisor at Tehran University. He is highly upright, scholarly, and tidy. May I suggest you entertain the notion of his offer?

——Original Message——

Date: 20 Sep 2003 12:06 PM
From: "Prof. H. R. Mostarshed"
Sender: TURKISH-ARCHAEOLOGY-INFO mailing list
Reply-To: "Prof. H. R. Mostarshed"
Subject: Housing Exchange, Istanbul–Paris
Comments:

Dear Colleagues,

I am seeking a two-month Paris–Istanbul housing exchange. I will be in France during October and November for archival research. My Istanbul apartment is large, with bath, office, kitchen, furnished, two balconies, one of which overlook Bosphorus view. The neighborhood is on the Europe side. Please write for more information and strong references.

Best regards,

Dr. H. R. Mostarshed, President of TOCSED
University of Tehran, Tehran, Iran
Visiting Professor of Archaeology
Department of Ancient Cultures and Languages
Istanbul Boğaziçi Üniversitesi

"Istanbul?" I wrote to Arsalan. "What's that like?"

"You would not write to me again that you are bored, my Claire, that I promise."

One Dr. Mostarshed wrote to me that evening. My apartment was just what he had been looking for, he said; the Place Dauphine was his favorite location in Paris, and Arsalan his favorite student. We determined that I would leave my keys with Monsieur Tubert. Dr. Mostarshed would leave his with the kebab restaurant beneath his apartment. He sent me detailed instructions for the care of his cactus, the special way his front door was to be locked, and what to do if the electricity went out.

I was on a plane one week later.

Strange sounds of Turkish on the plane. From the air, my first thrilling sight of the Bosphorus. Crowds pushing and jostling at the luggage carousel. A terrifying ride in a decrepit smoke-filled taxi, the driver weaving madly in and out of traffic. At last, Dr. Mostarshed's apartment—spacious, as promised, with a view of hills, water, domes, minarets.

A thrashing, maniacal bass guitar, wildly out of tune.

I set down my luggage in the bedroom and opened the window. Vibrations rattled the artifacts on the bookshelf. Where was that noise coming from? I looked out the other window and saw a large industrial building with a neon sign that read *MUSIK*. Was it some kind of recording studio? There were four more buildings like it within eyesight, each with the same sign.

Dr. Mostarshed hadn't mentioned *that*.

I closed the window again and lay down on the bed to test it. Immediately I heard a spooky cry, and then another. I had known that Muslims pray five times a day, of course, but I'd never known so much electric amplification was involved. Voice after voice joined the chorus. The bass guitar held its own, mingling with the muezzin and with traffic noise—Turkish drivers, it seemed, labored under the impression that the clutch and the horn must be used in tandem.

The guitar and the horns kept up throughout the evening, punctuated by outbursts of high-decibel piety, almost but not quite drowning out the sound of children kicking a soccer ball against the wall of Dr. Mostarshed's building while shouting at one another and blowing a traffic whistle. Hammering. Tapping. Drilling—from the apartment next door. Men bellowing at the tops of their lungs in the street. Every few minutes—car alarms. Jackhammers. Gulls shrieking. Cats in the alleyway mating and howling. A truck rattling over the cobblestones, blaring Turkish from a loudspeaker.

The sound on my computer, letting me know I had mail.

"Have you found everything you might need?" Arsalan asked the morning after my arrival.

I didn't answer him. I could barely keep my eyes open.

■ ■ ■

From: Arsalan arsalan@hotmail.com
Date: September 30, 2003 01:15 PM
To: Claire Berlinski claire@berlinski.com
Subject: Re: Groceries?

Yes, there is a famous open-air fruit and fish market up the hill, at Galatasaray, and surely too a small shop where you might purchase your coffee and milk. There is an excellent Persian bakery and confectionery down the hill by the Galata Tower. You should find the tower easily; it dominates the skyline. It was built by Genoese conquerors and used to send fire signals. This was part of a communication system devised by the Romans and inherited by the Byzantines. Should you pass by the bakery, do say hello to the baker, my friend Hossein, and sample his pistachio baklava. Even my mother agreed it to be of her exacting standards. Tell him you are my friend. Of course, you will wish to go to the Egyptian market for your spices. That is a wonderful morning's excursion, though you must be on the alert for pickpockets, I am afraid. I am sorry Dr. Mostarshed did not think to leave basic provisions for you; that was inhospitable of him.

I set out to buy groceries, wandering through the zigzagging, soot-covered alleyways around Dr. Mostarshed's apartment. Laundry and political pendants, strung on lines between apartments, flapped in the breeze; gulls swooped and laughed, playing in the rooftop gardens and balconies that overflowed with tangled vines and plants stuck not in planters but in disused drums of sunflower and olive oil.

I lost my way within minutes. I wandered through the twisting streets, passing *nargile* cafés full of Turks lounging on cushions, drinking tea from tiny cups with stained-glass patterns, drawing lazily on hookahs. The air was heavy with the smell of fruity tobacco. At last I found my way to the Bosphorus. The light in Istanbul wasn't bright or clear. It was as if the city had been shot in black and white. The edges of the mosques and minarets across the water seemed to fade slightly into the sky, as if smudged with a thick brush.

The Bosphorus itself was turquoise, teeming with massive, slow-moving quadruple-decker cruise ships, cargo vessels, fishing boats that sailed under a massive concrete bridge lined from end to end with fishermen, who cast their rods and reels into the Bosphorus and pulled them back glittering with fish. So many lines had been cast over the side that the bridge looked like some elaborate stringed instrument. Hawkers by the water were selling nuts and figs and bright red apples from horse-drawn carts; waiters tried to coax me into their restaurants, gesturing grandly at the fish displayed in their storefronts. The air smelled of charcoal fires, lignite, car exhaust, grilling meat, fog, fish, the sea. Cars honked, people shouted, motorbikes weaved in and out of traffic. I stood on the corner for nearly ten minutes, waiting for the traffic to stop. At last, a child of about eight came up to me, took my hand, and helped me across. "Where you from?" he asked.

"America."

"Very dangerous country!"

As I walked the crowds grew dense; the sky darkened. Faces surged by me—dark faces, light ones, broad flat Mongol faces, faces with high chubby cheeks, faces with magnificent thick mustaches; Turkish schoolgirls in seductive schoolgirl outfits, with short skirts and knee socks; fat women in *hijab*, their weight shifting slowly from hip to hip as they walked; Japanese tourists; a curvaceous round-hipped woman in a tight skirt, swaying on high heels, with her hair tucked modestly under a scarf. I saw heads reminiscent of paintings on Etruscan pottery, the caricatured hooked nose everywhere, the grape-black hair and cruel, dark eyes—eyebrows high and arched, lids round and sensual and languorous—but then I saw astonishing ebony-flecked blue eyes, peering out below eyebrows that were fierce and closely knit and feral.

I had forgotten to look for groceries.

Navigating by the looming tower, I walked home through a neighborhood of narrow streets and tea shops, where elderly men wearing caps sat on stools, smoking one cigarette after another under portraits of Atatürk, playing backgammon, their faces cracked and sunbeaten. A pack of young men stood on a corner, shouting at one another, surrounding a skinny fellow turning over cards from a deck. Everywhere men were hauling, pushing, carting, hammering things—there was construction everywhere, but the purpose of the construction was unclear, since nothing appeared renovated. I found the bakery Arsalan had recommended, or what remained of it. It was boarded up. It appeared to have long since been gutted by a fire.

That evening, I wrote long letters about what I'd seen to my friends.

From: Arsalan arsalan@hotmail.com
Date: October 1, 2003 04:15 AM
To: Claire Berlinski claire@berlinski.com
Subject: Re: Re: Re: Re: Re: Re: Impressions of Istanbul

That is the legacy of the Ottoman Empire, Claire. The faces of Istanbul are not Turkish only; they are Kurdish, Balkan, Azeri, Turkmen, Armenian, Anatolian, Persian, Avar, Qashqa'i, Arab, Bulgar, Pecheneg, Bosnian, Hungarian, Venetian, Pisan, Amalfitan, Genoese, Romanian, Albanian, Macedonian, Cretan, Bashkir, Georgian, Lâz, Circassian, Kazakh, Uzbek, Uighur. So you see blue eyes like that, perhaps, because some Anatolian village was sacked by a band of pillaging Cossacks who left behind nothing but their genes.

From: Imran Begum imranbegum@gmail.com
Date: October 1, 2003 06:45 AM
To: Claire Berlinski claire@berlinski.com
Subject: Re: Impressions of Istanbul

Sounds nice. Glad you are so excited. Very busy and happy with Larissa! Breathe deep and hydrate well. Love, Immie.

From: Samantha Allen allens@aol.com
Date: October 1, 2003 01:45 AM
To: Claire Berlinski claire@berlinski.com
Subject: Re: Istanbul

I'm off for the weekend—I'm going up to Big Sur to meet Lynne! xxxSam.

My mother didn't think Istanbul sounded safe. My father evinced only slightly greater interest. "Very much occupied with prebiotic chemistry," he wrote. "An absolutely extraordinary subject. Almost finished with the origins of life."

• • •

From: Arsalan arsalan@hotmail.com
Date: October 2, 2003 09:10 AM
To: Claire Berlinski claire@berlinski.com
Subject: Re: Istanbul

Claire, I am very pleased that you are so loving Istanbul. I love it too. I trust you have at least found groceries this morning? If you cannot find coffee to your European tastes in your neighborhood, you will surely find it in the bazaar behind the Yeni Mosque. If you visit in the morning, the crowds will not be too great. You will then be near the neighborhood of Fener, should you be curious to see elements of old Istanbul life that have vanished elsewhere in the city.

Fener, by the way, is where my friend Hossein the baker lived. Am I foolish to be concerned for him? He was most kind to my mother when she visited me during my sabbatical in Istanbul, and although fortune has robbed him of his position he is an educated, sensitive man who was before the Revolution a jurist. His bearing somewhat reminded me, I must say, of my late father. He invited me once to his home, where his wife cooked for me an excellent Persian meal. A difficult life for such a man. I cannot imagine how he would support his family without his bakery. Perhaps, if you do pass through Fener, you would look for his lavender-colored house, at the very highest block of Sadrazam Ali Pasa Caddesi, and tell me whether that at least remains?

And should you be interested in such sights only rarely seen by tourists, may I also recommend to you a visit by ferry to Eyüp? It is the site of Istanbul's holiest mosque, named after the Prophet's companion, who led an army to the city gates. His defeat gave rise to myriad eschatological prophecies concerning the significance of Constantinople's fall. This is why Mehmet the Conqueror, Selim the Inexorable, and Süleyman the Magnificent all believed they were the Messianic king who would unite the world and its religions beneath their aegis. . . .

Think, in this batter'd Caravanserai
Whose Portals are alternate Night and Day,
How Sultan after Sultan with his Pomp
Abode his destined Hour, and went his way.

Do let me know, when you return, what you have seen; I take great pleasure in seeing Istanbul again through your eyes—

Arsalan

I could see the Yeni Mosque from Dr. Mostarshed's window. I set out down the hill to find the market and its European coffee, for, as I had complained to Arsalan, Turkish coffee had proved a bitter disappointment. Before the wide steps of the mosque, men were bathing their feet in a fountain at the center of a courtyard surrounded by a forest of domes. Behind, in the bazaar, the alleys burst with restaurants and tea houses, covered in vines and open to the street, tables stuck outdoors along the alleys at odd angles. Men in the tea shops threw backgammon dice; televisions played in the background, all tuned to different stations, all blaring at top volume, the radio thrown in for good measure, all drowned out from time to time by wails of prayer from the loudspeakers of the mosques. Each intersection branched into more alleys bursting with shops. *Come in, lady, yes, good price!*—silver, turquoise, tea sets, silks, jeweled cushions, glazed Turkish pottery in azure and crimson—*Where you from, lady? Where you from?*—dates, figs, dried apricots, baklava with walnuts, small cakes of batter fried and soaked in syrup, semolina, *helva*—*Come drink some tea with me my friend!*—Vizier's fingers, rose jam, almonds, pistachios, pine nuts—*Please taste, just one taste!*—tins of caviar, scoops of spiced eggplant, vine leaves—*Lady, just come in one moment!*—spangled cushions, beaded curtains, lanterns, hookahs, candle holders—*Just to look, lady, please, no pressure!*—pyramids of flame-colored spices, of currants and cumin—*Come in, yes, you drink some tea!*—*Lady, come in*—*LADY, YOU COME IN NOW!*

I realized after purchasing my coffee that I was on the street Arsalan had mentioned. As I climbed the hill the neighborhood swiftly changed. The shops thinned out, replaced by gutted, collapsing wooden houses. Idle groups of loitering men stared at me in silence. Unwashed children played outside. I climbed up the narrow, winding street until I reached what seemed to be the highest block. The neighborhood was in a state of shambling ruin. There were buildings in something like a Victorian style, topped by onion domes, decorated with ornate iron gratings and metalwork, but they sagged in ruined weariness as if exhausted from carrying the weight of history—paint flaking, ironwork rusted and twisted and mad. They looked as if they'd gratefully finish collapsing if given so much as a gentle nudge.

Women in headscarves squatted over camp stoves, grilling corn and meat, sending plumes of charcoal smoke into the air. A young girl of perhaps nine with a hooked nose and wild staring eyes was beating a carpet in front of a lavender-gray house. I cast a glance down the staircase behind her. The interior of the house was filthy and wretched, a dank cave, poorly ventilated, with half a dozen dirty mattresses on the floor. It was lit only by a naked light bulb swinging from the ceiling.

"Hossein?" I said to her, and then added, uselessly, "a baker?"

She looked at me fearfully, then dashed inside.

• • •

From: Claire Berlinski claire@berlinski.com
Date: October 4, 2003 08:15 PM
To: Arsalan arsalan@hotmail.com
Subject: Re: Turkish

Oh yes, I've been trying. I bought a copy of *Teach Yourself Turkish* and I've been reading it, but the grammar is quite intimidating. I do like the way it sounds, but it might as well be Vulcan for all I understand. Can you recommend a better book, maybe? I so hate having to point at things in the shops.

From: Arsalan arsalan@hotmail.com
Date: October 4, 2003 08:30 PM
To: Claire Berlinski claire@berlinski.com
Subject: Re: Re: Turkish

Surely I can recommend to you a book. I taught myself when I lived there from the very fine Langenscheidt, *30 Stunden Türkisch: Ein Kurzlehrbuch für Anfänger.* I have a copy here; would you like me to send it to you? But don't worry, Claire. Turkish grammar is exceedingly regular. The difficult vocabulary and constructions were eliminated during Atatürk's *Öztürkçe* ("Pure Turkish") reform—along, alas, with the language's lexical depth. I am sure with your fine intelligence you will be speaking very well in no time. What is Vulcan?

• • •

From: Arsalan arsalan@hotmail.com
Date: October 5, 2003 09:16 PM
To: Claire Berlinski claire@berlinski.com
Subject: Re: Re: Re: Re: Re: Re: Re: Re: Turkish

Really, Claire, I think that you are making Turkish more complicated than it need be. You need only apply the dubitative suffix *miş* to imply some doubt in the sense of it seems and follow it all at the end with the verbal suffix *siniz; you are*—and it is simple, there you have it, *Siz türkle-ştiriverilemeyebilenlerdenmişsiniz.* Do you see?

From: Claire Berlinski claire@berlinski.com
Date: October 5, 2003 09:18 PM
To: Arsalan arsalan@hotmail.com
Subject: Re: Re: Re: Re: Re: Re: Re: Re: Re: Turkish

But of course. Gesundheit!

From: Arsalan arsalan@hotmail.com
Date: October 5, 2003 09:19 PM
To: Claire Berlinski claire@berlinski.com
Subject: Re: Re: Re: Re: Re: Re: Re: Re: Re: Re Turkish

No, no. It means, "I gather you are one of those people who is incapable of mastering Turkish."

From: Arsalan arsalan@hotmail.com
Date: October 5, 2003 10:27 PM
To: Claire Berlinski claire@berlinski.com
Subject: Re: Re: Re: Re: Re: Re: Re: Re: Re: Re: Re: Re: Turkish

Do not be offended. It is a lovely language. Suppose you were to sneeze: *"Açu!"* I would respond, *"Çok yaşayın!"*— "May you live many years!" You would then say, *"Sen de gör!"*—"And may you be there to see it!" Or perhaps I might say, *"Claire'im, çok güzelsin"*—"O my Claire, you are very beautiful." Then you must answer, *"Estağfirullah!"*— "I ask pardon of God (for you who praise me when all praise is due the Creator!)" Do you see?

• • •

As the days passed I learned to count in Turkish and order my
food. I adjusted to the noise in the apartment. I worked in the
mornings, then walked for miles, my imagination churning. I believed I could see conspiratorial Young Turks gathering behind
the elaborate wrought-iron doorways. I could sense the spirits of the drunken Crusaders; they were smashing relics, stuff-
ing their pockets with gold, belching, emptying their bladders
against the darkened walls, vomiting, wiping their mouths with
the backs of their filthy hands, then passing out, sated, in the
street.

Every night, Arsalan and I exchanged letters all throughout
the evening.

From: Arsalan arsalan@hotmail.com
Date: October 14, 2003 08:16 PM
To: Claire Berlinski claire@berlinski.com
Subject: (No subject)

Dear Claire,

I know that I have not answered your question about the
earthen goblet. I have not forgotten it. But I have not
known how to reply.

This goblet you saw was five thousand years old. On it
was portrayed a pattern of a goat and a leafy tree. When I
unearthed it, I noticed something of very great fascination.
If one were to spin the goblet, the goat would appear to
jump toward the tree and eat the leaves. I realized that it
was a form of prehistoric animation, the first in history. I
had made an extraordinary discovery. While excavating the
grave my team unearthed a skeleton. We believed that perhaps it belonged to the goblet's maker.

What I am about to tell you I have not told anyone else in the world. I do not quite know why I am about to tell you now. Perhaps it is because I can no longer live with this memory. I am not sure even how to tell you. You must, please, I beg, promise me that you will not tell another living being. *Wrap my secrets within your soul, and hide,* as Rumi said, *even from myself, this state of mine.*

Something so dreadful happened, Claire. I had been carrying the goblet to my car. And then I tripped. It happened so fast! It was in my hands; then it was on the ground, in shards. It had been safe in the earth for five thousand years before me.

I was stricken with horror, and I could not bring myself to tell my colleagues what I had done. I was alone, and I did a shameful thing. I took a knapsack from my car, put the broken pieces into the knapsack, and took the goblet home. It is hidden now in the bottom of my dresser drawer. When the item was discovered to be missing, I said that an investigation must be launched. Like a coward, I blamed the barbaric locals who would steal such a thing.

At night, I dream of it over and over. I see the moment in my mind, over and over again. How can I forgive myself? I cannot just say, "How clumsy of me." Clumsy, so clumsy, like Wollef! I cannot just say that. It makes me sick with shame.

Perhaps you will no longer respect me. But I consider you now a friend. I could not have this secret between us. I ask your forgiveness for disappointing you.

Arsalan

· · ·

· **From:** Claire Berlinski claire@berlinski.com
Date: October 14, 2003 09:36 PM
To: Arsalan arsalan@hotmail.com
Subject: Re: (No subject)

Oh, Arsalan.

If it's any consolation, it sounds exactly like something I would do.

My grandmother once gave me a letter to mail. It was important—something to do with the settlement she's supposed to receive from the German government for the property the Nazis confiscated from her family. It fell out of my handbag as I was walking home. I never told her. I never told anyone. You're the only one in the world who knows.

I will never tell anyone your secret, I promise, and you must never tell anyone mine.

Claire

When I think back upon our correspondence now, I notice an odd trick of memory—it's hard for me to remember exactly where it took place. I was in Istanbul, of course, alone in Dr. Mostarshed's bedroom, listening to the muezzin and the flapping gulls. Almost motionless, relaxed, I propped myself up against the decorative Anatolian cushions, my computer on my lap. The screen was the only source of light in the room. Arsalan's words swam up before me, and I replied. Time seemed almost to contract. But somehow I was *with* Arsalan. We were in *his* apartment, with its window overlooking the turquoise minarets of Isfahan, the muezzin calling the faithful to prayer. There were Persian rugs on the floor, a tea setting with a tarnished copper samovar, pomegranates on the table in a bowl of crystallized sugar. Once, as we wrote back and forth, I lost track of time completely, unaware that a whole night had passed until I heard the muezzin, looked out the window, and saw that the sky had turned pale.

. . .

Several weeks after my arrival, I wrote to him in the early evening, as I had every night since we began corresponding. There was no reply. As the next day passed with no response, and then the next, I became concerned, then anxious. I checked and rechecked the mail. By the next day, when there was still no response, I looked at the Persian news sites to see if something dreadful had happened in Isfahan. There was no news of note.

That night I dreamed of seeing Arsalan's face in the middle of one of Istanbul's massive crowds. Elated, I called his name, but he looked at me without recognition, and when I followed him, in the odd way of dreams, I found myself chasing an agile stray cat, who slipped repeatedly from my grasp. When I woke up, distraught, I wrote to Imran to ask for his interpretation. I doubted I'd hear back from him any time soon. He had cut back on his e-mail schedule; the forty minutes he usually allotted for daily correspondence had been halved; the other twenty minutes were now devoted to listening to jazz with Larissa.

As soon as I sent that e-mail, one from Arsalan arrived, to my great relief. "My electricity has been out for two days," he wrote. I began composing a response. I wanted to speak honestly. As I was writing the letter, though, carefully choosing my words, revising and erasing, my own power went off.

After that, I lost my nerve.

. . .

Beyond the ancient city walls on the south bank of the Golden Horn, Eyüp was flanked by massive cemeteries carved into the white hillside, cypress trees looming from the graves. I stepped off the ferry into a world of nacreous mosques, fountains, tombs, bathhouses, mansions, and pavilions, the mystical effect created by the noble architecture, the old trees, the flocks of birds, and the praying crowds only slightly diluted by the endless rows of stalls selling glow-in-the-dark clocks imprinted with verses of the Koran.

From the lively riverfront cafés and bustling markets near the shrine, I first thought the district to be comfortably middle-class, the kind of place to which people retired. But only minutes from the mosque, Eyüp turned into a shantytown of veiled women trailing children with dirty faces along streets strewn with garbage. Oddly, almost every collapsing shack had its own satellite dish. Walking along the unpaved roads, which smelled of raw sewage, I wondered why the residents of Eyüp were so eager to watch television that they would sooner buy a satellite dish than fix their sewage systems. Were they following the news? A favorite soap opera? I wished my Turkish was good enough to ask.

My electricity was still out; it had been out all morning. I wondered if, without a satellite dish, they felt as anxiously cut off from the world as I did without the Internet. I supposed they must, and I was hardly in a position to fault them for their priorities, for when I turned the corner, I spotted an Internet café and decided the sights of Eyüp could wait. It had been almost four hours, after all, since I had last heard from Arsalan.

I walked in to check my e-mail. Loud Turkish pop music was playing, and everyone was smoking—the air was thick with blue haze. A pack of teenage boys idled at the cash register; one of them pointed me to a free computer. I logged on to my e-mail account. There was nothing more from Arsalan, but Imran had written back, and he had written with terrible news.

He had been speed-dumped.

From: Imran Begum imranbegum@gmail.com
Date: October 22, 2003 02:05 PM
To: Claire Berlinski claire@berlinski.com
Subject: Re: Strange dream last night . . .

My dear friend,

It is over with Larissa.

I am not sure what happened, exactly. At some point last weekend, she just stopped feeling good about it. Fair enough. It means we were wrong for each other. Better to find this out after three weeks than three months or years. I thought we were right for each other, and we weren't. It was an illusion, caused by an insufficiency of time and knowledge. As surely as the tide rolls in, reality rolls in with time, and knowledge with it, like silt.

She was honest and decent, which helps. She even returned the gifts I gave her, not in a rejecting way but out of fair play.

Nonetheless, I am heartbroken.

As for your dream, you have developed a powerful romantic fantasy about this fellow. I suggest you be highly wary of transference. When you engage with a figure with no body language, tone of voice, or facial expressions, it is particularly apt to crop up. This is axiomatic in my line of work. We must be as blank a screen as possible so that our patients project onto it whatever film is playing inside their tortured minds. A computer screen is also a blank screen.

I must rush now to my bedroom and grieve before my next patient arrives. 24 minutes left.

Love,

Immie

The image of Imran heading home sadly with the pocket watches he'd given Larissa broke my heart.

The rest of his letter unsettled me as well. His concerns about transference did not come entirely as a surprise. I'd read Freud, too. In the course of treatment, Freud observed, female patients often fell in love with their analysts. Freud's lesser colleague Otto Breuer had observed the same phenomenon; he decided that his patients fell in love with him because he was so lovable. In Freud's modesty lay his genius. The patient's love, he concluded, was induced by the analytic relationship. This relationship, unlike any the patient had ever before experienced, allowed her to perceive in her analyst a transferred imago of her infantile attachments. Her vision of the analyst was a projection.

Of course, Freud remarked, this is also true of all romantic love—as Imran had discovered.

CHAPTER FIVE

The story was compelling—mostly because the characters and situations
were so believable. It almost reads like a nonfiction memoir.

—Customer review
of *Loose Lips* on Barnesandnoble.com

The waiter was babbling at me in Turkish, but I had no idea what he was saying. I kept repeating the only phrase I knew: *Coffee, please. With milk.* When a big-boned, cheerful blonde walked in, I assumed she was Turkish too, despite her appearance, because she spoke to the waiter so quickly and fluently. But upon realizing I was having trouble, she spoke to me in perfect American English. "He's trying to tell you he can't bring you coffee."

"Why not?"

"Because he's not the waiter. He's a chiropractor." I looked at the tables and wooden stools around me with puzzlement. "Don't worry; the waiter's coming," she said. "Here, sit with me," she said, gesturing at a table.

I didn't want to impose, but she assured me I wasn't. I sat down, and so did she, her body dwarfing the little wooden stool. I asked her how she'd become so enviably fluent in Turkish. "Oh, I'm *not*! The other day my neighbor took me aside and said, 'You know, Sally, you're a nice woman. You're really okay, for an American. But tell me—why do you keep calling my cat "pubic hair"?' " Her loud, friendly voice caused the chiropractor to laugh, even though he couldn't understand what she was saying. At last, the waiter came and took our order. "I got us some baklava, too," she said.

Sally was from Wisconsin, she told me when I asked, and she'd been in Istanbul for two years. She worked at the U.S. Consulate. She asked what I was doing in Istanbul, and when I told her I was a writer who had come to Istanbul on an impulse, her face lit up. "Really? No kidding. My husband's a writer, too." I was about to ask what he'd written when the chiropractor pulled two brochures from his breast pocket featuring sketches of da Vinci's Vitruvian Man before and after his spinal alignment and handed them to us. "I could probably use a chiropractor," Sally said, looking at the brochure, then rubbing her lower back. "My back is *so* sore from running on these awful roads."

"You run? Where do you go? The traffic here's insane."

"Yeah, no joke. We just had to repatriate the body of this poor guy from Baton Rouge who got whacked by a taxi."

"Oh, no!"

"Oh, yes! Cab hit him on the *sidewalk*." She shook her head. "Worst thing was he'd been with his girlfriend that night, and, you know, he shouldn't have *had* a girlfriend. So he didn't have his wedding ring on. We found it at his hotel when we went to collect his personal effects. We figured we better stuff it on his finger before we packed him up, but by then he's all bloated, and his finger's about ten times the size of the ring. Oh, man, it was horrible—we had to use pliers."

"That's disgusting!"

"That's not the worst of it." She lowered her voice. "I was pulling, and the other guy was pushing, and . . . whoa, Pop goes the weasel! His *whole finger* comes right off. Had to tell his wife it got sliced off by flying glass."

"Oh, my God!"

"Yep! What I do for my country. Anyway, so be real careful where you run." She looked at me. "Say, you don't know the city real well, huh?"

· · ·

I checked my e-mail when I returned to Dr. Mostarshed's apartment.

From: Arsalan arsalan@hotmail.com
Date: November 9, 2003 03:16 PM
To: Claire Berlinski claire@berlinski.com
Subject: Burnt City

Alas, Claire, my colleagues have received urgent reports of looting at the Burnt City. We have convened an emergency meeting by telephone, and concluded that a delegation, of which I shall be the ambassador, must go directly to the city and tour the surrounding villages. There we will meet local authorities and explain the significance of the city's treasures. We will show them what we do and teach them how we work, telling them in simple language that these beautiful things belong to their families and their ancestors. We will explain to them that these artifacts are their heritage and that honorable men do not sell their heritage. We will also explain that if we put these treasures in a museum, the tourists will come and bring them more money than they would make by selling them just once. We are hopeful this will diminish the looting. It is a very urgent matter.

Regrettably, I do not believe there will be access to the Internet in such villages, so for the moment, I shall not be able to look after your well-being with the care I should like. I have asked Dr. Mostarshed, however, to call frequently to make sure you have everything you might need.

I am quite concerned about Wollef in my absence. The maid has promised to feed him, but I am not sure she understands how much supervision the animal truly requires. I found him caught by his toenails in the curtain the other day. He would have been there all day if I hadn't freed him.

Until the day I return, dear Claire,

Everyone has someone, a friend to love,
And work, and skill to do it. All I have
Is a fantasy lover who hides
For safety in the dark of my heart's cave—

I shall be thinking of you.

Arsalan

• • •

The next morning was foggy and cool. Sally took me on a path where you could run on the sea wall, past fishermen bringing in the morning catch and the ruined hulks of old fishing boats listing in the water. As we ran we compared notes about our running injuries. We both suffered from runner's knee. She'd had a stress fracture over the summer and was only just now recovering. We ran about five miles, watching the city come to life as the sun struggled up the horizon. Afterwards, we were starving. She invited me back to her place for brunch: "My husband's making eggs Benedict and the best banana nut muffins in the world."

"That sounds great. I've just *had* it with kebabs."

"Istanbul will do that for ya!" She called her husband on her cell phone and told him to make a double batch.

She told me as we walked up the hill that her husband was from Wisconsin too—they had been college sweethearts. She had grown up on a dairy farm and looked it: you could tell at a glance that her childhood had involved wholesome fresh air, crisp red apples, and cheddar cheese. Sally was not so much fat as *large*—big hands, big feet, big head, big everything. Her upturned Episcopalian nose was splashed with freckles; her strawberry blond hair was cut in a sensible chin-length bob; and she had the kind of ruddy skin and huge, calcium-nourished teeth that say *American* as clearly as a blue passport with an eagle on it. When she smiled, her teeth looked as big as packs of cards.

She and her husband had been political science majors at the University of Wisconsin. They had both taken the Foreign Service exam, but only Sally had passed. "I nearly didn't take the job," she told me as we took the elevator up to their apartment, "because I didn't think Dave would be able to stand it, being just a house-husband, but he insisted I take it—he said if I didn't I'd never stop wondering what I missed, and it would give him an excuse to try writing the novel. He'd always wanted to do that."

The slight, mild-mannered man who opened the door to Sally's apartment wore a tie-dyed Cherry Garcia apron over his flannel shirt. His nose and John Lennon eyeglasses were dusted with flour, and his slightly graying hair was pulled into a ponytail. "Hey, gals," he said after introducing himself as Sally's husband. "Come here and look what I got down at the flower bazaar!" We followed him into the kitchen. He showed us a clear Pyrex bowl filled with water and leaves. "Aren't they cute? Hey, Claire, do you want a celery-ginger picker-upper? I just juiced it."

I took a closer look at the bowl. They weren't leaves. They had flippers. While pouring the picker-upper, Dave told us he'd gone down to the flower bazaar near the New Mosque to pick up some bug spray for his tomato plant. While he was there, he'd passed a pet stall with a tank full of squirming miniature turtles, each the size of a silver dollar. He was so enchanted by their cuteness that on an impulse he bought a pair as a surprise for Sally.

I wasn't going to be the one to tell him. This was something I had learned at the Department of Agriculture: miniature turtles don't exist. Those were *baby* turtles. They would grow to be the size of large dinner plates and live to the age of seventy-five.

Sally was looking at the Pyrex bowl with a puzzled expression.

"Dinner's almost ready!" Dave said, still staring at the turtles, who were scrabbling frantically at the sides of the bowl. "Whoa, fellas! Just look at you go!"

● ● ●

From: Samantha Allen allens@aol.com
Date: November 10, 2003 01:15 AM
To: Claire Berlinski claire@berlinski.com
Subject: Weekend with Lynne

Dear Claire,

Meeting Lynne was like coming home. It was like stepping into a warm bath on a cold day. There was no awkwardness. I had expected it to be strange at first, but from the moment I saw her I felt at ease. We began talking like old friends, and we never stopped, not for two weeks.

I'd booked a room at a hotel, but over our first lunch, she asked me to stay in her cabin—not to sleep in her bed, just on the couch, she said. Later that evening, I told her I wanted to wait. I lied. I said I wasn't into casual bed-hopping. I told her I needed to know a woman deeply before I could make love to her. She told me no man had ever said that to her before.

We took her dogs for walks on the beach. I helped her

renovate her terrace. We bought lumber together. I stained the wood. I built pedestals for her flowerpots, so she could see them from her writing desk.

I wasn't playing a role at all. I was completely myself, except that I tried to keep my voice extra-low, and I had to resist her, physically. It killed me. I massaged her shoulders. I kissed her fingers and the back of her neck. I smelled her skin. But when she put her hand on my cheek, all I could think was that she would notice that the stubble didn't feel the way it should. When she took my hand, I thought she might be noticing that my wrists are too thin. I kept thinking, *Now, now's the moment, tell her.* But I didn't have the nerve.

There's something about her, Claire. She's fragile. Like a flower. She's been married; I didn't know that. Her husband was some jerkoff anthropologist. Once she caught him with one of his students in his office. He told her he was reenacting tribal mating rituals. It kills me that someone could have hurt her that way.

I tried a thousand times to tell her the truth, but I couldn't do it. I hated lying to her. I didn't just hate it because I was nervous about being caught. I hated it because I don't want to hurt her. I don't want to be another man who disappoints her. She makes me want to be a better . . . man. I guess.

Sam

* * *

When Sally and I went running again two days later in the Byzantine Hippodrome, Sally hinted at a certain frustration with Dave and his novel. "Maybe you'll understand this better because you're a writer too," she said. "He started working on it when we went to Bulgaria, and it's been four years now, but he just can't seem to fin-

ish it—it's like he can't pull the trigger, you know? He keeps saying how he has to go back and change something. He has to
tighten up the section about the victim's grandmother, or the detective's voice isn't quite right . . . there's always some reason not to
show it to an agent. How long did it take you to write your novel?"

"Oh, a really long time," I said. "Novels are hard to finish."

It wasn't her only complaint. Sometime between brunch and
our run, Sally had discovered the truth about turtles. "They need
a pool bigger than our bathtub," she said. "They need a place to
swim. To wade. To hibernate. They need a basking area that's exactly the right temperature or their shells will rot. They need a
water heater. They need an expensive filter because they *crap* so
much. They need to have their water cleaned every day. They
smell bad. They bite. They carry *Salmonella*. They get maggots."
She had to stop—she'd run out of breath. She put her hands on her
waist and bent forward, panting. "And Dave's all excited because
on the Internet it says if we train them right they'll play tricks and
let us scratch their bellies."

"If you wash your hands after touching them I'm sure you'll be
fine."

"He's spent the last two whole days building them this green
plastic turtle house in the middle of the living room. I come back
from the office and there are all these rotten leaves on the living
room floor, and when I ask him why he says it's a vegetative
canopy. It's supposed to remind them of the Mississsippi Delta."
She got up and began running again, then stopped a few seconds
later. Her shoe had come untied again. "*Damn* it! How am I going
to take seventy-five years of this?"

I expected that since she spoke the language so well, Sally
would be able to help me understand some of the things that baffled me about Turkey, but in many ways she seemed just as puzzled
as me. While we were running, we passed another garden of satellite dishes rising from a neighborhood with no functioning sewers.
I pointed this out; I wondered what she made of that. "I don't

know," she said. "I guess they're like my mom and dad that way.
Mom and Dad watch about ten hours of television a day. Mom has
diabetes and Dad has high blood pressure. I started running because I didn't want to be overweight like them." Half a mile later,
she remarked that you could buy satellite televisions cheaply at the
Carrefour on the E5 highway. "You can get pretty much everything you'd get at Kmart there, really. It's great. I can take you
there if you need anything."

I had asked Arsalan the same question before he left for the villages.

From: Arsalan arsalan@hotmail.com
Date: October 23, 2003 03:16 PM
To: Claire Berlinski claire@berlinski.com
Subject: Re: Eyüp

This is a most interesting problem, Claire. Throughout
the Islamic world, society is viewed in concentric circles of
trust, starting with the immediate family and proceeding
outward through blood relations. People will not share
their family's precious resources with those to whom
they're not related—hence do we suffer from an almost
complete lack of public-mindedness. The tragedy of the
commons is multiplied. The Turks, moreover, are chroni-
cally afflicted with the Genghis Khan Syndrome. They are
not as clannish as the Arabs (or as sly as we Persians). But
in their hearts they are still nomads on the steppe, waiting
for the great khan to distribute the spoils. They expect the
sewers to be handed down from *Devlet Baba*, the father
state. Recall that in many Islamic countries, Turkey especially among them, public works have historically been the
responsibility of distant, centralized authorities. Note the
elaborate antique fountains still in use: they usually bear
the *tuğra* of the sultan or an inscription from one or an-

other pasha. And do not forget, in the Ottoman Empire, all land was technically owned by the sultan. A complicated system of leases and grants permitted people to buy and sell land after a fashion, but nowhere near as easily as in Europe, where one could obtain title. Public authorities could, and would, seize property at any time, so it made no sense to develop one's land overmuch. The consequence of this collective inheritance is the fatalism and resignation that leads the residents of Eyüp to buy satellite dishes rather than take the initiative, cooperate, and fix their own sewers.

After that, every time I passed an antique fountain, I stopped to look at it. Arsalan was right—the *tuğra* of the sultan was always just where he said it would be.

• • •

I was alone in Dr. Mostarshed's bedroom the next evening, trying for the third time to compose a reply to Samantha, when a giant bat flew in through the window and began flapping madly from wall to wall, squeaking frantically. I ran from the room, slamming the door behind me. When I poked my head in the door fifteen minutes later, it was still flapping and diving, crashing into the furniture, all huge and black and hairy and nasty. It was hard to say which one of us was more unhappy that it was trapped in my bedroom.

Sally had said, "Call us if you ever need any help with anything," and in a moment of womanish hysteria, that's just what I did, even though it was nearly midnight. "What should I do?" I asked.

"Don't worry, we'll come over," said Sally.

"What are you going to do, negotiate a consular treaty with it?"

"Moral support," she said. "Besides, Dave's a guy."

I tried to pretend they shouldn't inconvenience themselves, but I was grateful. I knew it couldn't hurt me, but there's a damned good reason no one wants a pet bat.

Fifteen minutes later, when they arrived—Dave bearing a loaf of pumpkin bread—the thing was still bouncing off the walls. The way it was knocking into everything wasn't much of an advertisement for sonar navigation. Dave poked his head in the bedroom door and blanched. "Yep, that's a bat all right," he said, shutting it again. He looked at Sally. She was staring at him with her arms crossed. His Adam's apple bobbed up and down.

"Well, I guess I should open the windows in there, and, uh, you know," he said. "Okay, here I go. I'm gonna open the window. Here I go." He dived into the room, ducking for cover, and raced over to the window. He opened the window all the way and ducked back out, slamming the door behind him. "Poor little guy; he's frightened."

Five minutes later, the squeaking stopped. Either the bat was gone, we figured, or it had knocked itself out against one of Dr. Mostarshed's antique vases. Dave opened the door: It was gone. "Thank God," I said. "You're my hero."

Since we were too keyed up with adrenaline to sleep, we made some tea and sliced up the pumpkin bread. We stayed up until about three in the morning, talking. Dave and Sally reminisced about the cockroaches in their hotel room in Costa Rica, which were evidently as big as human heads. I mentioned that I'd had trouble finding breakfast cereal in Istanbul, and Dave promised to bring me a batch of his homemade granola. "Exotic foreign food is great," he said pensively, "but you just don't want it for breakfast."

Before leaving, Dave checked the rest of the apartment to make sure all points of potential bat-entry were sealed. To thank them, I gave them the only copy of *Loose Lips* I had brought with me; they admired it appropriately and said how much they were looking forward to reading it.

Knowing they were there for me in an emergency made me

feel a little less alone. I was about to write to Arsalan about the bat, but I suddenly realized that he wouldn't receive the message.

Imran, at least, had replied promptly to my last letter.

From: Imran Begum imranbegum@gmail.com
Date: November 11, 2003 03:45 AM
To: Claire Berlinski claire@berlinski.com
Subject: Your concern

Dear kind friend who has been so generous with good wishes, thank you for your care; it means a lot to me, having no siblings and only one interested parent. Morale is adequate. I am consoling myself with Marie, age 43, petite and feminine with a 38E bust. She has convinced herself she's in love with me, and I'm not even trying to reason with her; no bloody point. I plan to begin speed dating again as soon as my *Larissaschmerz* is well boundaried, in three weeks time. Three new patients, so I'm flush as a bald eagle in a twister. I have purchased a new stereo amplifier to console myself for my loss, and I am endeavouring to eat more plaice, haddock, and cod for their mood-stabilizing omega-3 oils. Hydrate well, my good friend. Love, Immie.

Samantha had written, too, wondering why I hadn't answered her letter. She and Lynne had been speaking on the phone every night, she added. During their last conversation, Lynne told her that she had gone for an HIV test and hoped Sam would do the same. When the time came, said Lynne, she didn't want condoms to spoil their intimacy.

"They won't," Samantha said glumly. "I can *promise* you that."

She didn't know how to break the news. In a letter? In person? What should she do if Lynne became hysterical? She was so anxious that her therapist had urged her to titrate up the Paxil. She wasn't sure she should; last time she did that, it had made her so manic that she'd shoplifted three kilos of T-bone steak. "Then somehow I wound up in a nude photo session in front of about twenty people I didn't know on a red velvet couch with an albino python wrapped around me."

She didn't really need to hear that I had warned her, even though I had. God was already punishing her enough. I told her that she should stop agonizing about *how* to tell Lynne, and just *tell* her already—it didn't really matter how she did it; it wasn't going to be pretty under any circumstances. For her anxiety, I suggested, she should try eating more plaice, haddock, and cod: they contained a lot of mood-stabilizing omega-3 oils.

• • •

On Sunday morning, Sally called to say she was going to the Çemberlitaş hamam for a steam bath and a massage. Would I like to join her? In the taxi, she told me that she and Dave had finished *Loose Lips*. "We had to fight each other for it at night. We really enjoyed it."

"How are the turtles?" I asked.

She stopped smiling. "Dave's building them a webcam."

A pudgy, cheerful girl of about eight gave us towels and slippers at the entrance to the bathhouse. Sally showed me the lockers. We undressed and wrapped the towels around our waists, then passed through a cool room to the vast marble caldarium, lit naturally by crescent- and moon-shaped windows carved into the dome of the cupola. "We just sit here for a bit first and work up a good sweat," Sally explained, pointing to the heated octagonal slab of marble in the center of the steam room. We lay down on our towels, listening to the pleasant soft gabble of women's voices, the sounds of fountains and sluicing water. Shafts of misty light pierced the steam.

As we relaxed Sally asked me about *Loose Lips*. She wanted to know if I would write it differently now, after September 11. "The world's so hard to laugh about now. Don't you think?"

The warmth was making me drowsy. I noticed that the heads of the marble columns supporting the arches of the dome were diamond-shaped, like baklava. Amid that expanse of marble, the world did not seem such a bad place, but that didn't seem the thing to say, so I said something vague about it all being terrible, and yes, how serious it all seemed.

"Exactly, the world seems so serious. When I took my job, I had no idea how serious my responsibilities would be. I thought I would be looking at people's visa applications and asking myself, 'Is this person going to try to work illegally in the United States?' I never thought I'd be asking, 'Is this person going to try to kill my family?'"

"Do you ask yourself that every time you look at a visa application?"

"Every single time."

What a lousy job, I thought. I was grateful that I didn't have to make those decisions—and that I'd never have to shove the finger of some bloated corpse into a wedding ring. Sally adjusted her towel, then flipped onto her stomach. I did the same. "I keep thinking how I'd feel if it had been me who let Mohammed Atta into the country. You know, it's scary, sometimes, just working at the consulate. When I took the job, my mom was so upset because the U.S. embassies in Kenya and Tanzania had just been bombed. I told her, 'Mom, you can't spend your life worrying about random things like that.' I used to ski, and I told her I was sure that way more people died in skiing accidents every year than in terrorist attacks. Now every time I walk through the front gates in the morning I think how easy it would be to drive a truck with a bomb through them. I think about all these things now—how easy it is to get the most God-awful weapons, how badly they want us dead." A fat masseuse came over and gestured toward me. "Go ahead— you go first," Sally said, gesturing toward the edge of the slab. "Take your locker key with you."

"No, you first."

"Okay, if you insist." She slid over to the edge of the slab and lay facedown on the marble. The masseuse began pummeling her healthy pink Wisconsin flesh. I stayed where I was. Around the bathing area, cool cubicles with marble fountains were separated from the center by marble walls into which blossoms and Ottoman couplets had been carved. Round, dark-skinned women moved slowly from the marble slab to the fountains and back, pouring warm water over their soapy breasts and hips. A few minutes later, another masseuse came over, and I slid over to the edge of the slab. She scrubbed the dirt from my skin with a coarse cloth, then soaped me with bubbles squeezed from a billowing cheesecloth, then poured buckets of warm and cool water over my body, then massaged my back, then washed my hair. For a moment, time collapsed upon itself, and the women around me, Ottoman courtesans all, plotted their palace intrigues.

After the bath, Sally and I retired to the cool room to lie on the cushioned divans and drink sweet tea. Relaxed and drowsy, I closed my eyes for a moment and thought about Arsalan. I imagined him unfastening the clasp of my necklace, his fingers brushing against the back of my neck.

"It's a different place these days," Sally was saying. Her voice shook me out of my fantasy.

I didn't know what she was talking about. I realized she'd been speaking for five minutes and I hadn't heard a word. "Totally different," I agreed again, not at all sure what I was agreeing to, but fairly sure it was the right thing to say.

• • •

Although it was already November, Istanbul was rosy, the air soft. The temperature was perfect for jeans and a sweater. I had settled into a rhythm. I worked in the mornings, then wandered out for lunch at one of the neighborhood restaurants, where cooks sliced juicy pieces of meat off turning spits, then slapped them on thick bread with chili peppers and tomatoes and pinches of powdered spices. Sally and I went running every other day. She always invited me for dinner afterwards. Dave sent me home with leftovers in Tupperware.

Although Arsalan had said he would be away for *at least* a week, when ten days after his departure he still hadn't returned—or at least, he hadn't written—I was disappointed. However remote these villages were, surely one of them must have an Internet café? The news was full of stories about the rapid penetration of the Internet in Iran. It was apparently a threat to the authority of the regime. One article I read stressed that the Internet was exposing rural areas to outside influences to a previously unimaginable degree. Surely that meant that the Internet was *accessible* in rural areas, did it not?

From: Samantha Allen allens@aol.com
Date: November 20, 2003 01:15 AM
To: Claire Berlinski claire@berlinski.com
Subject: Re: (No subject)

Of course it does. Sorry to tell you this, but a guy who wants to be in touch will find a way to be in touch, even if he has to train a carrier pigeon. If he hasn't written, he's just not that into you. You know all those women I was writing to before I met Lynne? I just can't get rid of them. If I haven't answered their e-mails in two weeks, you'd think they'd figure *he's just not that into me.* But they keep forwarding me these dumb Internet jokes and sending me e-cards. With these awful spelling errors, too. It's really a turnoff.

I wasn't sure she was right. Los Angeles was one thing, but Iran was another. I found myself studying news reports and blogs from Iran to better assess the penetration of the Internet into obscure Iranian villages. The news on these sites seemed oddly incongruous with the tone of Arsalan's letters. It was hard to reconcile the urgent communiqués from the International Atomic Energy Agency with Arsalan's melancholy Persia of Sufi poetry and Safavid miniatures. Iranian authorities were torturing prisoners of conscience, hanging dissidents, acquiring the materials to make nuclear weapons, and funding terrorists, but Arsalan's world seemed entirely remote from any such concern. To judge from their weblogs, most educated Iranians looked out their windows and saw democracy protests. Arsalan saw peacocks: "A male and a female," he had written to me the day before he left. "Perhaps they wandered over from the local bird sanctuary? Wollef was enthralled. We watched them for fifteen minutes or so, with Wollef chattering away. Then just as mysteriously as they arrived, they disappeared again. I wish you could have seen it."

He and I had exchanged letters about politics, but I never sensed that he found these issues passionately interesting, at least not in the way he found ruins and relics interesting. I thought I recognized his strain of political detachment; I had seen it before in my mother and in the musicians who came to play at her summer chamber music festival. My mother took an almost perverse pride in her indifference to current events. "Politicians come and go," she had shrugged once when a friend asked her why she wasn't watching the presidential debates. "They're all the same. Music lasts forever."

Arsalan, it seemed to me, shared something of this attitude. Once I had asked him how he viewed President Khatami and the reform movement. "They're all the same," he had written back. "Persian art has depicted the same palace intrigues for the past two millennia. Here's a nice example, by the way, from the Moghul era, commissioned by Emperor Akbar, circa 1551–53." He had attached to his message a reproduction of a Rajasthani miniature, detailed as a Persian rug, depicting a gold-flecked city of refulgent rose and lapus lazuli, the roofs and edges of the buildings forming loops within ribbons within swirls. Guards with elongated Indian features dozed lazily in the parapets and turrets, oblivious to the enemy assassins climbing up the palace walls, knives in hand.

I liked the picture so much that I made it into wallpaper on my computer. I was looking at it again over a breakfast of Dave's homemade granola, wondering about the man who had sent it to me, when the phone rang. It was Dr. Mostarshed. It was Dr. Mostarshed *again*. Dr. Mostarshed was proving to be a first-class pest. At first he had written repeatedly because he couldn't figure out my apartment. He couldn't find the switch to the bathroom light; he didn't know how to use the microwave; the key was stuck in the mailbox lock. I didn't mind answering those messages. But then he called to say he'd left a notebook of critical bibliographical information on his bookshelf, and would I mind reading him the handwritten notes he'd made on page three, or perhaps it was page five? Over the past few days he had been calling over and over again, asking me to read passages from the various notebooks he'd forgotten. He was driving me nuts, especially since he could never remember which notebook held the information he needed or what page it was on.

In fact, I was beginning to wonder what kind of man was inhabiting my charming little studio. There was a photograph on the wall of a nerdy Iranian man who I assumed was Dr. Mostarshed, shaking the hand of a nerdy official at some kind of nerdy award ceremony—the Nerd of the Year award, maybe, who knows; the banner behind the dais was written in some nerdy language I couldn't understand. I'd assumed from his humorless expression, his apartment's reserved interior decor, and Arsalan's description of him that he would be a sober, responsible tenant. But when I looked through Dr. Mostarshed's music collection, it gave me pause to ponder. It contained the most extensive collection of Bob Marley bootlegs I had ever seen. Then the owner of one of the neighborhood electric guitar stores stopped me in the street. He wanted to know whether Dr. Mostarshed would be going to the Rainbow Gathering this year. They were really hoping Doctor M. would make it again for the fire dance.

Dr. Mostarshed wanted me to look for a folder in the drawer of his desk, in the study. "I apologize for disturbing you again," he said to me in his heavily accented English. "I think the reference I need is in the margin notes on the fourth or fifth page of a yellow notepad in a file marked 'Elmah Coins, Spring 2001.' " I opened the drawer and looked around. "By the way," he said, "something a bit strange happened here a few nights ago."

"Yes?"

"A man came by, quite late. He was singing outside your door. I opened the door and asked him to quiet down. He became rather belligerent. He said he knew you. He was quite drunk."

"I see." I felt my stomach flip a bit. "Did this man by any chance have an Irish accent?"

"He was hard to understand. I'm not good with accents in English, I'm afraid."

"Did he say anything else?"

"He said you had his coat, and he wanted it back."

So Jimmy was still alive, I thought when I hung up. I wondered what he had really wanted. I noticed to my great surprise that I was curious, but not *desperately* curious. Jimmy seemed distant, both geographically and emotionally. Only a few months before, I would have spent a whole day trying to plumb the deeper meaning of Jimmy's behavior. I would have written to Samantha—do you think those were *love* songs he was singing? I would have written to Imran—why can't he admit that it's not the *coat* he wants back? But oddly, I didn't feel the need. Istanbul, I supposed, was a good place to recover from a broken heart. I was glad of this, but also slightly uneasy: I had been convinced, not that long ago, that my feelings about Jimmy were profound.

I felt a bit embarrassed that Dr. Mostarshed had been disturbed, but I didn't think of it again until, several days later, I found a message from someone named Mária Dehelán-Dörömbözi in my e-mail in-box. It took me a second to place the name; then I remembered. It was on the mailbox near mine on the Place Dauphine. The message must be from the elderly Hungarian woman who lived below my apartment. How had she found my address, I wondered? She hardly seemed the technically savvy type. In any event, she was *irate*. Her letter was written in a screedy eighteenth-century French. Apparently she'd had some kind of run-in with Dr. Mostarshed. He was, she said, disturbing *la calme* of the entire building. It was not *just* his loud music, day and night. Unsavory people, bad people, *des louches*, were coming and going at all hours! The Place Dauphine, she wrote, was not a cheap hotel!

Wow, I thought. I guess I didn't need to worry about Dr. Mostarshed being disturbed by Jimmy—he was probably already awake.

The next part was the best. She had knocked on my door that morning to tell this disgraceful man that she had not slept *one wink* the previous night, thanks to his nocturnal escapades. She was, she had told him, *exhausted*. *"You're* exhausted?" he had replied before slamming the door in her face. "Madame, imagine how *we* feel!"

When I read this I nearly choked to death laughing. Then, when I thought about it, I began to get a little worried. It must have been pretty extreme, whatever he was doing in my apartment, to prompt her to go to the trouble of calling my landlord for my e-mail address and writing to me. I mean, the man was welcome to entertain whomever he wanted, but he was *not* welcome to get me evicted. And actually, he *wasn't* welcome to entertain anyone he wanted. I had just replaced the carpet at my own expense. I did not want to come back and find cigarette burns in the rug because he'd been hosting coke-fueled *échangiste* parties.

I made myself a cup of coffee while I considered the situation. I had been *very* careful with his apartment—I'd been watering his cactus faithfully, I had replaced a teacup that I'd broken with one just like it, and I had even scraped the pigeon shit off his balcony, which clearly no one had done for quite some years. It wasn't really all that funny that he was treating my place like a cheap hotel.

The phone rang. "Yes," I said, in a flat, unfriendly tone, preparing to tell Dr. Mostarshed that *primo*, I was *not* his secretary, and *segundo*, I had better come back to find my carpet immaculate.

"Hello," replied a man whose voice I didn't recognize. "Is this Claire?"

"Speaking."

"This is Arsalan."

• • •

"I wanted to make sure you were well," he said.

I didn't answer for a moment. I was too taken aback—not that he had called, but by his accent, which was not at all what I had expected it to be. I had expected him to have a Persian accent, or perhaps an English accent characteristic of the London neighborhood in which he had grown up. But it was neither English nor Persian. It was impossible to place. It was elegant and formal, almost queerly so. His consonants were crisper than any native speaker's, and he pronounced each word with great precision, as if he had studied English from a computer—or perhaps from a Martian.

It had never occurred to me that we could call each other. Iran somehow seemed like one of those places that was *too far away* to call. But of course he could just pick up the phone and call. He had Dr. Mostarshed's phone number; why shouldn't he have used it?

"I'm fine," I said at last. "When I picked up the phone, I thought you were Dr. Mostarshed. He's been calling and calling." For a moment, we were both silent, waiting for the other to speak, and then we both spoke at once.

"You first," we both said at the same time. He waited a moment and I spoke: "How was your trip?"

"I'm not back yet. I'm in Sistan-Baluchistan, near the Afghan border." The connection was absolutely clear, as if he were next door. His voice was deep. It was resonant and rough-edged from years of smoking Caspian tobacco. "I'm calling you from a satellite phone. It belongs to a doctor at the Afghan refugee camp. There are no regular phones here. I should speak only for a few minutes, since it isn't my phone."

That, I supposed, answered my question about why he hadn't stopped in an Internet café to drop me a note.

For a second, an absurd thought occurred to me. I was so in the habit of making mental notes of my daily experiences to recount to Arsalan that I imagined writing to Arsalan to tell him that Arsalan had called, and that Arsalan had sounded very different from the way I had thought he would. Two Arsalans existed in my mind simultaneously—Arsalan, my imaginary best friend, and Arsalan, this curious man with a Martian accent who was for some reason calling me and talking to me as if he knew me.

I told him that I was doing just fine and studying Turkish. I tried out a few Turkish pleasantries, to which he replied in kind. His Turkish sounded absolutely fluent, which only added to my disorientation—the mind has a fierce need to categorize people by their language and accent, and his linguistic shape shifting wasn't making things easier.

I asked him to tell me more about his trip. It had been a success so far, he thought, though exhausting: Sistan-Baluchistan was the most impenetrable—and the strangest—region of Iran. It was a notorious corridor for drug smuggling; undeveloped, drought-stricken, desolate, and poor; populated by pastoral nomads who spoke a ghastly dialect of primitive Persian. He and his two colleagues had trekked nearly two hundred fifty kilometers, first passing overland on a dusty plateau, then taking a boat through a network of lakes. They had stopped in several dozen villages, spreading the word about the importance of preserving the villagers' heritage.

They had planned to begin their return two days ago, but a vicious dust storm had swept over the region, making travel impossible. They were stuck now in the middle of nowhere, keeping company with six hundred dysentery-riddled Afghan refugees, two physicians from Médicins sans Frontières, and a trigger-happy unit of the Imam Ali battalion of the Revolutionary Guards, who had come to settle a score with an elusive Baluchi tribesman. "I thought I should get in touch with you," said Arsalan, "since I know you're alone there. I wanted to make sure you weren't having any difficulties."

See, Samantha? There was a perfectly logical explanation for his silence. Why, he'd just been caught in a raging dust storm in an Afghan refugee camp in Sistan-Baluchistan! How many women throughout history, I wondered, sitting and waiting by a phone that never rings, had hoped that was the problem?

As he spoke, I tried to perform an internal simultaneous translation: I tried to imagine *reading* the words he was saying, to see if they sounded like him. The effort made it hard to focus, and I realized he had abruptly changed the subject. "I knew they were native to the region," he was saying, "but I never expected to encounter one."

"You saw *what*? Where?"

"Right here. A bit higher up in the mountains. But it shouldn't have been here at all—the drought has killed everything here, except for a few scorpions. I have no idea what she was doing here. Looking for food, perhaps?"

"What did you do?"

"I didn't do anything. I've never seen one before, not even in a zoo. She had massive paws and yellow eyes, and the most intelligent, thoughtful face. I looked at her and she looked at me—at least I *think* she was a she. We were both absolutely still, just looking at each other. And then—I don't know why, it just seemed like the right thing to say—I said, *Hi, kitty.* Very softly. Just like I say to Wollef when he comes over to say hello in the mornings."

Arsalan repeated the words he had said to the animal, and oddly, he said them with a different accent—he pronounced the words tenderly, with a Persian inflection. *Hi, kitty.* He said it almost the way I would have imagined him saying it, with a low, hypnotic gentleness. "Were you frightened?" I asked.

"We were both surprised, but neither of us was frightened. I don't know why I wasn't. They're dangerous, very dangerous, and there's nothing to eat up here. She must have been hungry. But I was so mesmerized that it didn't occur to me to be frightened."

"What happened next?"

"I said it again . . . *Hi, kitty. Hi, pussycat.* She flicked her tail and made a rasping noise—*huggg, huggg, huggg, huggg.* Then she sniffed the air—just like Wollef does—and I suppose she decided I didn't smell like something good to eat. She cocked her head to the side and she said something important—*huggg, huggg, huggg*—but I couldn't understand it. I thought she looked discouraged by my response, or lack of it. As if she found me disappointingly limited. At last she shrugged, or at least I believe that's what she was doing, and then very slowly, very casually, she turned around and softly padded away."

He might have not have the accent I expected, I thought, but whoever this man was, he wasn't boring.

• • •

I heard from Arsalan next when he wrote to me two days later from Zabol, the capital of Sistan-Baluchistan. The dust storm had made a long overland journey impossible, so he was waiting to catch a plane back to Isfahan. The flight left only twice a week. He had just missed the last one. There were plenty of Internet cafés in Zabol and nothing to do but use them. "This city," he wrote, "is known for its processed foods, livestock feed, processed hides, milled rice, bricks, reed mats, and baskets. Occasionally a bomb goes off. I'm so bored here that I'm vaguely hoping for that."

I was stuck in front of my computer as well. The reader may have noticed that I had not spent much time in Istanbul working on my book. Unfortunately, so had my editor. Hours after Arsalan's phone call, he had sent me a terse, terrifying note: "Claire. Checking to make sure we're on schedule for timely delivery. yrs, B."

I had been working on the same chapter since my arrival. Stricken with anxiety and guilt, I resolved to remain at my desk until finishing it or death, whichever came first. By the time Arsalan's first message from Zabol arrived, I had been sitting dutifully before my computer for seven hours, writing and erasing the same paragraph over and over and checking my word count every ten minutes. Each time, to my dismay, the number seemed to decline.

The arrival of my editor's note had prevented me from dwelling at great length upon the significance of Arsalan's call, although I had, of course, dropped a note to Samantha about it.

From: Samantha Allen allens@aol.com
Date: November 22, 2003 01:15 PM
To: Claire Berlinski claire@berlinski.com
Subject: Re: Eek! He called!

I take it back. He's way into you. He must have missed you a lot if he called all the way from there.

From: Claire Berlinski claire@berlinski.com
Date: November 22, 2003 01:30 PM
To: Samantha Allen allens@aol.com
Subject: Re: Re: Eek! He called!

Well, he probably just wanted to know if I was okay.

From: Samantha Allen allens@aol.com
Date: November 22, 2003 01:45 PM
To: Claire Berlinski claire@berlinski.com
Subject: Re: Re: Re: Eek! He called!

Of course *you're* okay. *You're* in civilization. *He's* the one in wherever-the-fuckistan. Anyway, don't worry about his weird accent. That's a superficial thing to get hung up on. Like gender. Look, you can't tell much from someone's voice. I think we reveal ourselves more completely in letters. Especially since so many people are born into the wrong bodies; you know what I mean? If you'd spoken to me on the phone before meeting me, you would have assumed I was a man. Most people do. But I think you know me—the real me—quite well. Better than many people who have met me in person. I mean, Lynne just sent me a bottle of aftershave, for God's sake.

She was right, I thought. Some people *are* born into the wrong bodies; that's for sure. I thought of my brother's closest friend in high school, Pearl Wu. Her face and figure told the world she was a diligent engineering student—the kind of girl who would make good grades, go to an excellent university, then marry another hardworking dullard, perhaps an equally earnest dentist. But her face and figure were *quite* mistaken. That girl with the nondescript features of a Chinese Communist Party propaganda poster was meant by destiny to wear a tight-bodiced crimson dress with stiletto heels and enormous gold hoop earrings; she was meant to hold a single red rose between her teeth; her *real* eyes were black like coal and flashed like lightning; her *real* calling was not engineering but the lambada. When her guidance counselor proposed that she study advanced math and physics, she told him she had other plans, *muchacho,* and repaired to the city's grittiest Hispanic nightclubs, squandering her youth on salsa, sangria, and the secret hope that jealous men would call her *Chiquita* and grab her ass as if there was something there to grab. When she was a sophomore at UC Davis, my brother had told me, Pearl encountered some pistol pocket from Guadalajara in a chat room on the Internet. After corresponding with him for three weeks, she told the world she was in love, dropped her classes, quit her job at Jamba Juice, and flew down to Mexico to spend the winter in his arms. I wonder what he thought when he met *her* in the flesh?

Whatever my reservations and whatever the truth, between Arsalan's boredom and my unfinished chapter it was easy to pick up our correspondence right where we left it. Despite the odd sensation I'd felt speaking to him on the phone, I found it just as natural to chat with him by e-mail as before, so much so that I told him how surprised I'd been by his accent.

From: Arsalan arsalan@hotmail.com
Date: November 22, 2003 03:16 PM
To: Claire Berlinski claire@berlinski.com
Subject: Re: Burnt City

Yes, and I had imagined you with a French accent.

From: Claire Berlinski claire@berlinski.com
Date: November 22, 2003 03:20 PM
To: Arsalan arsalan@hotmail.com
Subject: Re: Re: Burnt City

A *what*? Where did you get that idea? Why would I have a French accent? I'm American.

From: Arsalan arsalan@hotmail.com
Date: November 22, 2003 03:26 PM
To: Claire Berlinski claire@berlinski.com
Subject: Re: Re: Re: Burnt City

I don't quite know. You live in Frnce, I suppose. I pologize for my spelling. This keybord is covered in dust, nd the first letter of the lphbet is so filthy tht it is sticking. This whole miserble city is covered in dust. I have just been served stew of sheep ft and dust. I'm covered in dust. I cn't wsh it off becuse the wter here is rtioned.

Moreover—ah, banging sharply on the keyboard seems to fix things!—I have just received an e-mail from my colleague, the director of a team of archaeologists working near the Burnt City. The team arrived at the site yesterday only to discover that smugglers had looted seven graves. Each grave contained twenty to eighty artifacts. I can safely say there are no comparable artifacts anywhere in the world. This trip has been a complete waste of time. It's simply not enough for a few hapless archaeologists to traipse from village to village speaking slowly to these thieving rural idiots. We need armed guards at the site, day and night. But the officials haven't implemented a single security measure, damn them.

I was—perhaps a bit naively—puzzled to hear this. Several nights before, I'd picked up a book from Dr. Mostarshed's bookshelf and had been reading it since with great interest. It was a study of Shi'a Islam and the intellectual origins of the Iranian Revolution called *The Mantle of the Prophet*, written by a professor of medieval Eastern history at Harvard. I was struck by the author's account of the ordinary Persian's sense of history. It seemed, from the way he described it, that Iranians viewed the ancient past as something fully relevant to their daily lives, a source of passionate pride and burning grievances. The Shah repeatedly likened himself to Cyrus the Great, commissioning lavish banquets to celebrate himself as his heir—which is, when you think about it, quite strange; it is hard to imagine Jacques Chirac, for example, positioning himself in an election campaign as the sacred heir of Vercingetorix.

From: Claire Berlinski claire@berlinski.com
Date: November 22, 2003 03:44 PM
To: Arsalan arsalan@hotmail.com
Subject: Re: Re: Re: Re: Burnt City

But Persians are known for treasuring their past, aren't they? I would have thought protecting the nation's archaeological heritage would figure prominently in the government's priorities.

From: Arsalan arsalan@hotmail.com
Date: November 22, 2003 03:56 PM
To: Claire Berlinski claire@berlinski.com
Subject: Re: Re: Re: Re: Re: Burnt City

You would think so. But you would be dead wrong. Not only do they do nothing to protect it; they're actively destroying it: building proud, stupid dams across the country that will cause untold damage to thousands of priceless sites. We will never even know what will be submerged. Thousands of reliefs, graves, ancient caves, and other remains from the Elamite era are already underwater. The dams threaten the remains of Pasargadae, the capital of ancient Persia. Cyrus the Great's mausoleum is at risk. It survived looting by Alexander and wave after wave of invaders who descended upon Persia from the shores of the Caspian, from Central Asia, from Arabia. Innumerable wars were fought, towns fell, their inhabitants massacred, and yet the ruins remained. Its excavation, in the 1930s, was one of the great triumphs of modern archaeology. And now it faces burial under mud. It sickens me and robs me of my sleep.

I was sorry to hear about it—it surprised me, in fact, how much it disturbed me, although I'm not sure whether it was because of my own sentimentality about the ruins or because I felt so sorry for Arsalan, who reminded me of a man helplessly watching a member of his family drown. It seemed to me a grievous crime, in any event. Archaeological ruins are like the giant pandas; they are particularly poignant when endangered. It's terrible to think that once they're gone, they're gone forever, and no amount of regret will bring them back. I had been outraged by the Taliban's destruction of the Great Buddhas. So had Arsalan. "I had never seen those Buddhas," he wrote. "And now I never will."

I did not hear from him again for the rest of the day, nor the day after. But on the following morning, there was a message waiting for me when I opened my e-mail.

From: Arsalan arsalan@hotmail.com
Date: November 24, 2003 07:56 AM
To: Claire Berlinski claire@berlinski.com
Subject: The Veil

Dear Claire,

I know your time in Istanbul is coming to a close. I have returned to Isfahan, and have found, waiting for me, an invitation to the UNESCO conference in Paris next month. I would not ordinarily go to such a thing, but if you would only beckon me to come, I shall accept.

When shall it come to pass, ah when,
That suddenly, beyond our ken,
We shall succeed to rend this veil
That hath our whole affair conceal?

I await your word.

Arsalan

· · ·

I reread the poem. I wondered if he realized that were the veil to be rent at that moment, he would see me with dirty hair, sleep-swollen eyes, and a red splotch on my cheek where my pillow had been. When he imagined me, did he see me as I was now, wearing an old stained Appalachian State University Athletics sweatshirt my mother had found at a thrift store, my toenail polish flaking off, surrounded by unwashed dishes I'd been too lazy to carry to the sink?

I did not answer right away.

From: Samantha Allen allens@aol.com
Date: November 24, 2003 04:15 PM
To: Claire Berlinski claire@berlinski.com
Subject: Re: He wants to visit!

I hate to be the killjoy here, but isn't it a bit odd that he's sending you romantic poetry even though he's never even met you? Have you considered the possibility that he's a desperate weirdo?

From: Claire Berlinski claire@berlinski.com
Date: November 24, 2003 04:19 PM
To: Samantha Allen allens@aol.com
Subject: Re: Re: He wants to visit!

No, I think that's totally natural in Iran.

From: Samantha Allen allens@aol.com
Date: November 24, 2003 04:27 PM
To: Claire Berlinski claire@berlinski.com
Subject: Re: Re: Re: He wants to visit!

Exactly my point.

She could be right, I thought. I was more concerned that we simply wouldn't care for each other in the flesh. Or that we would. I thought of Jimmy's lavish declarations of eternal devotion, the way his eyes had moistened with briny Irish tears when we first kissed, how he'd sworn that he would lay down his life for me, *Och aye*, he would.

I sent a reply to Samantha promising her that I would think it over carefully, but several seconds later, the new mail icon swished up. *Message undeliverable. Recipient's mailbox is full.* I sent it again and received the same rejection. How very annoying. I was sure she didn't realize it. Lynne had probably sent her another two dozen high-resolution photographs of her dogs, Casper and Weinberger, chasing the Frisbee on the beach.

Samantha had sent me her phone number once when I was distraught about Jimmy; she had told me to call if ever I needed to talk. I hadn't used it—I don't really like talking on the phone. I scrolled through my old messages, found it, then dialed. A man picked up. "May I speak to—" I began, then realized it was a machine.

"This is Samantha Bryant," said the recording. *Holy shit*, I thought. *She really does sound like a man.* I don't know why that surprised me; she had said so repeatedly, but it did, completely. I knew she screened her calls. If I spoke, she would probably pick up. But I was suddenly shy about speaking to her; I didn't want to discuss this with some man I barely knew. I hung up without leaving a message.

The sun was setting. Imran would be home soon. I sent him a note. What did he make of Arsalan's suggestion? I asked. I made myself some tea, then sat quietly with my thoughts, looking out the window as the evening light illuminated the Golden Horn. Despite myself, I felt a reservoir of suppressed emotion begin to overflow. I hadn't realized how much dormant yearning I had in me.

I finished my tea, then busied myself. I tidied, brushed my teeth, washed my face. Imran replied punctually.

From: Imran Begum imranbegum@gmail.com
Date: November 24, 2003 06:45 PM
To: Claire Berlinski claire@berlinski.com
Subject: Re: Should I say yes?

Dear Friend, I would advise you to meet this man in person, yes. A confrontation with reality will do you no harm. No use living in a phantasy world. But do keep your expectations low, dear friend! Remember how little you know

this man. Letters are not relationships. Patients who cannot see the person to whom they are speaking will readily
confess their most private thoughts. Letter-writers, too!
Don't be misled by this. It is the relief of confession—and
the acceptance offered afterwards—that causes you to believe you've found a kindred spirit. Little to do with the
person to whom you're writing, I'm afraid.

A patient threw up this morning. I briefly considered
moving. All septic cheese.

Much love,

Immie

He was right, I thought. I would never stop wondering about
the Lion if I didn't meet him. There was, to be sure, a chance I
would be terribly disappointed, but if I didn't meet him, there was
no chance I wouldn't be.

And with that thought, I gave in to my hope: I wrote back to
Arsalan and said, *Yes, come.*

CHAPTER SIX

The sound of the phone broke through my earplug barrier. Thinking it might be Arsalan, I rushed to answer it, but it was only Sally. She hoped she wasn't disturbing me while I was working— Dave had poached and chilled an *enormous* salmon in a lime-ginger reduction. "He got it at the fish bazaar. He didn't mean to get such a big one, but he got confused with his numbers, and by the time he figured it out they had it all packed up." There was just far too much for the two of them; should she bring over a care package with some zucchini fritters, too?

I looked at the clock. It was 8:30 in the morning. "Maybe a little later?" I asked.

"I have to go to work. Can I just pop over right now?"

"Yeah, I guess," I said, wishing I were assertive enough to say no. I didn't want to be ungracious when she was trying to be generous. I told myself I would probably appreciate the fish come dinner time.

Sally rang the doorbell twenty minutes later. She was dressed in her blue pinstripe consular officer suit. "Special delivery!" she said, holding out a mountain of salmon under Saran wrap.

"Wow. Thank you." I had no idea what I'd do with that much fish.

"Can I come in just for a jiffy? These shoes are pinching my feet so bad. I just need to put a Band-Aid on my toe."

"Sure," I said, rubbing the sleep out of my eyes and wondering why people assume that if you work at home, you're not really working.

She walked into the kitchen and settled herself on one of the wooden stools, taking off her navy pumps with a sigh and massaging her toes. "Damn. I've run my nylons. How's the book coming along?" She nodded in the direction of my computer. It was sitting open on the kitchen table. I preferred to work in the kitchen—it was a bit quieter than the bedroom, and the Egyptian death mask in the study gave me the creeps.

"Okay, I suppose. Slowly. *Lots* to do," I said meaningfully.

"Wow, this apartment is really noisy," Sally said loudly. "Is it hard to concentrate?"

I closed the kitchen window. "Nearly impossible." *Especially with you here.* I stood up to make some coffee. Sally looked even more annoyed by the noise than I was. "I was hoping for a few minutes of quiet time with you," she said. "I'd like to talk to you about something important."

My heart sank. From her serious expression, I could tell she was aching to have a long conversation about her marriage. However sympathetic I was to Dave, I could see why she might be exasperated. After two years in Istanbul, it did seem that the man should be able to speak Turkish well enough to avoid coming home with a fish the size of Moby Dick. Still, I didn't want to hear about it right then. "Well, have some coffee; the prayers will be over soon." I resigned myself to getting no work done that morning.

She glanced out the window. "It's a nice balcony, though." She struggled to project her voice over the traffic and the muezzin without shouting. "I wish we had one like that. You could grow a beautiful garden there. It's too bad the guy who lives here doesn't do anything with it."

"I don't think he's the gardening type."

When at last the muezzin stopped, Sally put down her coffee. "Claire," she said again, "I'd like to talk to you about something really important." Again, she glanced at the balcony, and suddenly I had a suspicion. *No way*, I thought. *I'm not taking the turtles.* It wasn't even my apartment—I couldn't exactly leave them there as a surprise for Dr. Mostarshed.

"Why, what's up?"

"Let's step out on the balcony, okay? I want to see what the view's like." *It's the same as it is from the window*, I thought. *And it's staying turtle free.* But it was a sunny day, and if she was going to talk my ear off, I figured we might as well get some air. I opened the door to the balcony. Sally stepped outside and sat on one of the uncomfortable canvas chairs. "This is wonderful," she said. "Imagine how you could fix it up in the summer—a hammock, tiki torches—anyway, sit, sit; I want to talk to you." She motioned toward the chair opposite her. I sat down reluctantly.

"So what's up?" I asked her again, trying to get comfortable on the little chair. It was so low that crouching on it instantly made my leg ache. It was the one I'd injured in the motorcycle accident. The leg only hurt me in certain positions, but that was one of them.

Sally leaned toward me, placing both elbows on her knees and clasping her hands. "Well, let me start by saying that I think we've developed quite a good friendship here." Her tone of voice, I thought, was peculiar. She'd suddenly become almost formal. "And over the time we've spent together, I've come to respect and trust you. I've been impressed by your character and your intelligence and your common sense."

"Well . . . thank you." Although everyone likes to be praised, I was a bit puzzled. I wasn't sure what I'd done to impress her that much. We hadn't really known each other that long.

"I think you may already have an idea what I'm going to say to you." I wasn't sure. Somehow this seemed a bit too heavy to be about the turtles. I hoped she wasn't about to tell me she was thinking of leaving Dave.

She looked at me as if she wanted me to encourage her to continue. "No idea; tell me," I said. My neighbor started hammering something. *Whack, whack, whack.* Sally looked in the direction of the noise. I turned up my palms. "I don't know why he's hammering. He hammers all day. It's just what he does. You want to go back in?"

Sally took a deep breath and shook her head "No, this is great out here. Okay—" A car with an unmuffled engine roared up the street and squealed to a halt below the balcony. The driver leaned on his horn. Everyone on the street began shouting in Turkish. I cupped my hand to my ear to indicate that I couldn't hear a word she was saying. She rolled her eyes and waited for a few seconds, then tried again, speaking loudly. "Okay. As I was saying, I've been impressed by you. You're extremely knowledgeable and clear-minded about foreign affairs. When we've spoken about my job at the consulate, I've sensed that you understand what's at stake— how serious it is." The honking and shouting stopped, but the hammering continued. I missed a few words. "—the kinds of challenges we face since September 11," she finished. I cast my mind back over the conversations I'd had with Sally. We had discussed politics only a few times, and I didn't recall saying anything particularly incisive.

Her expression was distinctly odd, I thought. I'd never seen that look on her face before. I tried to figure it out. Her face was *professional*. As if she were explaining that my visa application had been rejected because I had failed to provide legible photocopies of the supplementary documents requested on the nonimmigrant visa application form. She leaned over farther, then she reached over and put her hand on my knee—the knee that hurt. The warm gesture seemed incongruous with her expression. "Claire, as you've probably guessed, I have some special responsibilities at the consulate."

"Huh?"

"Because of your expertise and your contacts, our government has asked me to ask you for your help. You're in a unique position to assist us." *Whack, whack, whack.*

"What on earth do you mean?" Her hand was still on my knee.

"You have a friend we need to speak to. We'd like you to help us meet him. I can tell you we wouldn't ask this if it wasn't critically important to national security."

"What are you talking about, Sally?" Her hand was making me quite uncomfortable, and so was her weird, rehearsed tone of voice. Was she kidding? Or was Sally kind of nuts, like poor Mad Bob Popovich? Mad Bob was one of Imran's classmates in medical school. He seemed absolutely normal in every way, save his conviction that the KGB had placed hidden cameras in the traffic lights to track his every movement. "Who do you mean by *we*?" I asked.

"I mean that I'm authorized to speak on behalf of the U.S. government. We understand that you're in regular contact with an Iranian national named Arsalan Safavi. We urgently need to speak to him in person. We need your help to make that happen."

I stared at her. I had never said a word to her about Arsalan. The hammering seemed to grow louder and louder. *Whack, whack, whack, whack, whack.* "You're kidding me, right?" I said. "You're fucking kidding me, aren't you?"

She wasn't smiling at all.

· · ·

My neighbor was still hammering. A driver began honking, and then, like neighborhood dogs who begin howling just because the first dog started it, every other driver in the vicinity began honking too. Sally's hand was still on my knee. I shifted to the side to dislodge it. "Are you telling me that you work for the CIA?" I asked, needing her to say it out loud.

"Yes, I am." She put her hand back on her own knee. She was still leaning close enough that I could smell her chewing-gum breath.

"You've been lying to me this whole time?"

"The only thing I haven't told you is that. Everything else I've told you is a hundred percent true. And you understand why I couldn't tell you that."

"You've been reading my *mail*? You can't do that. It's against the law. I'm a U.S. citizen."

"No, we haven't been reading your mail. I promise you."

"Then how do you know we write to each other?"

"We've been reading *his* mail."

"Oh, well—no *problem* then! I'm sure that's just what Congress intended you to do! Do you rip off the parts of the letters I wrote before you pass them around the whole fucking federal government?"

"Claire." Sally's voice was calm. "I know this is upsetting, and of course I can understand how you feel. I want to assure you that we're doing this for a reason—a very good reason. You and I both want the same thing. We both want a world where people don't hijack planes and fly them into the World Trade Center. The people we're trying to learn about aren't Boy Scouts. You *know* there are people in the world who want to see us dead. A lot of them live in Arsalan Safavi's neck of the woods. You saw those towers collapse like everyone else. Can you think of anything we need more these days than good intelligence? Do you really think we're doing this because we just like reading other people's mail?"

"Who is he? Why do you want to talk to him?"

"Unfortunately, Claire, this is going to be the hard part for you. I can't tell you much about that."

"You can't tell me?" I could hear my voice rise and end in a squeak. I made myself take a deep breath. "How can you not tell me?"

"The fact that I can't tell you should give you confidence that we take operational security very, very seriously. It should reassure you that we're professionals and we know how to keep both of you safe."

Keep us safe? This freckled, button-nosed woman with teeth like piano keys—a woman who couldn't even keep her own husband from building a turtle hutch in the living room—was going to *keep me safe?* From *what?*

"Is he a terrorist? Is he in Hezbollah? Why the hell has he been writing to *me?*"

"No. No. Relax. He is definitely not a terrorist. He's not a bad guy at all. You don't need to be afraid of him. We just need to talk to him."

"About *what?*"

"About things U.S. policy makers need to know to keep us safe. I wish I could tell you more than that—I understand how frustrating it must be to hear this—but I know you understand why I can't."

"Why has he been writing to me? Why me?"

"I can't tell you that, unfortunately—"

"*Oh yes you can.* If you don't tell me that, I'm getting on the next plane out of here. And as soon as I've done that, I'm writing to him and telling him everything you've just told me."

She blanched. "Claire—that would be a really bad move. You seem to know the law pretty well, so you probably know the laws about divulging the identity of an undercover operative."

She's *threatening* me now? Some recruiting technique. I stood up. "It's time for you to go, Sally. Or whatever your name really is." I opened the door to the kitchen and pointed her toward it.

"Wait. Wait. I'll tell you this, okay? It's just a coincidence. We think it's just a coincidence. He just happened to start writing to you. Your involvement in this is a complete accident. But it's a happy accident, as far as we're concerned, because we know you're a patriotic American who understands something about this world."

I stood there with my hand on the door. "He just *happened* to start writing to me? You expect me to believe that?"

"He really loves spy novels."

"How do you know that?"

"We know what he looks at on the Internet. He reads a lot of reviews on Amazon.com."

"Sounds like you have your proctoscope way the hell up the poor guy's ass, so why don't you just contact him yourself?"

"We don't want to cause trouble for him. We need to meet him outside of Iran—for his safety. We know he's coming to see you—"

"You know that already? You don't waste a *minute*, do you." It suddenly dawned on me that she had insisted on coming out to the balcony because she thought Dr. Mostarshed's apartment was bugged. Who did she think was listening? I wondered. The Iranians? The Turks? "So why don't you just meet him by accident in a coffee shop, the way you met me?"

"Well—I don't want to get into details, but Iranians are very suspicious. They have to be. They live under a brutal government. We think an introduction from someone he trusts would go a long way."

"So I'm supposed to invite him for a romantic weekend and then say, 'Hey, baby, by the way, my friend Sally from the CIA will be joining us'?"

"Actually, we'd ask you not to mention that to him. We'll disclose our status when and if we feel it's appropriate."

"Let me get this straight. You want me to lie to my friend, invite him to Europe under false pretenses, and put him at grave risk without his consent. Do you know what would happen to him if he got caught meeting an American spook? They'd hang him. *No way.* I can't do that to him. I won't do it."

"We're going to make sure that doesn't happen. We're professionals. We know how to do this securely."

"Like you handled that guy who got hit by the taxi? *No way.*"

"Hold on a second, Claire. What makes you so sure he wouldn't want you to introduce us? Don't you think he has the same concerns about the world that we do?"

I was caught short by that question. I wasn't sure how to answer it. Finally, I said, "He's an archaeologist. I think I know him well enough to know that whatever you've got in mind is the last thing he wants to be mixed up in. The last thing either of us wants to be mixed up in."

"Don't be so sure. Do you think living the way people live in Iran is easy? Do you think he likes living in a medieval theocracy? Do you think he supports their foreign policy? You know, *Death to America*?" She paused. "And if you think that, why would you protect him?"

I stood there with my hand on the door. She gestured toward the chair, as if urging me to sit back down again. I remained standing. "What exactly would you want me to do?" I said at last. "I'm not saying I'll do it."

"We want you to keep writing to him just as you have been. We want you to encourage him to visit you as soon as possible. And when he does, we want you to invite a few friends around to your home in a natural, nonalerting way. I'll be one of those friends. That's all we need. We'll take it from there."

I didn't know what Arsalan would want me to do. "I need to think about this. I can't make this decision on the spot."

"Why not?" Clearly, she had expected me to be more cooperative. Perhaps she'd thought I would be cowed by the mystique of the CIA. Perhaps she'd thought I would unquestioningly accept that this mission was vital to national security. Perhaps she'd thought that after September 11, there was nothing I wouldn't do for my country if asked.

And perhaps she was right about all of that. I just needed to think.

"I'm not going to make a decision this big without thinking about it. I'll call you when I've thought it over."

She rubbed her forehead wearily as if she were getting a headache. "Well, that's fine. Think it over. I understand this is a lot to take in all at once. But it's best if we don't use the phone from now on. We want to take every possible measure to assure your confidentiality. So let's meet in person."

My confidentiality? Did she mean my safety? Who did she think was listening to my phone? "Fine, whatever."

"Let's meet tomorrow evening at 7:30, in Üsküdar." Üsküdar was on the Anatolian side of Istanbul. I had never been there. "Take the ferry to Üsküdar from Eminönü. When you get off the ferry, turn right. Walk up the boardwalk about half a block. If you look left, across the street, you'll see a large Ferris wheel. Meet me at the base of the Ferris wheel."

"Why Üsküdar?" I asked, expecting some cloak-and-dagger explanation.

She sighed deeply. "Because," she said, "the only reptile vet in Istanbul is in Üsküdar, and I've got a turtle with shell rot."

• • •

I caught the crowded ferry to Üsküdar just as the boat was leaving. There were no seats left, so I walked to the bow of the deck and stood outside. The boat took off at a surprisingly fast clip, rising and falling on the black water, illuminated by a golden harvest moon, trailed by wheeling gulls. Droplets sprayed over the bow, splashing my face with cool mist. On the shore in every direction gigantic mosques and minarets glowed like fire. The great Topkapi Palace, in the distance, reminded me of those old comic book advertisements for Amazing Live Sea-Monkeys Magic Castles. I'd

been fascinated by those ads as a child, but even at the age of eight
I was a sufficiently savvy consumer to guess that if I ordered a
Magic Castle, it wouldn't look quite the way I imagined it. Still, I
always wondered if anything in the world really looked like that.
Now I knew.

The strait was quiet and as smooth as black ice. A pimpled
teenaged waiter in a white uniform came around to the deck with
small glasses of tea as we neared the shore. Atatürk, somber as a sea
captain, presided over the stairwell. Atatürk always dressed for the
occasion. In restaurants, he was a dignified headwaiter. He became
a striking martial figure at police stations. In schools he was a patient headmaster. The Turks saw in him whatever they needed to
see, and who was I to laugh?

I still had not decided what to do.

The boat reached Üsküdar at 7:25. I stepped out into Asia,
which looked, apart from the Ottoman architecture, like Coney Is-
land. The boardwalk was packed with revelers. Merchants hawked
festive food near the ferry dock: an elderly man was selling cotton candy from a churning vat built into the trunk of his car;
ice cream scoopers made dramatic shows of waving their ladles,
dipping cones into molten chocolate and nuts. Popcorn was pop-
ping; kebabs were sizzling; everyone was shouting—*balıkbalıkbalık*,
balıkbalıkbalık, fishfishfish, fishfishfish. For three lira you could
rent a plastic gun and shoot the colored balloons bobbing in a row
in the Bosphorus, or throw a ball into a rubber basket for a prize.
Hawkers selling live bunnies and chicks plied their wares beside
hawkers peddling fake wooden snakes on strings. The bunnies and
chicks looked freaked out by the snakes. I was sympathetic: they
did slither in a disturbingly lifelike way.

Sally was at the Ferris wheel at precisely 7:30, dressed in denim
overalls that made her look as if she'd just arrived from milking the
cows. She was carrying a miserable-looking turtle in a plastic bag
filled with water. When she saw me she waved, then walked up
to me. "Hey," she said softly. She gave me a light pat on the arm.

"Glad you found it okay. How are you?" Her gentle tone of voice took me aback. I wasn't prepared for that: I'd been expecting a brisk, professional, spylike encounter.

"I'm okay," I said. The turtle was hurling himself frantically at the sides of the plastic bag, paddling his flippers like a windmill. His little reptile face looked more furious than frightened.

"This must be tough on you," she said.

I searched her face for any sign of insincerity, a cold mask behind those sympathetic words, but I didn't see one. "I'm fine." I shrugged. I didn't want to talk about my feelings.

"Want to walk a bit?" she asked.

"Fine." I wondered if she wanted to keep moving so she could see if anyone was following us, then wondered how the hell you'd ever know in these crowds. There were thousands of people on the boardwalk, strolling and eating and inspecting the goods strewn across the pavement—clusters of *nargile* pipes, yo-yos, toy cars, balloons, carpets, plastic dolls, cheap crap of every variety.

"How are you feeling about what we talked about?" she asked as we walked.

"I want to know more about what he does on the Internet."

"Beg pardon?" Once again, it was hard for us to hear each other. Across the street, a huge mob had gathered for an open-air concert with acrobats; parents lifted their children onto their shoulders to see. Through the windows of some kind of club overlooking the water, I could see men in uniform entertaining women in strapless dresses.

"You told me you knew what books he looked at on Amazon. What else does he do?"

"I don't remember, off the top of my head. He looks at a lot of archaeology stuff. Why?"

"Is he writing to anyone else?"

"You mean, the way he writes to you? Are you asking if he has another girlfriend? No. He doesn't."

She had no reason to lie about that—not one that I could think of, anyway. If Arsalan was corresponding with other women, she would probably tell me. It would make me less likely to care what happened to him.

We walked without speaking for a few moments. The stairs between the boardwalk and the water were covered with woven carpets and embroidered cushions. Teenaged girls—some in head-scarves, some in tiny tight sweaters—had come out to flirt with the teenaged boys who were hanging out on the steps, playing Turkish folk songs on their guitars. "Let's sit down," I said, spotting two empty cushions.

Sally acquiesced, setting the turtle beside her. Across the black water, I could see the turrets and clock tower of the massive Haydarpaşa train station. Arsalan had once told me the train to Teheran left from that station once a week. From Teheran you could connect to Isfahan.

"What makes you so sure he wants to speak to you?" I asked. I wasn't sure what I expected her to say.

She looked as if she were thinking it over, trying to decide what she could tell me. Finally she said, "He needs our help."

"With *what*?" What kind of help could he need? Was he in trouble?

"I'm just not at liberty to discuss that."

"How do you know he needs your help?"

"Claire—" she said, and didn't finish. At last she asked, "What difference would it make?"

It would make all the difference, I thought. But I knew she wouldn't tell me. I watched the families who had come out for the evening with their children to sit on the cushions and watch the view. Near us, a woman swathed in a black *hijab* was trying to keep her hyperactive toddler under control. He was picking up and flinging the contents of his diaper bag with loud gleeful shrieks.

I didn't know if I believed her. I had no faith in the competence of the CIA. I had no idea what Arsalan would want me to do. It was not *his* fault that the Iranian regime was barbaric. It was not *his* fault that his government hated us and was building the Bomb. I studied Sally's big freckled face. "Claire," she said, "I can promise you—"

Suddenly, the toddler shrieked piercingly, and we both turned in the direction of the noise. "Oh, *no!*" Sally exclaimed. He had picked up the bag with the turtle. *"No! Hayir!"* She reached out to grab it back, but she wasn't fast enough. It all happened in a split second. The child hurled the bag to the ground. The bag exploded. The turtle skedaddled. "Shit—find him!" Sally cried, dropping to her knees. The child's mortified mother grabbed him by the hand and began shouting at him while apologizing plaintively to Sally in rapid Turkish, getting right in Sally's way. The kid started crying hysterically. Sally was on the ground, feeling around for the turtle, but in the dark and the crowds and the chaos, she couldn't see him; he was too small and too fast. I couldn't see him either—he was probably in the Bosphorus already. At last, after crawling and patting the ground in every direction, she looked up at me. "Where could he have gone?" she asked helplessly. I noticed again how big her teeth were. She had never looked more to me like a giant rabbit. I watched the whole incident with horror, realizing that my fate and Arsalan's would be in the hands of this frantic, incompetent woman who was on the ground on all fours searching for an errant reptile. I looked around too, but it was hopeless: the turtle had taken the Midnight Express.

So why, you might ask, did I agree to help her?

I agreed because however much I disliked Sally, she was right. I knew what was at stake.

THREE

BACK IN PARIS, AGAIN

I have been Your lover and been with You a thousand times;
Yet each time you see me, Your question is always "Who is he?"

—HAFEZ

CHAPTER SEVEN

Is the Central Intelligence Agency really as bursting with ninnies as is thought by many, including, it would seem, by Claire Berlinski? . . . It's hard to believe America could have averted another 9/11 or similar calamity—so far, at least—if our intelligence providers had been quite as dimwitted as the book suggests.

—DAVID KLINGHOFFER,
reviewing *Loose Lips* for *National Review*

Imran was nearly a half hour late, which irritated me immensely, not only because Imran, I well knew, was carrying seven time-pieces but because he had promised to bring an eggbeater with him on the Eurostar from London. I would have called him, but he didn't carry a cell phone. Imran refused to carry anything made of plastic. The other guests would be arriving in thirty minutes. The lasagnas were in the oven—one meat and one vegetarian, for Lynne—and the Caesar salad needed only to be dressed. The wine was chilling. The table was set. But I hadn't even started on the mousse. It seemed to me urgent beyond measure that I begin whipping the hell out of those egg whites.

I checked myself in the mirror again, then looked out the window at the scurrying umbrellas on the Place Dauphine. The cobblestones were slick and shiny. It had been raining implacably since my return to Paris four days earlier, and the Seine was foul and turbid. Dr. Mostarshed had left my apartment in seemingly immaculate condition; nonetheless, I had spent every minute since my return scrubbing and sterilizing it. When I took the sheets Dr. Mostarshed had used to the Laundromat to boil them, a car had rounded the corner and sprayed me with puddle-mud; I had returned with my jeans soaked.

Samantha and Lynne had been in Paris since that morning, staying at a romantic hotel on the Île St.-Louis. I had not yet met them. It had been easy to convince Imran to come; for him, it was only a three-hour trip, and he always enjoyed coming to Paris to shop for badger-hair shaving brushes. Samantha had required a bit more coaxing. Paris, I suggested to her at last, would be the ideal place to break the news to Lynne. It was the City of Love, after all. Lynne was sure to be too overwhelmed with the romance to focus on the little details. Samantha, grasping at any hope, thought it might be worth a shot; she had frequent-flier miles she had to use before they expired, anyway. She invited Lynne, and Lynne accepted, coyly telling her she would bring her best lingerie.

I would be the only one at the table who knew why Sally was really there. As far as everyone else was concerned, she was someone I'd met in a café in Istanbul who had come to Paris for a weekend holiday. Nor did anyone but me know the truth about Samantha. (Except for Imran, to whom I'd written about her, and Arsalan, to whom I'd also written about her, recounting the whole story, and Sally, to whom I'd also told the story, on one of our runs. So I suppose, actually, everyone but Lynne knew. But Samantha didn't know they knew—I had promised to keep her secret. How was I supposed to know we'd all wind up like this together?)

The doorbell rang. *About time*, I thought, wiping my hands on my apron and preparing to chastise Imran for his tardiness. But when I opened the door it was Sally, which infuriated me. "You're early," I said pointedly. She was also inappropriately dressed. She was wearing that dowdy blue pinstripe consular officer suit again. This was a dinner party in Paris. Why did she look like some frumpy government employee? Didn't they teach them anything about fashion at the Farm? Charlene, I thought, would never have made that mistake. I was wearing a black silk chiffon party frock with tiny rhinestones on the lace-up corset bodice, chandelier earrings, and my highest-heeled black sandals. Not only did Sally look matronly; she had succeeded in making me look overdressed. "You look wonderful," she said, and handed me a bottle of wine. It was something cheap. I thanked her and stuck it under the sink.

"What a nice apartment," she said. "It's so cozy."

"Yep." I busied myself lighting the candles on the dinner table. She looked out the window. The doorbell rang again. It was Imran, at last—in a Haggarts tweed shooting suit with a waistcoat and matching tweed cap. "Where have you been?" I hissed. "You were supposed to be here ages ago."

"There was a holdup on the train. Some grizzled chain-smoking multiple addict with anxiety up to his ears threatened to immolate himself in the station." He kissed me on the cheek and handed me a bag with an eggbeater in it. "You look lovely."

I looked at him, baffled by his outfit. "Are you going fox hunting?"

"Don't you like it? I just bought the waistcoat today in St. James. I ordered a Gladstone bag in Havana brown from my luggage maker to go with it." He spotted Sally, who had come to the door. "Hullo, I'm Imran," he said in a basso voice, extending his hand.

"Sally," she said. They pumped hands. "How do you do."

"Very well indeed," said Imran, smoothing his thick black hair. "An enjoyable day at work. Six compassionate hours. And you?"

"Fine, thanks," she said, and smiled her friendly rabbit smile. "What kind of work do you do?"

"I run an entity called The Applied Philosophy Centre." He said this grandly. "Which is, essentially, my Harley Street consulting room. The Centre offers cognitive, gestalt, psychodynamic, and philosophical approaches to emotional wellness. I am founder, chairman, treasurer, decanter filler, and dustbin emptier, with special responsibility for purchasing tissues and air freshener." He raised himself slightly on his toes. "I hope to be promoted next year." He lowered his spectacles and peered over them curiously. "And you?"

"Oh, I—"

"Why don't you both sit down?" I interrupted. "Come in, come in. Just leave the umbrella in the hall; no one will take it. Can I get you a glass of wine?" I ushered them toward the old futon I'd dragged up from my storage room. I'd put it on cinder blocks and propped it up against the radiator to serve as a couch. With the futon, the folding table, and all the extra chairs I'd borrowed from my father, my studio looked cramped and tiny.

"Yes, and I'll take a jug of water, too, thank you," said Imran. "At least two pints." Imran took hydration very seriously.

"I'd love a glass of wine," said Sally. I went to the kitchen and opened the Gewürztraminer. When I returned, Imran was explaining to Sally his schedule for the coming eighteen hours. From 10:00 the next morning, when the stores opened, until noontime, when he would pause for light refreshment, he would look through the Marais for a particular shaving brush, one with bristles from the *neck* of the badger, not the back, gently tapered to a wooden grip made with finely grained Finnish pine and oiled to ensure its water resistance. After refreshing himself, he would shop for marigold-scented shaving cream at his favorite bespoke perfumer, whose boutique was orthogonal to the rue St.-Honoré. "You sound quite the collector," Sally said politely.

"Quite. My mother was an exceptionally anhedonic woman. She refused to spend money on luxury consumption. No meals out, no theater tickets, no vacations. I make a point now of spending an amount *more* than appropriate to my income bracket on shaving equipment, antique watches, and handmade shoes. It's a compensation for her inadequate mothering."

"It is? Does it work?" asked Sally, with what sounded like genuine interest. Before he could answer, the doorbell rang again. My heart was thumping so stridently that I was amazed Sally and Imran could hear each other over it. From the bathroom I overheard a snippet of their conversation; Sally was saying, "I must say she sounds quite a bit like my father. My father—"

Sam was standing on the doorstep holding a bouquet of carnations mixed with baby's breath. His arm was draped lightly over Lynne's shoulders. *"Bonsoir!"* they said in unison, his voice deep and resonant, hers high and girlish.

I was stunned. They didn't look weird at all.

• • •

When Samantha had written to me about Lynne, I had asked myself repeatedly, *How could this woman be so obtuse?* I had thought it impossible that any normal woman could fail to notice, upon close inspection, that her boyfriend was in fact a girlfriend. But Sam did not seem to me, as he had in his photographs, even slightly effeminate. He must have practiced a lot since they were taken. He was a head taller than Lynne, fleshy but not fat, dapper in a navy suit with a red tie and suspenders. He looked every bit a man—from his shoes and his watch to his posture and his short gelled hedgerow of hair. His facial hair looked just like a real five-o'clock shadow. And were those Samantha's real eyebrows? Not only were they bushy in a masculine way, they *wriggled* like male eyebrows. "Sam! Come in, come in!" I remembered to urge, and turning to the angular woman beside him added, "You must be Lynne. I'm Claire." I kissed her cheek, and then Sam's. His stubble felt just like stubble—he even smelled like a man; in fact, he smelled just like a British naval officer with whom I'd once had a summer fling.

Lynne was even more consumptive than she'd appeared in

her photograph, a pallid, goose-bumpy creature with insect limbs, dressed in a short plaid skirt and pointy-toed alligator boots. "Come in, have a seat," I urged again. "How thoughtful of you," I said to Sam, taking the carnations. "Let me take your coat," I said to Lynne. "Who wants wine? We all do, don't we. I'll get us some. It's just about chilled. German. I have a French wine, too, if anyone wants one. Well, of course we do; we're in France. So much good wine here. Not like Istanbul—that's not a great wine-drinking city! I'll just pour us a few glasses. You must still be so jet-lagged. Air travel is the worst. I'm always a zombie for days after that flight. I can't sleep on planes, ever; I always look at people who seem to be sleeping so soundly in those little seats and wonder—"

I realized how I sounded, and shut up.

Lynne sat down on the edge of the sofa, placing one of her feelers on Sam's thigh; Sam sat next to her, stretching out his legs and hooking his thumbs underneath his suspenders. They looked perfectly natural together. I went to the kitchen to get the wine and noticed that the glasses had spots. I gave them a quick rinse. By the time I came back out, Imran had taken control of the conversation.

"—a new patient, a stammerer who's a 37-year-old virgin—"

Sam and Lynne were looking at him with bewilderment, but Sally seemed fascinated. I was grateful for her social skills. "Here's the wine!" I interrupted. I passed out glasses and poured to the rim. Sam downed half of his in a single gulp. I followed suit. I looked at my watch: it was 7:15.

Arsalan had promised to bring caviar, and I had planned to serve that as the hors d'oeuvre. I'd put out crackers, hard-boiled eggs, and crème fraîche, but the caviar hadn't arrived. Everyone looked hungry. I rummaged around the kitchen cabinet and found some peanuts. When I placed them on the table, Lynne flinched, visibly.

"Oh, *God*," whispered Lynne, looking up at Sam.

Sam looked at me as if I'd just set out a bowl of maggots. "Claire, Lynne's allergic. If that gets in her food she'll die."

"Oh," I said, quickly taking them off the table. "I'm so sorry."

"You couldn't know," said Lynne. She turned to Sam and whispered. "Didn't you tell her?"

Given a choice between admitting to Lynne that he hadn't and making me look like a murderer, Sam chose the latter. "Of course I did," he whispered back to Lynne, loud enough for everyone to hear. Lynne pursed her lips and gave me the look you'd give to an idiot who'd tried to dry her cat in the microwave. Sam put his hand on Lynne's insectoid thigh and scowled at me protectively.

Well, I thought. *This is getting off to a great start.* Imran looked as if he just might be gearing up to ask me why I felt so much rage toward my guest that I'd wanted to kill her. "I'm just going to whip the egg whites for the dessert," I said and scurried off to the kitchen.

I applied myself to the egg whites. The eggbeater was stiff, and the eggs didn't whip well. I beat them and beat them, but all I got was mild foam. Where was Arsalan? I poked my head out of the kitchen and saw Sally looking at her watch. Sam was gazing longingly at Lynne, who was listening to Imran with intense concentration on her face. I didn't know what Imran was saying, but I feared it might be something that would prompt Lynne to go into a neurotic reaction—she looked to me like the sort. God, I hoped he wasn't telling her that anaphylactic shock was in fact typically an expression of repressed rage and internal conflict about achieving orgasm.

Whatever was going on, I supposed I ought to head it off at the pass. "So," I said, striding out of the kitchen. "I'm sorry to interrupt, but who here is good at beating egg whites? They're not whipping up the way they're supposed to. Lynne? Are you a good cook?"

"Hopeless, I'm afraid."

"Anyone?" I asked.

Sally looked at her watch again, and looked at me.

Imran cleared his throat. "Sally," he said in his low, slow, psychotherapist voice, "I've noticed that you've checked your watch several times since we sat down. Are you waiting for something?"

Sally looked startled but recovered quickly. "No, no," she said breezily. "I was just wondering what time it was."

"I see." Imran leaned in her direction, adopting an active-listening posture. "Were you aware that when I asked you that question, your body language changed?"

"It did?" asked Sally.

"Yes, and it just did again. Your shoulders tightened, and you crossed your arms and legs more securely." I felt my shoulders tightening too.

"Really?" Sally uncrossed her arms and legs. "I wonder why?"

"May I offer a thought?" said Imran. This seemed like dangerous territory, but I was too curious to see where he was going to try to stop him. "I've noticed that when I consult a timepiece repeatedly, it's often because I feel anxiety." *No shit, Imran.* "It's quite normal to feel anxiety in new social situations. In our modern safe world, you see, the survival fear has transmogrified into the popularity fear. Social survival is the new *survival.* I would suggest that when you feel the urge to consult your watch, you instead focus on deep, steady breathing and good posture instead."

Everyone looked at their watches.

"You might find it helpful," Imran continued, "prior to entering a new social situation—" The doorbell rang. Sally and I both whipped our heads around.

"I'll get it," I said, leaving them to discuss Sally's anxiety. Before opening the door, I took a deep breath and stood up straight.

"Hi there," said Arsalan, smiling broadly. His arms were full of things—a carry-on bag, a hanging bag, a plastic box with a handle. "Sorry I'm late. Those fools at customs convinced themselves this must be some kind of weapon of mass destruction. I told the inspector, 'You really don't want to put your hand in there, my friend; trust me,' but he didn't believe me." He lifted the box slightly and gestured toward it with his head.

"What is it?"

"Wollef, of course."

. . .

Our eyes met. For a moment we just stared at each other—I wasn't sure what to say. I had imagined him so many times, and now, at last, here he was in front of me. He looked just the way I'd pictured him. He was plump and slightly cross-eyed, and his ears stuck out straight to the side, like Yoda's. At last, I found my voice. "Well *hi*, Wollef," I said. "Hello there, pussycat. You've had a long trip, haven't you, sweetheart?"

He glared at me. He really looked like Yoda. *Cat am I. Patronize me do not dare.* Finally, he sneezed.

Wollef, said Arsalan—who also looked as I'd imagined him—had not cared for the cramped conditions of air travel any more than the rest of us generally do. He had tried taking him out of the box to comfort him, but a flight attendant had come over and had told him to put the cat back: if he went berserk, she warned, it would be a safety hazard. Wollef howled plaintively in his box until Arsalan snuck him out again, put him under his shirt, and stuffed him like a lumbar support in the space between his seat and the small of his back, where the cat had remained, mercifully silent, for the duration of the flight. The flight attendant had not noticed the whiskers and the tail poking out from underneath the armrest.

Arsalan had produced all the appropriate vaccination certificates at customs, as well as his invitation to the UNESCO conference. Nonetheless, he had aroused the inspectors' suspicions. "It happens to me everywhere I go these days," he said without rancor. "I can't really blame them; I'd look closely at Iranians too if I were them. But any idiot could see there was a cat in there." Wollef had by that point been tired, confused, and frightened. Not surprisingly, when a gigantic hand in a rubber glove began probing the interior of his box, he did what any cornered animal would do: he opened up a gigantic can of whup-ass on the glove.

The inspector had yanked his shredded hand from the box. "*Oui, ceci est un chat,*" he concluded hastily, and summoned first aid. Miffed, he had detained Arsalan and Wollef until a Persian translator could be found to vouch for the authenticity of Wollef's rabies certificate.

"We should give him some water," I said to Arsalan, "and something to eat. He'd probably appreciate a litter box, too. You should have told me he was coming. I would have had everything ready for him."

"Well, I didn't know until this morning. I wasn't planning to bring him. The maid's daughter was supposed to care for him— her mother is visiting her sister in Teheran, you see. But fifteen minutes before I was supposed to leave, she still hadn't shown up. She's totally irresponsible. And I just couldn't leave him without being sure, so—"

"Of course. Why don't we take him into the kitchen and see what we can fix up for him? He'd probably be more comfortable alone in the kitchen than outside with all those strangers, don't you think?"

"I think both of us would be, really," he said gently.

I looked at him and suddenly felt awful about the awkward dinner party to which I was about to subject him. He must be so tired after a long day of traveling with an anxious cat. I didn't allow myself to think of the other reasons I might feel guilty. "Hullo," boomed a jovial voice behind me. I turned. Imran looked well into his cups already. "Sorry to interrupt; must go to the loo," he said, undoing his belt buckle. He squeezed past me and into the toilet by the front door. He closed the bathroom door, banged up the toilet seat, loudly unzipped his fly, and began urinating with a great sigh of pleasure. He was, from the sound of it, having no problems with his prostate. Then, still urinating, he began singing the chorus from the "Ode to Joy."

Freude, schöner Götterfunken, Tochter aus Elysium—Whush!
Whush! *Wir betreten feuertrunken, Himmlische, dein Heiligtum!*
Whush! Whush! Whush! It sounded as if Secretariat was in there
taking a leak with Caruso. Whush! Whush! Whush! Wollef
started howling. *Deine Zauber binden wieder,* Imran sang grandly. I
looked up at Arsalan, whose eyebrows were drawn together in puzzlement. Imran kept pissing. Arsalan could not have looked more
confused. Finally, he leaned over and whispered in my ear—I
could feel the warmth of his breath—"That's astonishing! No
wonder the other one can't tell!"

For a moment I had no idea what he meant, and then I understood his confusion, and despite everything I started laughing
uncontrollably—I mean, *completely* uncontrollably. I started laughing and I just couldn't stop. Arsalan looked even more confused. I
finally managed to choke it out. "No, no, that's *Imran,* not Samantha. Imran really *is* a man." When he understood, he started laughing too, which made me laugh even harder. Neither of us could
stop. My face was contorted with the effort of trying to stop.
Imran's stream slowed to a dribble, and for a moment we both
managed to get ourselves under control. Then it started again. *Wo
dein sanfter Flügel weilt!* I doubled over. So did Arsalan. I started
making weird snotty snorting noises; he began choking and
coughing; so did I; he slapped me on the back.

We were both still convulsed in hysteria when Imran emerged.
"Hullo, I'm Imran," he said, offering his hand to Arsalan.

Arsalan smiled at him. He had a truly joyful smile. I hadn't
been expecting that; he hadn't been smiling in his photograph.
"Arsalan. Nice to meet you." They shook hands.

"Looks like you two are making good initial contact. Keep
bonding," said Imran. He clicked his heels, spun around, and
walked back to the others.

I looked at Arsalan again. He had looked intimidating in his
photograph, but in person he looked warm. I was absolutely certain this man planned me no harm. I wondered how long it would

take for everyone in the living room to leave, and whether, perhaps, if we locked ourselves in the kitchen and refused to feed the guests, they would just give up and go away.

"Come on," I said, taking him by the arm. "I'll introduce you to the others."

. . .

Arsalan refrained admirably from staring at Sam. Sam stared at Arsalan. Sally exchanged a pleasant, professional handshake with him, making pleasant, professional eye contact. Lynne cringed at the sight of Wollef—she was allergic to cats, too—but evidently she was not *mortally* allergic to them; she would be fine, she said, if she took a Claritin. I poured everyone more wine. I put the caviar on the table: Arsalan had brought the largest tin of it I'd ever seen. Everyone exclaimed that this was a very wonderful thing for him to have done. I took Wollef to the kitchen and gave him a bowl of water and a plate of tuna fish; he rejected both and bolted, ending up under my bed.

Arsalan looked pained. "I didn't realize he'd hate traveling this much," he said, taking a small finger of tuna, getting on his hands and knees, and trying to coax Wollef back out with it. He spoke to the animal in Persian in a low, gentle voice. Wollef remained under the bed.

"He probably feels safe there. Maybe we should just let him stay there until he feels more comfortable?" I suggested. "We can put some food and water under the bed for him." Arsalan reluctantly agreed; I could tell he was feeling guilty. "We can put some blankets under there too." My only concern was a litter box. I turned one of the lasagnas out onto a serving plate, washed the baking tin, and filled it with soil from a dying houseplant—Dr. Mostarshed, alas, had overwatered it. "There," I said, putting it under the bed. "He should be fine." I got down to look. Resentful eyes glittered back at me.

Arsalan and I were side by side, on the ground, looking under my bed. My shoulder brushed against his. He noticed and I noticed. Neither of us said anything. Neither of us moved.

"Arsalan and Claire!" Sally sang out from the table. "This caviar is fantastic! Come have some before we finish it all!" Arsalan, obviously wondering if it would be ill-mannered to crawl under the bed with his cat, stood up reluctantly to take his place at the table. I followed suit.

Arsalan pulled out my chair, then sat down next to me—directly opposite Sally. "So, Arsalan—" Sally began, but was interrupted by Lynne, who with a great whooping convulsion began sneezing. She sneezed about ten times in a row. "Excuse me," she said, and ran off to the bathroom. She came back with toilet paper in her hand and a very red nose.

"Are you okay?" Sam and I asked simultaneously.

"Ibe fide. Id's just the cat." She wiped her nose and rubbed her eyes.

"Don't rub," whispered Sam. "It will make it worse." Sam looked tense. Apart from saying hello to Arsalan, he'd barely spoken since I put out the caviar. I topped up his wine glass. Lynne reached over and rubbed his thigh affectionately; he smiled at her, but it was a thin-lipped half smile. I wondered if something was bothering him, other than the obvious. His letters had been so lively. Was he always such a drip in person?

I got up to clear the plates and fetch the lasagna. When I returned, Arsalan was making small talk about the museums of Paris with Lynne, who was wiping her running nose and dabbing her watery eyes. Imran was talking to Sally about her father. "That does sound hurtful," Imran said while loading a huge mound of caviar onto his cracker. "I would attribute your dad's comment to envy. I see it as a psychic eructation of pain. Parents also have failings and neuroses—"

"Claire," said Sam quietly, beckoning to me with his index finger. I walked over to him. He stretched up to whisper. "Would you happen to have any Tylenol?"

"Oh sure. Follow me." He followed me into the bathroom; I opened the medicine chest. "Will ibuprofen do?"

"That's fine." He grabbed the bottle and shook out a few pills, then gulped them down with a swig of water from the tap. Standing up, he winced in pain.

"Headache?" I asked sympathetically.

"Time of the month."

Before I could respond, Lynne opened the bathroom door without knocking. There was no lock; I'd broken it long ago and never fixed it, since it would have been expensive and I lived alone, anyway. I jumped so high my head nearly hit the ceiling, but Sam didn't even flinch. I had to hand it to him; he had balls of ice. "Honey?" Lynne said. "Are you okay?" She looked nervous and fluttery. I wondered if she might be jealous; Sam had, after all, whispered something in my ear, then disappeared with me to the bathroom. I wondered how he had explained our relationship to her.

"Yeah, I'm fine. Just a real stiff neck from that flight," he said, stretching his neck from side to side.

"Oh, you poor thing! Come over to the table and I'll give you a neck rub." Sam cast me a helpless glance and followed Lynne's pointy boots back to the table. Lynne turned her chair toward him and began rubbing his neck, digging her bony thumbs into his trapezius muscles like a manic Roto-Rooter. If he didn't really have neck pain before, he certainly had it now.

"Neck pain?" Imran asked Sam.

Sam nodded manfully. "Old baseball injury," he said. Arsalan caught my eye; he looked as if he were trying not to laugh, which made me worry I was going to start laughing again, too. I bit my lip hard. I had to look away from him. I busied myself by making sure everyone had enough lasagna and salad.

"In my experience," Imran offered, "neck pain, like gastric distress, is often related to suppressed emotions. I notice that I suffer from neck and joint pain when I'm holding in my feelings too tightly."

I suddenly noticed that my neck was aching, and stretched it side to side.

"Neck pain?" Arsalan whispered to me. I nodded. He put his hand on my neck and rubbed it gently.

"Really," said Sam at the same time, looking as if he might like to inflict neck and joint pain of the nonsomatic variety on Imran.

"Oh, very much so," said Imran. "I also notice that your energy and mood have changed over the course of the evening. Are you feeling fatigued?"

"Jet lag." Terse.

"I'll offer you a thought," said Imran in the paternal voice he uses when addressing highly disturbed people. "The more emotionally expressive I am, the less tired I feel. I've found this to be true for many of my patients."

"You don't say."

"I do indeed. Secrets are tiring. Suppressions and repressions, too." He looked meaningfully at Sam. Sam looked at me with alarm. I shrugged as if to say, *I have no idea what he's talking about.* I looked meaningfully at Arsalan. He raised an eyebrow. He stopped rubbing my neck but left his hand on my back. Sally looked meaningfully at Lynne, who didn't seem to notice. The room was suddenly very quiet. I heard a scratching sound and looked in the direction of the noise. *Scratch, scratch.*

"What's that?" asked Sally.

"Wollef," said Arsalan and I simultaneously, with great relief. *Scratch, scratch.* Soil came flying out from under the bed. "Well!" I said. "Looks like he's feeling right at home! Who wants more lasagna?" *Scratch, scratch.* A *lot* of soil came flying out.

Lynne's coat was on top of the bed. She looked at the flying clumps of soil. Her skin, pale to begin with, turned white as the interior of a radish. "No, thanks," she said weakly. "I'm fine." Wow, I thought. If a little bit of used kitty litter skeeved her out so much that she lost her appetite, I really wouldn't want to be there when Sam explained how the rest of their romantic weekend in Paris was going to go down, so to speak.

"I'll have some more," Imran boomed cheerily, holding out his plate. "It's delicious." *Scratch, scratch*. I put another large helping on his plate. "More wine, too, please. Did I tell you that I bedded an ex-nun the other day? A more virginal middle-aged woman you could not imagine. Sadly she's 'fallen in love' "—he made mock quotation marks in the air—"so playful pokes are now *ausgeschlossen*."

"A nun, Imran?" I said. "A *nun*?"

"An *ex*-nun. She orgasmed very easily, especially when I taught her to breathe slowly and deeply into the pleasure, diaphragmatically. I would guess this is why she 'fell in love' so deeply and quickly. She mistook my devotion to her orgasm for devotion to her. A shame."

Lynne looked stupefied. Sam looked revolted. Sally looked fascinated. Imran dug into his meal with relish. "Mmmmm," he said. "Well done with this lasagna, really. It's just lovely."

• • •

"I coated the cylinders of my Jag in polytetrafluoroethylene last week," Imran offered the table. "It's been noticeably quieter and more economical since. Almost thirty to the gallon."

"Really?" said Arsalan. "That's Teflon, isn't it?" I noticed that we needed more wine; I got up to get some from the kitchen. Sam was looking miserable. Lynne was still sneezing. Wollef was still scratching.

As I reached the kitchen, I overheard Sally. "Arsalan," she said brightly, "I understand you're an archaeologist. That is *such* a coincidence."

I froze at the kitchen door. I had an impulse to run back to him and shout, *No! Don't talk to her!* I stood there with the empty lasagna tray in my hand, listening.

"It is?" said Arsalan.

"Yes, it's such a coincidence, because I really need an archaeologist's advice."

"Why; will you be needing to be mummified?" Arsalan asked politely.

"I'm sorry?" said Sally.

"I've just never heard anyone say they really needed an archaeologist's advice before." He sounded more curious than suspicious—and, alas, he sounded flattered.

"Yes," said Sally, "it's such a coincidence—and especially because you're from Iran. I'm so glad I ran into you this evening. I just found out this morning that I'm going to be managing a fund earmarked for Iranian archaeological conservation projects. I could really use your thoughts about the projects that would most benefit."

"A fund for Iranian archaeological conservation projects?" His voice registered surprise. "What kind of fund?"

"We received a bequest from an anonymous donor. I suspect it's probably a wealthy Iranian American. The donor asked the State Department to manage it, and since of course we don't have an embassy in Iran, we're going to manage it from Turkey."

"That's odd; why would he give it to the State Department? Why wouldn't he ask UNESCO to manage it? Or give it directly to a university?"

"You know, I don't even know who he is, so I couldn't tell you exactly, but I can tell you that it isn't that uncommon. In our country, many people don't really feel comfortable with the United Nations. For some Americans, it has a bad reputation—you know, for corruption, mismanagement, that sort of thing. And perhaps he didn't want to be in direct contact with Iranian universities. Maybe he's someone who has a troubled relationship with your government. Maybe they wouldn't be allowed to accept money from him directly. That would be my guess."

"And you're going to be deciding where the money goes? How much money is involved?"

She certainly had his attention now. I felt helpless, as if I were watching a bus stall on the railway tracks as the train came barreling down. I wondered if she'd thought of that approach herself or if the idea came from headquarters. I was still standing frozen at the kitchen door with the lasagna tray in my hand. "There's an initial bequest of $25,000, to be renewed annually if he's satisfied the money is being used appropriately," she said.

Is that all he's worth to you? I thought, and then realized that by Iranian standards, that was a lot. Waving too much money around, I supposed, would arouse suspicions—not just Arsalan's but those of everyone around him. I looked at his face. He looked serious and thoughtful, but not dubious. "Is there any particular kind of project you're looking at?" he asked.

"Well, the donor specified that he's particularly concerned about historic sites that are threatened with flood damage. Because of the dam projects, you know. He knows time is running out for those salvage operations. So that's his priority."

Arsalan nodded thoughtfully. "Yes, of course. Yes, certainly I can make some recommendations. I—"

Sally interrupted. "That's wonderful! I'll tell you what: I don't have all the papers here with me. I'd like to show you the brief I've received with the donor's precise specifications. But fortunately, I brought them with me—I wanted to read them on the plane. They're back in my briefcase at my hotel room. Can I invite you to have lunch with me tomorrow so I can show them to you?"

"Well—" Arsalan glanced at me. "Tomorrow's quite a busy day—"

"Just coffee then, perhaps? Somewhere convenient for you?"

"I suppose I could do that."

"How would eleven o'clock work for you?" asked Sally. "Do you know the café at the Musée Guimet? Would that be convenient?"

"Of course, sure." How sensible, I thought. No one would find it odd to see Arsalan visit the Asian art museum.

"Wonderful. I'm so glad. How wonderful that I ran into you. What are the odds of that?"

I caught Arsalan's eye. He smiled at me. It was a warm, trusting smile.

She did it, I thought as I put the serving plate in the sink and filled it with water so the lasagna wouldn't stick. Quite effortlessly. The mission of the dinner party was accomplished. My role was over. I'd done my duty to my country.

I found another bottle of wine and came back out. Arsalan was chatting with Sam. Lynne was wiping her nose.

Sally was sitting quietly. Her head was bowed, her shoulders sloped, and her hands crossed primly in her lap. But the corners of her mouth were turned up in an enigmatic little smile.

●　●　●

"Then, forty-seven days after entering the tomb, Lord Carnarvon died in agony at the Hotel Continental in Cairo," Arsalan said to Lynne and Sam. He had placed his hand on my shoulder again when I sat down. Lynne was still sneezing and sniffling. Sam had brightened a bit; he seemed to be listening to Arsalan with interest.

"My suggestion is that you tell your father the truth fully and calmly in simple sentences," Imran said to Sally. "No melodrama— just facts, figures, wishes, and needs." Sally nodded thoughtfully.

"In 1972, Dr. Gamal Mehrez, who was the Director-General of the Egyptian Museum in Cairo, insisted that he didn't believe in the curse," said Arsalan. "He said, 'All my life, I've had to deal with tombs and mummies. I'm surely the best proof that it's all coincidence.' "

"Needs are legitimate and okay when they're not neurotic, and yours are not neurotic," said Imran.

"But four weeks later, as workers were moving the mask to transport it to London, Dr. Mehrez dropped dead of circulatory failure," said Arsalan.

"Wow," said Lynne, squeezing Sam's hand. "That's so weird."

We had emptied nearly seven bottles of wine. Sally, I noticed, had started knocking it back as soon as she concluded her business with Arsalan; she and Imran had been discussing her father ever since. I hadn't known about the subtle way her father had tried to undermine her self-esteem.

I got up to try to rescue the dessert. I could hear laughter from the table, punctuated by sneezing. I threw out the egg whites that hadn't whipped properly, washed the bowl, and separated a fresh batch of eggs. Sometimes egg whites won't whip if there's a particle of oil in the bowl. Perhaps that had been the problem. I tried beating them again, this time with a fork. I had been beating them for a few minutes when Arsalan came into the kitchen and closed the door behind him.

"I'm trying to get these to whip up," I said.

"Let me help," he said, his voice low. My hand was on the fork. Standing behind me, he put his hand on top of mine.

"Hullo!" boomed Imran. "Just looking for a top-up. Don't mind me. Is the wine in the fridge?"

"Yep," I sighed. Arsalan removed his hand, stepped away from me, and leaned against the counter. "Help yourself," I said.

"Don't mind if I do. You know, I quite fancy her!"

"Who?" I asked.

"Sally. She takes good responsibility for her emotions. I do wish her breasts were a bit bigger. She has Protestant breasts. Oh well, can't have everything. Anyway, you two carry on. Cheerio!" He left without closing the door again.

I looked at Arsalan. "She's *married*," I said. Then I heard a loud, indignant *meow*.

"Well hello! You've come out!" said Arsalan. Wollef was looking up at him. He began rubbing against Arsalan's legs.

"Hi, kittycat," I said, reaching down to stroke him. "How are you feeling?" Wollef meowed again—loudly and insistently.

"He's hungry." Arsalan picked him up and cradled him, stroking his belly. Wollef stretched out in his arms like a human infant and began purring.

"Didn't he like the tuna?" I stroked Wollef's head.

"I don't know. Usually he likes fish. Maybe he doesn't want to eat so close to the litter box?"

"We could try feeding him in here. Hold on." I went over to the bed and fished the tuna out from underneath it.

Sam flagged me down on my way back. "Do you mind if I take some more of that ibuprofen?" he asked.

"Of course not. Help yourself. You know where it is."

Sam got up. Lynne caught my eye and quickly motioned for me to take his empty seat, putting her finger against her lips to indicate I shouldn't say anything. I sat down, still holding the tuna fish, wondering what she wanted. She looked buzzed. "Hi," I said softly. "You doing okay?"

"Can I ask you a question?"

"Sure," I said, thinking that Arsalan was waiting for me in the kitchen. Imran and Sally were deep in conversation. "Your father *needs* to hear that to keep growing and developing as a man," Imran was saying.

"You and Sam are pretty close, right?" Lynne asked me, sotto voce.

"I guess, sort of—why?"

"Is he attracted to me?" Her eyes were a bit wild. She was definitely drunk. I looked at the kitchen. I did not want to be having this conversation. Arsalan stepped out with Wollef in his arms, saw me, and brought him over; I thanked him mentally.

"Hi, Wollef," I said gratefully. "You must be *starving.*" I put the tuna on the floor beside me. Arsalan set Wollef down. Wollef sniffed the tuna, turned up his nose, and began rubbing against my leg, then Lynne's.

"Oh, no, go away, kitty," said Lynne. "I'm allergic to—" She began sneezing violently, her whole body racked with spasms. She patted the table, looking for something with which to wipe her nose, but couldn't find anything. She sneezed again in a projectile explosion, getting snot all over herself. She got up and rushed to the bathroom. I couldn't stop her.

We all looked at one another in horror.

Seconds later, the screaming began.

. . .

"Her anger management skills are *execrable*," said Imran primly, shaking his head disapprovingly after Lynne slammed the door behind her.

"Here, put this on it," I said, handing Samantha the package of peas I kept in the freezer to put on my shin splints.

"Thanks." She looked stunned. "I don't understand why she didn't knock. Why didn't she knock?"

"Almost certainly because at some level she knew the truth already," said Imran.

"She certainly *sounded* surprised," said Sally.

"Well, she might not have known the *details* of the truth. But I'm sure she knew she was being deceived," said Imran.

"Do you think?" said Sally.

"Oh, yes. We usually do," said Imran. I looked at Sally.

"If it's any consolation, I didn't think she was that great," I said. "She seemed really high-maintenance."

"She didn't seem at all like Voltaire," Arsalan agreed.

"You told him that?" Samantha looked at me accusingly. "Did you keep *anything* I told you to yourself?"

"Well, no, actually." I didn't see any point in lying now. "I'm sorry. I have no excuse. I personally would never trust me with a secret. I mean, I wrote a book called *Loose Lips*. Hell, most of my friends don't even invite me to surprise parties anymore."

Sally's face froze.

"Of all the ways for her to find out," said Samantha despondently.

"Samantha," I said, putting a hand on her shoulder, "I am absolutely certain—one hundred percent certain—that no matter how she'd found out, it wouldn't have changed anything. Also, you would never have had the nerve to tell her. It had to happen this way." Everyone else nodded in agreement.

"If I'd only told her right from the start."

"It wouldn't have mattered," Sally said firmly. "She would never, ever in a million years have slept with you."

"Yeah, come on," I agreed. "You heard the way she said *coochie*."

"*Highly* gynophobic," Imran offered.

"Although she might not have been quite so angry if you'd told her a bit sooner," said Arsalan. "Wollef, no! Get away from that!" He walked over to scoop up the cat. "Here. If you're hungry, have some tuna fish."

"We need to clean that up," I said. We all looked at one another. I hated to make Samantha do it; she was already so upset, but it *was* sort of her fault.

"At least it's mostly on the tile and not the carpet," said Sally sensibly.

"Yeah, but that tomato sauce will stain. So will the red wine." I waited for Samantha to volunteer, but she was staring glumly into space. I went to get a bucket and some detergent.

"I ruined your party," said Samantha when I returned. "I'm so sorry."

"Don't be silly," I said.

"I feel so awful," she said.

"Well here." I handed her the bucket and the paper towels. "Clean that up. It will make you feel much better."

. . .

"Thank you so much," said Sally at the door. "I had a lovely time."

"Are you going to be okay?" I asked Samantha.

"I think I'm all right now," she said, sniffling a bit. Imran had been helping her work through her grief for the past half hour. He was magnificent in a crisis.

"How are you going to get back to the hotel?" I asked Samantha.

"I'll walk. It's not far."

"Where's *your* hotel?" Imran asked Sally.

"Up in the Sixteenth, by the Arc de Triomphe."

"What a coincidence! So is mine. Shall we share a cab?"

"Oh, what a good idea," said Sally, flashing him a flirtatious rabbity smile.

We all exchanged handshakes and cheek-kisses. I told Samantha to call me in the morning. I wished Imran good luck finding the shaving brush he needed. "It was a wonderful meal," said Sally before they headed for the elevator. She was weaving just a little on her sensible navy consular pumps. "Kudos."

I closed the door. I was alone with Arsalan. Wollef was sleeping on the futon, snoring softly. A half bottle of red wine was left on the table. The candles had burned low, dripping wax in pretty patterns over the winelights, casting flickering shadows on the wall.

CHAPTER EIGHT

I'm starving," I said.

"Me too. Ravenous," said Arsalan. The sun was beginning to come up.

"There's nothing to eat but leftover lasagna."

"Can't we call room service?"

"Good idea. Have them send up some fresh-squeezed orange juice, some croissants?"

"Scrambled eggs, toast, hash browns—"

"They have hash browns in Iran? How do *you* know about hash browns?"

"I don't, actually. I've always wondered what they were."

"They're fried potatoes. Grated, fried potatoes."

"That's all? I thought they'd be something more American."

"What could be more American than that? They're delicious."

"I've had fried potatoes before, though."

"Have you had blueberry muffins? That's very American. Bacon, sausages—"

"No pork."

"You don't eat pork?"

"How revolting! You do?"

"Sure. But we can have them send up a steak this time instead."

"All delivered on a tray with a rose. I'm really starving. Should we go out?"

"I don't think anything's open yet. You want some leftover lasagna?"

"I can't feel the same way about it after last night."

"I know what you mean. I have some canned soup. And some rice. Oh! I could make pancakes! Do you have those in Iran?"

"Of course. We invented them. We invented everything."

"What else did you invent?"

"The windmill."

"What else?"

"The Internet. Come here."

. . .

"When did you realize you were in love with me?"

I thought about it. "I think it was when your electricity went out, and I didn't hear from you. Remember that? I realized it then. What about you?"

My head was on his chest. He stroked my hair. "About six hours ago, I think. I think I was only in love with the idea of you before that. But I was *very* in love with the idea of you."

"You're better in person."

"So are you."

"I wish Wollef liked me more."

"You can't really blame him for being jealous. He's never had to share me with anyone before."

"Really? There's been no one?"

He hesitated a bit. "No one who matters."

I wished I hadn't asked.

. . .

"Damn, it's 10:30 already, I should get going," he said. "I should probably go over and register for the conference afterwards. Will you be here this afternoon?"

"Of course. If I'm out, it's just because I'm getting groceries and kitty litter. I should return the chairs to my dad, too. Should we arrange a time to meet so you can get back in?"

"Yes, but I don't know how long the registration will take."

"Then take the spare key. Top drawer of my desk. Come back whenever you want."

"Well, it shouldn't be that long, anyway." He yawned. "A nap sounds wonderful. I should show my face at the reception this evening, but may I take you out for dinner afterwards?"

"I'd love that." I wondered what he would be feeling and what he would say when he came back. I had managed to put Sally out of my mind all night.

"Will you make reservations somewhere for about nine o'clock?" he asked.

"Sure; what are you in the mood for?"

"Whatever you like. A nice bistro. A place where I don't have to wear a tie."

"Okay, I'll think of something."

"Great. I'd best go," he said, pulling on his jeans. "How do I get to the Métro from here?"

"Go out, turn right, go to the bridge, turn right. You'll see it."

"Bridge, turn right. Okay, now where's my wallet? Oh, there it is. Wollef, you be good." He scratched the cat's ears; then he kissed me. "See you this afternoon," he said, and kissed me again, on my forehead, on my neck.

As soon as I closed the door behind him, Wollef began trying to poke his paw under it, and when he realized his paw was too clumsy and fat, he sat down and began meowing. "Shhhh, shhhh kitty," I said. "It's all right." I reached down to pick him up, but he squirmed out of my arms. "Okay, have it your way. I'll be in the bathroom if you need me." He was still meowing—loudly—an hour later when I got out of the bathtub.

There's no way to nap when a cat is crying in your apartment.

"Wollef, Wollef sweetie, *please* be quiet," I begged. I tried putting the pillow over my head, but I could still hear him, and I couldn't sleep like that anyway. I had given him water and more tuna fish; he wanted neither. Was he unhappy with the litter box? Did he want something else to eat? I didn't have anything else to give him. He wouldn't let me pick him up.

At last, desperate, I got dressed. I grabbed my father's chairs and lugged them back to his apartment. "You look hungover as hell," my father astutely observed. I declined his offer to share his home-cooked onion sandwich on white bread with ketchup. "You sure?" he asked. Then I walked over to one of the pet stores on the right bank of the Seine. The bright sunlight made my head ache. I stood outside the window of the pet store for a few minutes watching the puppies scrabble and wrestle in their cages. I looked at my watch: Arsalan had met Sally about an hour ago. I wondered what she had said to him and what he would say when he came back. I bought a dozen cans of wet cat food, the kind that always puts my father's cats to sleep. I bought a litter box and some proper kitty litter. I bought a little cat toy—a birdie attached to a rod and string. Then, since I was out anyway, I picked up some groceries, and after that I stopped in a café and ordered an omelet with some fresh-squeezed orange juice, hoping it would help my hangover.

"Here you go, Wollef," I called out when I returned. "Special delivery!"

He didn't come. "Wollef? *Woooolllllleffffffff!*" I looked under the bed. I wasn't worried—cats tend to hide themselves well.

Then I realized that the apartment didn't look right.

• • •

I checked quickly: My jewelry box hadn't been touched. There was no sign of forced entry. Nothing belonging to me was gone.

But his suitcase—gone. His hanging bag in the closet—gone. Wollef's toy mouse—gone. Everything he owned—gone.

No note. No messages on my answering machine. No e-mail. No Wollef.

I didn't know the name of Sally's hotel. Despite her warnings not to contact her by phone, I called her number in Istanbul. No one answered. I called her cell phone number. It rang and rang.

I sat down on my bed, bemused, verifying and reverifying that yes, every trace of Arsalan was gone. I didn't even know what narrative to ascribe to this turn of events. Was it a matter for the police? I imagined trying to explain it. *See, I met this guy from the Middle East on the Internet, and he said he loved me, right, and I slept with him on the first date, and now he's disappeared without a trace, and I'm not sure why, but I'm worried he's in some kind of trouble—or maybe he just dumped me, I don't know.*

And if I tried to explain that the CIA was mixed up in it? *'E 'as been missing for 'ow long? I see. And 'e 'as stolen nuzzing from you, but zee CIA 'as taken 'ees luggaige and 'ees pet cat. Vaire peculiaire . . .*

Maybe Sally had said something that so panicked him that he rushed back, grabbed his things, and got on the next flight out of Paris? But why would he not even leave a note?

Should I be worried about him? Furious at him? Was there a logical explanation that in my sleepless state I was overlooking? I tried to imagine what could have transpired at his meeting with Sally that would have prompted him to do this. Had she told him his life was in danger?

Was his life in danger?

Maybe he had become furious at me when he realized that she was really a CIA case officer, and that I had lured him to Paris under false pretenses. Had he become so angry that he had resolved never to speak to me again—and if so, could I blame him?

I called Imran. "Hello," he answered in his calming psycho-therapist's voice, the one he used for suicidal patients, since only they would interrupt him in the middle of the therapeutic hour.

"Imran, Arsalan's disappeared. I went out and when I came back he was gone, and so was all his stuff. What's the name of Sally's hotel? I need to find her."

"Arsalan has disappeared." He said it slowly. "How painful."

"Yes, very; where is Sally staying?"

"Sally? Why would he be with Sally?"

"He wouldn't be. But she would have been the last one to see him. They were supposed to discuss that donor aid."

"Claire," he said patiently, "are you planning to contact Sally to press her for details about your ex-lover? Because that would be neurotic. Compulsively seeking explanations is a way of not accepting that it's over. I advise you to grieve your fantasy properly instead."

"I'm not sure that it *is* over—" I thought about trying to explain, then thought better of it. God knew who was listening to my phone calls.

"Of course it is. Disappearing is rather an unequivocal message, don't you think?"

A vagrant memory came to mind. In graduate school, my friend Floyd had been dating a South African girl who was keener on him than vice versa. They went dancing one night at a club with UV strobe lights, and as the lights flashed, illuminating his white shirt, Floyd leaned into Violet and remarked, "I love UV!" To his horror, Violet threw her arms around his neck and screeched, "Oh, Floyd, I love you too!" He was so appalled that he excused himself to go to the men's room, stopped at the coat check on his way, grabbed his coat, and disappeared into the night. He was scared to answer his phone for at least a year. Didn't seem to me like the best way to handle the situation, but men and women think differently. Men usually can't figure out why I think the best way to deal with a flat tire is to cry helplessly. At last I said to Imran, "I'm worried he might be—might have been in an accident."

"Very unlikely, Claire. It's painful, but it doesn't sound as if Arsalan had much respect for you. Sounds as if he made good use of you, said what was necessary to say to open the tap, then moved away easily when he'd had his fill. I see men doing this to women all the time."

Would he even believe me if I told him the whole story? I wasn't sure anyone would. "Yes, you're probably right. But I need to speak to Sally because . . . well, I just do."

"I see." He sounded dubious. "Well, she'll have left the hotel by now, I suspect. She was going back to Istanbul right away, she told me."

"What happened between the two of you?" I asked.

He cleared his throat. "I helped her process her emotions more fruitfully."

"If she gets in touch with you, will you let me know?"

"I don't think she will. I advised her not to, in three separate five-minute speeches about what I could and could not offer. I'm sorry you've had such a painful experience with Arsalan. I'm surprised by his behavior. Very cowardly. Alas, this kind of pain is part of life. At least *you* had the courage to try. Grieve fully and well. I must return to my session."

I hung up and tried Sally again. No answer.

Arsalan had never sent me his phone number in Isfahan. I called Dr. Mostarshed's number in Istanbul. No answer. I looked up Isfahan University on the Internet and called their main line. "Hello; do you speak English?" I asked when a man answered in Persian.

"A little," he replied, to my surprise.

"Could I please have the phone number for Dr. Arsalan Safavi?"

"No," he said suspiciously, and hung up.

I tried Sally again. I tried Dr. Mostarshed again. I let both numbers ring and ring.

I called and asked to be connected to the organizer of the conference. The receptionist put me through to a woman named Isabelle. I said that I was an old friend of Arsalan Safavi's. Had he registered? "One minute," she replied. She put me on hold. When she came back, her voice was strained, or perhaps I was imagining it. "Madame? Monsieur Safavi has had to leave. There has been a personal emergency."

"Did he leave a phone number where he can be reached?"

"Not at all," she said, and hung up on me.

. . .

From: Samantha Allen allens@aol.com
Date: December 6, 2003 01:26 PM
To: Claire Berlinski claire@berlinski.com
Subject: Re: Re: Back home

Sorry about Arsalan. I hate to tell you this, but the only reason he'd act like that is that he wasn't that into you. I have to say, I didn't think he was that great. He's kind of pompous. And that accent makes him sound like an android; you were right.

Anyway, I get home and there's a letter from Lynne. She's really angry, but she had a lot of questions, like— *When was I planning to tell her? How could I have lied to her like that?* So I wrote back as well as I could. I mean, I don't really have any good answers, do I? I didn't figure I'd hear from her again, but fifteen minutes later, I get another letter from her. She still doesn't understand, she says—*Was she just some lab subject? Was I just planning to use our whole relationship as a chapter in my book?* It's weird: we've been writing back and forth all night, except now she's sending me hate mail instead of love mail.

From: Claire Berlinski claire@berlinski.com
Date: December 6, 2003 01:32 PM
To: Samantha Allen allens@aol.com
Subject: Re: Re: Re: Back home

I'd say it sounds as if Lynne is finding it hard to let go. Compulsively seeking explanations is a way of not accepting that it's over. I'd advise her to grieve her fantasy properly instead.

• • •

"*Sweet Jesus.* Back-alley-Sally? They had her handling an Iranian? That's incredible. That's a goddamn disgrace is what it is—"

"So you know her?"

"Yeah, you should have asked me about her before you got mixed up in this. Why didn't you call me before? She was one of the white chicks who *didn't* get fired."

"For what?"

"You calling me from your own phone?"

"Yes—"

"Well, maybe I'll tell you someday. Not now. Trust me, if a black woman had done what she—"

I interrupted. "What do you think happened to him?"

"Well, I wouldn't have the first clue now, would I? Not like they tell me anything these days. But they put *her* on an Iranian! Jesus! That really chaps my hide. Man, knowing her she's probably left his whole file in a taxi or something by now. Hope the wrong people didn't find *that* like they did last time. If his people got wind he was talking to the CIA, by the way, he's dead. Those guys have no sense of humor. And she'll get another damned administrative warning just like she did the last time, and—"

"*Dead?*"

Charlene heard my voice wobble and catch. "Oh, don't worry,

honey. Look, maybe he was a bad guy anyway. Maybe *we* made him disappear. He's in Gitmo or something. I reckon they don't have e-mail there."

"My God. Would we really do that?"

"Sure. We live in a bad world. That's what happens to bad guys when we get our hands on them."

"But Sally said he *wasn't* a bad guy."

"Well, of course she did. You wouldn't have invited him into your home if she'd said he was some kind of head-chopping terrorist, would you?"

"I'm *sure* he wasn't. Isn't it possible she recruited him? That he agreed to work for the CIA?"

"Sure. Sure it's possible—"

"But then why would he have disappeared?"

"Maybe they told him to. They don't want their assets sleeping with someone who writes books called *Loose Lips*. Can't really blame them, either, can you? Hold on, honey, gotta take this call." She came back on the line a minute later. "That's my conference; I gotta run. But I wouldn't worry about it. Really I wouldn't. In my opinion, it's most likely that he just wasn't that into you. Happens all the time. Guys are pigs."

• • •

From: Claire Berlinski claire@berlinski.com
Date: December 09, 2003 02:20 AM
To: Arsalan arsalan@hotmail.com
Subject: (No subject)

Arsalan,

Please—just let me know that you're okay. I won't contact you again, if that's what you prefer. Just let me know you're alive.

Claire

From: Mail Delivery System
Date: December 09, 2003 02:20 AM
To: Claire Berlinski claire@berlinski.com
Subject: Mail delivery failed: returning message to
  sender

This message was created automatically by mail delivery software.

A message that you sent could not be delivered to one or more of its recipients. This is a permanent error. The following address(es) failed:

arsalan@hotmail.com
  SMTP error from remote mail server after RCPT TO: <arsalan@hotmail.com>:
  host mx4.hotmail.com [65.54.244.104]: 550 Requested action not taken:
  mailbox unavailable

From: Prof. H. R. Mostarshed hrm86@farsinet.com
Date: December 21, 2003 09:20 AM
To: Claire Berlinski claire@berlinski.com
Subject: Re: Arsalan Safavi

Dear Ms. Berlinski,

I apologize for not replying more promptly to your many messages. I have been away on a dig in Eastern Turkey. I am sorry but if Dr. Safavi's e-mail address does not function, I do not know how else to reach him.

By the way, I believe that perhaps I have left a yellow file folder marked "Hittite Empire" in your apartment. Have you by chance come across it? I would be most grateful if you were to return it. You in turn have left a beige garment here, which I shall be happy to return to you should you wish.

Kind regards,

Dr. H. R. Mostarshed

. . .

"U.S. Citizens Section; how may I help you."
    "May I speak to Sally Melill, please."
    "Who's calling, please?"
    "Claire Berlinski."
    "One moment, please." A clicking on the line, then a different voice.
    "Hello, Sally Melill is no longer with us."
    "Where is she?"
    "She's gone back to Washington pending a forward assignment."

"Department of State."
    "Hello, may I speak to Sally Melill, please?"
    "Do you know which section she's in?"
    "I don't, no."
    "Could I have that name again please?"
    "Sally Melill, M-E-L-I-L-L." A rustling of papers.
    "Miss Melill is unavailable right now. May I take a message?"
    "I've left half a dozen already. Is she going to call me?"
    "I'm sorry, ma'am, all I can do is give her the message."

"Directory assistance, what city?"
    "Washington, D.C."
    "What listing?"
    "Sally Melill. M-E-L-I-L-L."

"One moment please . . . I'm afraid there is no listing available."

"What about Dave Melill?"

"No, sorry, nothing under that, either."

From: Mail Delivery System
Date: December 22, 2003 12:20 AM
To: Claire Berlinski claire@berlinski.com
Subject: Mail delivery failed: returning message to sender

This message was created automatically by mail delivery software.

A message that you sent could not be delivered to one or more of its recipients. This is a permanent error. The following address(es) failed:

arsalan@hotmail.com
   SMTP error from remote mail server after RCPT TO:
   <arsalan@hotmail.com>:
   host mx4.hotmail.com [65.54.244.104]: 550 Requested
   action not taken:
   mailbox unavailable

• • •

I tried every number on the Isfahan University website. At last I reached someone who spoke halting English and told me that Dr. Safavi was on sabbatical; he did not know where he could be reached or when he would return. I wrote to every journal that had ever published an article by Arsalan, asking if they had contact information for him. I received only two replies, both suggesting I write to him care of Isfahan University.

On the day after Christmas, ancient Bam, the jewel of Iran's heritage, was destroyed by a massive earthquake. More than forty thousand people were killed. I scoured the Internet for a sign of him. Perhaps he had gone there. Perhaps he had commented to the press about the catastrophic archaeological loss. But I found nothing.

At last, no longer knowing where else to look, I stopped looking.

It turned bitter cold in Paris, and then it snowed. I worked on my book and finally finished it, submitting it months late. I wrote an article for a travel magazine about the muezzin of Istanbul, and another one for *Runner's World* about Istanbul's hidden running trails. I wrote a short story about a man who buys a cheap tattered book in a flea market in Istanbul, then discovers he is in possession of an undiscovered volume of poetry by Hafez. It was an idea Arsalan had given me. I worked on it for weeks, but the story seemed silly to me in the end. I never showed it to anyone.

On some nights, I reread his letters. I remembered walking through the melancholy streets in Istanbul, past the weary sagging houses, past the *tuğra* of the Sultan on the old fountains carved with Ottoman script, practicing my Turkish pleasantries in the shops. Arsalan and Istanbul were one and the same for me—even though we had never once been there together, he and I. Nonetheless, he was woven into my memories of the ruined streets, the roving packs of dogs, the men pulling wooden carts up the hill, the glowing mosques at twilight, the massive, dignified ships churning slowly down the Bosphorus.

From: Imran Begum imranbegum@gmail.com
Date: January 23, 2004 01:45 PM
To: Claire Berlinkski claire@berlinski.com
Subject: Re: Re: (No subject)

Dear distant Claire on the other side of the Channel, I am sorry you are finding it difficult to let go. There are no ointments for disappointments. Only grieving gets the sadness processed. Pick up a cushion and scream into it when the Arsalan-related feelings, really about early forgotten experience, come up. Do some hitting too. Scream and hit until you sob or feel exultant.

Avoid creating an extreme interpretation of the events! Do not scapegoat him or yourself as bad objects. Difficulty with nuance and degree is a factor that many of my most challenging patients have in common. As I grow older I begin to venerate the nuance, the shades of gray, the moment of hesitation between the Fascism of Alpha and the Communism of Omega!

1:40 p.m. Three done and lunch introjected. Must run, time marches on as relentless and unapproachable as the Wehrmacht. Much love and care, Immie.

The sun had given up trying to make it over the horizon. The cafés served hot chocolate and winter meals—pork knuckles with lentils, coq au vin, hearty red wines. The Pakistanis on the street corners stood over their big coal braziers, selling chestnuts wrapped in cones made of newspaper. Occasionally I searched for Arsalan on the Internet. I never found him. I did, however, find a forum on the Internet where women who had been disappointed by online romance came to share their stories.

"You're just looking at a computer screen, with no voice, animation, or even handwriting to connect you to a real person. This means you're already in a fantasy. This is not the real world, but many people can't see the difference. . . ."

"It was exotic and magical. It happened so fast. It was so intense. . . ."

"Women are much more affected than men by the written word. Women can much more easily become prey to a man who is just a clever writer. Women need to be very, very careful before they lose their hearts over the written words on a screen. . . ."

"Our local psychologist's office says his business is booming with women who've had their hearts broken on the Internet. . . ."

"As for finding out the true reason for his sudden departure from this romance, it is possible that you will never know. He may be too embarrassed or too ashamed to ever tell you. Now it comes to living with the unknown and not allowing this to influence your enjoyment of subsequent relationships. . . ."

"The illusion of romance on the Internet is dangerous. A man can pose as a compassionate lover, when all he really wants is sex. Once he's slept with the woman, he wants her to disappear as easily as when he logs off at night. . . ."

I added my story to theirs.

· · ·

At last the weather turned mild. The crocuses began to peer up in the gardens and parks. An American man I met in a bookstore invited me to dinner, and I accepted. He worked for IBM, and he had an apartment near the Pompidou Center. But the magic of the Lion wasn't there, and after a few weeks he stopped calling me and I stopped calling him.

Samantha and I kept writing to each other, and weirdly, Samantha and *Lynne* kept writing to each other. They never saw each other; they just wrote, page upon page, every single day. Lynne could not give up the correspondence and neither could Samantha.

Samantha finished her book and submitted it to her editor.

Imran dated a policewoman named Meg, 37; an advertising executive named Alexa, 44; and a Jehovah's Witness named Anne-Marie, 40.

As time passed I wondered what had happened to Arsalan a little less, although on some days I wondered a little more. His birthday passed, and mine. They were two days apart. I remembered this, and I wondered if he did too. On the day, despite myself, my heart beat a bit faster when I went to the mailbox, but there was no card from him. The doorbell rang in the afternoon, and when I looked through the peephole I saw a delivery man with an enormous bouquet of flowers. I opened the door and ripped open the card even before speaking to him. They were from my brother and his girlfriend.

I followed the news from the Middle East closely, especially the news from Iran. It made no sense to me, not, at least, when I tried to view the man I thought I knew through that prism: how did Arsalan, a passionate archaeologist with a needy, cross-eyed cat, fit in among the hardliners, the moderates, their intense insane doctrinal squabbles? Spokesmen for the Islamic Republic, wearing turbans, addressed note-scribbling Western journalists who asked them questions about the Iranian nuclear program. I would read the transcripts of these press conferences on the Internet and wonder how I could ever have thought I knew the man.

Yet I had, hadn't I?

CHAPTER NINE

... the witty dialogue and insights and observations about
the CIA are so detailed they sound autobiographical ...

—Customer review
of *Loose Lips* on Amazon.com

Spring turned into summer. Nine months had elapsed since the
Lion's disappearance, and I no longer lunged for the phone when
it rang. So when the phone did ring, I assumed it was my father
calling to complain again about the repetitive stress injury he had
developed from his compulsive StairMaster regimen. He had
called me every morning recently to tell me about this. "Hi, may I
speak to Claire?" said a man—not my father—with an American
accent.

"Speaking."

"Oh! Claire? Claire, um, hi," said the man. "This is Dave,
Dave Melill, from Istanbul?"

I had imagined receiving a phone call from someone who might have news of Arsalan for so long; yet when it finally happened I was unprepared. "Dave?" I said stupidly. "*Dave? My God*—where are you?"

"Well, I'm in Paris, actually? I'm—"

"In Paris? Where's Sally? Is she with you?"

"Um—" he hesitated.

"Where is she? What happened to Sally?"

"I don't know. Sally and I are—separated now. Separated. She's—I don't know where she is. I haven't spoken to her in three months."

"Why are you calling me? Do you know where Arsalan is? Do you know what happened to him?"

"What?" He sounded confused. "I'm sorry?"

I suddenly wondered whether he even knew what Sally was—I had heard of CIA employees who never told their spouses. "Dave, where are you, exactly."

"I'm in a hotel? Near the Bastille?"

"Okay. What's the name of the hotel?"

"Um, hold on. It's on the stationery. It's the Comfort Hotel Bastille."

"What's the address?" He read the address to me. I made him repeat it, and made him give me the phone number and his room number, too.

"Dave, where the hell has Sally been for the last nine months? She disappeared after I last saw her. I've been trying to find her ever since. I've left message after message after message for her. I called your apartment in Istanbul over and over. Why wouldn't she talk to me?"

"Um," he sounded hopelessly confused. "I . . . maybe . . . um, I was calling because do you want to have lunch maybe?"

"Dave, stay there, okay? Stay right where you are, and I'll come to the hotel and find you, right now, okay? Don't leave; don't move. Okay?"

"Well, yeah, I mean, yeah."

"And you're not going to leave?"

"Yeah, sure, Claire. I won't leave."

"Okay. I'll be there in twenty minutes. Hold on. Bye."

. . .

Dave was speaking so slowly I wanted to reach into his throat and pull the words out with my fingernails. We were sitting in the bright summer sunlight at an outdoor café by the Bastille. He was mired in the dazed, miserable self-absorption characteristic of everyone going through a divorce. He had obviously not been eating well; he looked at least ten pounds lighter. He had cut off his ponytail. There were dark circles under his eyes. "She didn't leave me, you know. I left *her*. I would have forgiven her for the affair. Anyone can make a mistake." He shook his head. "But it was all the lies. That's one reason I wanted to see you, because I have to know what really happened."

"And you think *I* would know?"

"Yeah. Because everything changed when she came to Paris that weekend. She met someone. I'm sure of it. She came back so different. She was all distant, and she wouldn't even talk about seeing a marriage counselor anymore. She just said, 'Those head-shrinkers are fucking quacks.' " He shook his head and brushed his hair out of his eyes nervously. "I want to know who she was with. Who did she meet."

"Dave, I don't have any idea what happened to her that weekend. Believe me, I don't. I've tried to find out too." For the fourth time, I asked him what he knew about Arsalan. When I said "CIA," he looked shocked. "You knew?" he said.

I began trying to fill him in, but he stopped me. "I . . . I can't talk about that stuff. I could get in trouble," he said. It was the first hint he'd given me that he might be capable of thinking about anything but his broken heart. "She's, the CIA, they have their attorneys trying to keep me from publishing my novel. And I'm not supposed to talk about anything related to that."

"What novel? Dave, just—can you please tell me if he's alive?" The waiter interrupted us, bringing coffee and croissants. I paid no attention to the food. "Dave? Is he alive?"

He looked at a flyer for a Chinese take-away on the ground, then began rubbing it in circles with his feet. He took a deep breath. "I don't know . . . I'm not allowed . . . I don't know for sure she didn't tell me too much about that stuff." He said it quickly, mumbling into his Phish T-shirt and running his words together.

"Where is he?"

"I don't know. I really don't know."

"How can I get in touch with Sally?"

"I don't know. Even I can't. We only talk through our lawyers now."

"Why is the CIA trying to keep you from publishing your novel?"

"It's—well, they can't. They have no legal right. My attorney says no way can they stop me. I never signed a secrecy agreement; *she* did. They're just trying to intimidate me."

"What's in that novel?" I had thought he was writing a detective story.

"It's about a guy who's married to a CIA officer. And it's about how they lived in all these places, and he's totally faithful to her even though there's all these opportunities not to be, and he *cooks* for her every day, and he watches her lie to everybody else in the world but he thinks she would never lie to him. And then he finds out that she's cheating on him, and she's using all this spy shit to cover her tracks, but he's not as stupid as she thinks, and he starts spying back because he has to know the truth."

"But this isn't the novel you were working on in Istanbul, is it?"

"No. It's a new one."

"How long did it take you to write it?"

"Six weeks."

"I see."

"Anyway," he said, "the novel's what I really wanted to talk to you about? Because I thought maybe your agent would be interested. Because it's a little like your novel, you know, the same themes, except mine is maybe a little more realistic. And mine has recipes?"

"Recipes?"

"Yes, because I thought that would help it sell. Recipes from all the places we went together."

"You went to Bulgaria and Turkey, right?"

"Yeah. But the recipes are mostly American, because Bulgarian food is really awful. It's recipes for those muffins you liked, and the apple-pumpkin pancakes. A lot of baking. Because that's what it's like, being married to a spy. You do a lot of baking." All at once he started crying, right there in the café. "You do a lot of baking while that lying *whore* makes a fool of you," he wept, shaking, with his face in his hands. The hungover French couple at the table next to us pretended not to notice. They looked pointedly in the other direction, embarrassed.

"Dave, shhhh, it's okay," I said helplessly. "You'll make it through this. You'll be okay."

"You do a lot of baking, and you get pet turtles to keep you company because she's away so much and you're so lonely, and you love them but she just *loses* one while she's out doing some goddamned *spy* thing, and then one day you go visit your mom in Wisconsin 'cause she's sick, and while you're home you check the turtlecam and you see your own wife, your own wife, screwing her boss right there on your living room floor."

"Oh, God, that's awful, Dave."

"It's so awful," he sobbed. "It's so awful. I loved her so much."

. . .

I was reading Dave's novel in the bathtub. The spiral-bound manuscript was more than two hundred single-spaced pages. The hero was an American from Wisconsin named Bob who was married to a CIA case officer named Jane. "I knew Jane was the woman I wanted to marry the instant I laid eyes on her." Those were the first lines of *Diamonds Are Supposed to Be Forever, You Lying CIA Bitch.* "Little did I know when our lips first met that this was the beginning of a wild ride—one that would have me preparing an eight-course meal for the acting director of the Bulgarian National Intelligence Service, a man they called the Venus Flytrap."

I could sort of see why the CIA didn't want him to publish this.

It wasn't easy, I learned from the introduction, to find real maple syrup—the key ingredient in Vermont maple dumplings—in the Balkans. But it was worth the effort. The Venus Flytrap ate seconds, then thirds. "I made roasts and sauces, casseroles and pastries," he wrote. "Once, I prepared a cream of pigeon soup while taking mortar fire. I baked cinnamon swirls to fortify an eight-man surveillance team during their stakeout of a notorious PKK safe house. I did it all out of love for my country, and love for one very special woman—a woman who turned out to be a lying, two-faced slut."

Dave devoted the first three chapters of the novel to Bob's wooing of Jane, in college, and the fourth, unfortunately, to the consummation of their courtship, in a moist scene involving a lot of gasping and shuddering. "Her body began to tremble, and my name broke from her lips in a high squeal. Afterwards, she worried—it was a small town, where a girl could get a bad reputation. I told her I would tell no one. It was the first of many dirty secrets I was to keep for Jane."

Then followed chapter after chapter about Bob's loneliness. While his glamorous wife jumped out of planes at the Farm, Bob baked butterscotch Toll House cookies. In Bulgaria, Bob learned how to use a professional chef's torch to crisp the tops of the mocha crème brûlée while Jane disappeared for weeks on end without calling. "When she came back, she was starving. She couldn't tell me where she'd been, but she said she never even wanted to *look* at a ploughman's lunch again."

While she was away, he played tennis with the other diplomats' spouses. "Ivana, the beautiful wife of the Czech ambassador, was lonely too. One day, while we were playing doubles, Ivana invited me back to her apartment. She asked if I would teach her to make real American hamburgers. She was wearing a tiny tennis skirt that showed off her long tanned Warsaw Pact legs. I knew from the look in her eyes that the American meat she wanted didn't come from a cow. Firmly, I told her, 'Ivana, I'm a married man, and I love my wife. All you do is take some ground beef; add salt, pepper, and a dash of Worcestershire sauce; and throw it on the damned grill.' I would have never lied to Jane. Oh yes, I knew that Jane herself was a trained professional liar. I'd seen her in action. She could look a man in the eye and tell him that two plus two equaled five. She'd make it sound like God's own truth. But I had known Jane when she was still a girl. I knew the innocent vulnerable core in my wife. And I thought what we had was pure—so pure that even the sinister cat-and-mouse world of international espionage could never corrupt it."

All this talk of cooking was making me hungry. It didn't seem to me that the CIA needed to lose sleep over Dave's determination to publish this. It wasn't going to be igniting any literary bidding wars anytime soon. I wondered how I could get out of giving it to my agent.

In the next two chapters, Jane scored triumph after triumph in Bulgaria, earning praise from her superiors and admiration from her colleagues. Little did they know that the secret ingredient in her success was real vanilla bean, procured by Bob on the black market from the rebellious teenaged daughter of a Tahitian diplomat. "Jane presented the Russian arms dealer with my tempting vodka-soaked real-vanilla-bean cake with real-vanilla-bean *crème anglaise*. It was, she told him, a token of her deep respect. But Ivan didn't know our secret: the cake pan contained a listening device, which I had baked right into the Teflon and covered with a rosette of decorative icing. It worked to perfection. Jane listened to him smack his lips all night long. Then, just before he passed out, sated, he began mumbling, confirming her suspicions. Those helicopter gunships weren't destined, as he had insisted, for a Bulgarian Army recruitment video. They were going directly to embargoed Liberia." The recipe for the cake followed, with both metric and imperial measurements, so you could follow it in any country.

Bob did the baking; Jane got the credit. "I was proud of my wife and proud of the role I played in the wings, making America safer and stronger. My admiration for her only grew and grew." I yawned and shifted around in the tub, accidentally getting the bottom of the manuscript wet. I supposed I could tell him that I thought his work was too edgy for a timid conservative agent like mine. *She couldn't handle a firestorm like this, Dave. She's establishment; you know? Your work is too honest, too raw. You need a visionary. You need the kind of agent who would have handled William Burroughs.*

At last, midway through the book, the action moved to Turkey. "Jane and I were thrilled when she learned we would be stationed next in Istanbul, the legendary world capital of espionage. At first, the city of minarets straddling the mighty Bosphorus was a dream come true. We decorated our apartment with colorful carpets from the exotic bazaar. Jane was a natural at bargaining—and not just for carpets. Within two months, she had wooed and won the trust of an elusive target, a Syrian diplomat stationed in Istanbul on whom the Agency had long had its eye. The homesick diplomat cracked when Jane brought his sick wife a pot of my authentic Aleppo lentil soup.

"But at home, increasingly, Jane seemed troubled. Her trips abroad lasted longer and longer. I suspected the War on Terror was taking its toll. For the first time, I watched Jane pick at her food. She said she was trying to lose a few pounds: she had taken up jogging. I tried to ignore the misgivings I felt deep in my heart.

"Then one day, my cousins from Wyoming came to Istanbul. We took them out to dinner. Cousin Bill told Jane he was an avid golfer. 'Oh, I *adore* golf,' Jane replied. When she said that, I began to shake. For I knew the truth. Jane *loathed* golf. That was when I could no longer push the awful thought out of my mind: my wife didn't lie to other people because she had to. She did it because she liked it."

Their marriage took two long chapters and nine more recipes to go south. I thumbed through the pages with impatience, thinking about getting out of the tub and fixing myself some lunch. *What the hell*, I decided; *I'll just send it to my agent. Let this be her problem.* I was about to put it down when I saw the first words of the next chapter: "One weekend, Jane announced she was going to Paris. She was after an archaeologist who worked in the ruins near an underground Iranian nuclear weapons bunker."

I turned off the tap and turned the page so fast I gave myself a paper cut.

"When she came back, she was different. I had prepared a lamb *tandir* for her, roasted in a traditional Turkish wood oven." The recipe followed. "But she said she wasn't hungry. I asked her what was wrong. Had there been a snafu in the operation? Not at all, she told me. It had been a textbook recruitment. The Iranian had fallen into her lap like a piece of ripe fruit. In fact, it had gone better than she had dared to hope.

"Then what was it, I asked?

"That was when she turned to me and in a voice that chilled me to the core, said, 'Bob—I'm not in love with you anymore.' "

My cut finger was bleeding into the tub, and the water had turned cold, but I turned the page, and then the next. There was nothing else about the Lion. The rest of the book concerned roast duck, creamed spinach, and Bob's heartbreak at discovering, to his surprise but not mine, that Jane was actually a lying, conniving whore.

The book's conclusion, however, was rather unexpected. Evidently, in one of those bizarre fifteen-minutes-of-fame flukes, Jane's turtlecam appearance had been discovered and recorded by a devotee of hot webcam amateurs, who posted it on his website, giving it a "five-horn" rating, leading to its widespread reproduction, distribution, and ultimate recognition as a minor classic among connoisseurs of the genre—who numbered, unfortunately for Jane, one very interested employee of the CIA's internal security division. She was fired unceremoniously, not for sleeping with her boss (she was actually on line to be promoted for that) but for having failed to notice she was under video surveillance. This, apparently, was one security blunder too many.

And that was how it ended: "I lost my wife and she lost her job—all because the CIA turned her into a cheating skank with the morals of an alley cat who tossed my heart in the garbage like yesterday's pot roast."

■ ■ ■

I got out of the tub and bandaged my paper cut. Then I lay down on my bed and tried to figure out how it must have happened.

. . . *"Arsalan," said Sally, "I have to say I was fascinated by what you told me last night about the ruins at the Burnt City. I very much admire your intellect and your commitment to scholarship. It sounds as if your work is truly remarkable."*

"How kind of you."

"What I'm about to say may come as a surprise, and I'm afraid to say it may disturb you."

He raised an eyebrow and took a sip of coffee. "Mmmm?"

"Well, as you know, I work for the United States government."

"Yes, of course."

"I was so impressed with what you had to say last night that I called Washington immediately to tell them that I believed we had found a perfect consultant—someone truly knowledgeable. And I learned something that I'm going to tell you in strictest confidence. Something that I think you have the right to know."

Puzzled, he tilted his head.

Sally leaned in closer to him, lowering her voice. "It's come to our attention that your government is hiding weapons—very serious weapons—in a bunker near the Burnt City."

"What?" He put down the coffee and looked around the café. "How do you know? Why are you telling me this?"

"Don't worry, Arsalan, no one is watching. I made sure of that."

"You did what? Who the hell are you?"

"I'm someone with access to very high policy makers in the United States. And I'm someone with responsibility for this kind of question."

"My God . . . you're a spy! Why are you telling me this?"

"I'm telling you this because I know you care about the Burnt City. And because I've been authorized to ask you to help us."

"That's insane! I don't want anything to do with you."

"Wait! Wait, Arsalan; hear me out. Just listen to what I have to say. Sit. Please sit." He froze, half out of his chair. "We need to know what's down there. We don't know where the bunker is, exactly. We can't take the risk of missing it. If we don't know where it is . . . well, figure it out for yourself. Thousands of innocent people will get hurt. The Burnt City will be destroyed. But if we know exactly where it is, we can target it. We can save it . . . and everyone around it."

"You're going to bomb us."

"You can't be surprised to hear that it's an option we won't take off the table. Look, I don't know what's going to happen— that's up to your government, not mine. But we're going to stop this insane regional nuclear arms race, one way or another. You know we need to do it, and you know we will do it. The only question is how."

Arsalan stared at her. "What are you asking of me?" he said at last.

"My government cares deeply about human life, and it cares about those priceless artifacts. We have precision-guided missiles. They have been tested extensively, and they work—but they work only when we have accurate targeting information. If we know exactly where the weapons are, we can take them out without even touching the ruins. But if we don't know what we're looking for . . . well . . ." She tore her napkin into little pieces then let them rain down on the table. "Use your imagination . . ."

But how had they found him in the first place? I supposed it hadn't been difficult.

. . . HQS SUGGESTS TARGETING PFMOONRAY ARCHAEOLOGIST WITH ACCESS TO PFQUICKSAND ARCHAEOLOGICAL SITE FOR RE-CRUITMENT. HQS HAS OBTAINED LIST OF SUITABLE CANDIDATES AND HAS INSTRUCTED MXFREEWAY TO BEGIN SURVEILLANCE OF PHONE AND E-MAIL RECORDS TO BEGIN SUITABILITY ASSESS-MENT . . .

. . . HQS NOTES THAT (IDEN A) HAS EXCELLENT ACCESS TO PFQUICKSAND. HIS WESTERN BACKGROUND AND HOSTILITY TO PRMOONRAY REGIME MAKE HIM A GOOD CANDIDATE FOR RE-CRUITMENT. (IDEN A) HAS BEEN CORRESPONDING WITH (IDEN B), A US CITIZEN WHO COULD BE USED AS ACCESS AGENT . . .

. . . HQS WISHES C/O TO REMEMBER THAT (IDEN B) IS A NOVELIST WHO HAS WRITTEN ABOUT TQDEATHSTAR AND AS SUCH IS A MAJOR OPSEC RISK. C/O SHOULD ENCOURAGE (IDEN A) TO END RELATIONSHIP WITH (IDEN B) BY EMPHASIZING RISK TO HIS OWN SAFETY . . .

So Arsalan had not been targeted in error. He had not been kidnapped and handed over to Jordanian torturers, nor had he been taken to Guantanamo Bay. He had not been assassinated by Iranian hit men. Nor was Arsalan was some insignificant scalp Sally was collecting to impress her promotion panel. She had been telling the truth, for once, when she said my cooperation was vital to national security.

Could I really blame Sally for telling Arsalan that if he were to work with them, he must not contact me again? For telling him that he—and the operation—would be at risk if he did? Given the stakes, had I been in her position I would have done the same. If I read in the newspaper that the CIA had shared the details of a sensitive and critical intelligence operation with the author of a tell-all book about the CIA called *Loose Lips*, would I not be aghast at their recklessness and incompetence?

And could I blame Arsalan for agreeing to help her? After all, what was our relationship compared with a five-thousand-year-old city and all the living creatures above it?

I lay silent on the bed, my mind wandering. *But I've got a job to do, too. Where I'm going, you can't follow. What I've got to do, you can't be any part of. I'm no good at being noble, but it doesn't take much to see that the problems of two little people don't amount to a hill of beans in this crazy world. Someday you'll understand that. Now, now . . . Here's looking at you, kid.*

I saw Arsalan, elegant in a white suit, lifting his glass of gin from afar, toasting me from his window against the azure minarets of Isfahan.

He was telling me that we would always have Paris.

• • •

Later that summer, I visited my brother in Turin and spent many hours with him discussing the novel he was writing and its characters. There were quite a number of them, and vivid they were, too, all living in the small apartment he shared with his girlfriend, who had developed an intense personal rivalry with one of the more minor players. (She wasn't sure *what* my brother was doing with that character while she was at the office, but she knew she didn't like the sound of it.) Since the novel was set among an animist hill tribe in Thailand, they lived as well with each of the protagonists' nine souls and a goodly number of jungle spirits. Much like Princess Diana's marriage, that apartment was a bit crowded. When I left, my brother was murmuring darkly about the difficulties of finding a competent exorcist in Italy, one who was not *always* on strike.

Inspired by my brother's creative example, I banged out a proposal for a new novel of my own and sent it to my agent. I sent her Dave's manuscript, too, with the passages about Arsalan excised. I told her she needn't even read it if she didn't feel like it, but could she please do me a favor and send him a very tactful rejection letter. She assured me she'd had a lot of practice sending very tactful rejection letters. Dave went back to America. He said he was going to apply to study at the Culinary Institute of America. I told him to keep in touch, but he didn't.

Samantha and I continued to correspond. Her book was published at the end of the summer, shortly before mine. It was ecstatically well received. Michiko Kakutani called it "pathbreaking," and Universal bought the film rights. It sold so many copies in its first three weeks that Samantha's publisher eagerly snapped up Lynne's companion memoir about falling in love with a man who was in fact a woman, and rushed it into print to capitalize on Samantha's wave of popularity. The two women had not seen each other in person since their trip to Paris. Lynne claimed never to have forgiven Sam—but they continued to write to each other eight or nine times a day.

In October, Sam appeared on the *Today Show* as both Sam and Samantha. When she told Katie Couric the story of Lynne, viewers across the country were moved. Lynne opened her e-mail the next morning and found herself deluged with letters from romantic Americans who urged her to see what was right before her eyes: whether or not Sam was a woman, he loved her; he truly *loved* her.

Lynne's publicist begged her to reconcile with Sam, preferably in public, better still on *Oprah*, and Lynne, worn down by the barrage of letters accusing her of heartlessness, agreed. Shortly afterwards, *Vanity Fair* ran a nine-page spread of photographs of the reunited couple, posing in a series of *faux*-domestic tableaux. After that, I didn't hear from Samantha for a while; she and Lynne went to Cozumel to get away from all the attention.

I realized sometime during the autumn that I had not heard from Imran in a while. It was unlike him to be out of touch in such an unscheduled way. I sent him a note, asking why he'd been so silent, and received no reply. I called him. The message on his answering machine told me that he was out of town; if this was an emergency, I should call an ambulance. I supposed he must be on vacation.

I kept up with my Internet surfing, reading the news from Iran with special care. I had searched Arsalan's name on Google many times in the months since Dave's visit, but so far had found no news of him. From time to time I searched Sally's name as well, but she seemed to have disappeared into the great void of the ungoogleable.

Shortly before the winter holidays, I searched them both again, but as usual, I found nothing. Out of idle curiosity, I tried Dave's name. I had never found any reference to him on the Internet before, but this time his name popped right up. He was in *The Book Standard*. In fact, he was their top headline.

RAW TALE OF CIA SPOUSE SPARKS BIDDING WAR

December 03, 2004
By Donna Weinstein

Dave Melill, 36-year-old author of *Diamonds Are Supposed to Be Forever, You Lying CIA Bitch*, an edgy, brutally honest look at the secret life and recipes of a betrayed CIA spouse, has signed a three-book deal with Knopf, the winner of a spirited bidding war.

The deal has sparked rumors that the advance was the largest ever paid for a book about the CIA.

"We can confirm that we have signed a world rights deal," said Paul Daugaard, Knopf's Executive Director of Publicity, Promotion, and Media Relations. "We're very excited to welcome him to our publishing family."

Bravely resisting the impulse to rend my garments, I picked up the phone and called my agent, who, unusually, took my call—the receptionist must have been a temp. "Well, I guess things worked out really well with Dave," I said to her. I didn't mean to say what I said next; it just sort of came out. "Why is *he* getting that kind of advance? I mean, I write edgy, brutally honest books about the CIA, don't I?"

"Well, Claire," she said, in an I've-got-a-lot-of-practice-being-very-tactful tone of voice, "thing is you're a *highbrow* kind of writer. You're more *literary*."

Was she *nuts*? I am *all about* commercial popular fiction. After telling her that I knew a *lot* of recipes, I hung up the phone. I decided I should call Dave to congratulate him, but when I dialed his number, a woman with a Slavic accent picked up. She was his personal assistant, she told me. No, he was not available to take my call.

I hung up. Now I was really depressed. I saw my new mail icon swish up, and opened the message. It was from Imran. Oh good, I thought dully; he's back safely.

I had to read it twice to convince myself that I'd read it right the first time.

Imran had eloped.

. . .

Imran was writing to me from Bishkek, Kyrgyzstan, where he had flown to marry his new bride, Gulmira Beknazarova, eighteen, and to adopt her three children: Nurbek, four and a half; Bogdan, three; and Nurdeen, seven months.

Imran had met Gulmira on the Internet two weeks before. I am not sure how he found the link to www.amoreinkyrgyzstan.net; he declined to explain. When he saw her ad, he told me, he knew he had to write to her. He sent me the link to her profile so I too could admire the wonder that was Gulmira. "This lady is seeking marriage with a man from the West," read the words above her photo. "Why not make this beautiful lady *your* wife?" Gulmira fl6186 was posed in gold satin hot pants and a matching halter top. I hadn't realized that Kyrgyz women wore such colorful native costumes. She looked too young to drive.

I read the ad.

GULMIRA FL6186

Height: 156 cm ~ 5 ft 1 in
Weight: 43 kg ~ 94 lb
Eye color: brown
Hair color: brown
Build body: slim
Smokes: No
Zodiac: Capricorn
Marital status: widowed, divorced
Languages: English, Level 1, very little knowledge,
    needs all letters translated
Seeks partner: 35–75 years old
Introduction: 4 credits

I am very kind, have open mind and never lie because I hate when somebody lie. I dislike coldness and onion. This not game for me and I am very serious about marriage in near future. I am ready for my love man make everything only good. I am have very tender character, always sincere, I am like beautiful things, flowers, cook food tasty, very love travel but never be in another country, only can see in TV this, and have dream about someday visit beautiful places in world. I one year ago have finished institute, and now I work in the insurance organization by the bookkeeper. At leisure I am engaged in sports and domestic colors. Like to have rest on nature in company of friends. You are brave, kind, undertaking, like dancing, small-arms-firing, swimming. I dream to meet my big love, for whom I can give all my passion, love, and tenderness. I dream to meet man with nice soul, who can be for me best friend and for my children nice and kind father. I can be naughty and affectionate like fluffy kitten, or enigmatic and charming like lioness of fashion. I can be calm and cozy like warm of fire-place in frosty evening or merry and bracing like fresh spring water in hot afternoon. I'm fragile and defenseless exotic flower, which wait for his own ray of sun and ready to bloom for him and always give happy and joy to him. Family it is the most important things for me. Every days and night which we spend with my beloved man, will be happiest time. I wish to live and to breathe only for him.

"Without hesitation," Imran explained, "I wrote a letter to her that flowed directly from my heart." If he felt nervous when he hit the send button, his heart nearly stopped when he checked his computer the next day and found a reply. After a whirlwind correspondence, he called her three days later at her grandmother's apartment. Hers was the sweetest, most angelic voice he had ever heard. With the help of his English–Kyrgyz phrasebook, he managed to communicate his bravery, kindness, and undertaking. He caught a flight two days later to Bishkek.

The next ten days were written directly from the pages of a beautiful novel, he wrote, and proved that true romance is alive and not just for songs or movies. They took a tour on horseback of scenic Issyk-Kul'skiy Zapovednik (which was easier done than said), and on their fourth day together, Imran asked Gulmira to join him forever in marriage. "She has," he wrote, "given my life new meaning." Yes, he acknowledged, there was a difference in their ages, but women in Kyrgyzstan grew wise to the ways of the world early.

I had no doubt.

Imran said nothing to suggest what, precisely, he found so compelling about Gulmira. He seemed to think it obvious, and perhaps it was.

He reported that fermented mare's milk was much better than one might expect.

• • •

The weather turned miserably cold, the kind of windy, penetrating cold that makes it seem as if nothing would be worth leaving the apartment for. And so I didn't, for days. On one particularly frigid morning, though, I realized in the worst possible way that I was out of toilet paper and that yes, some things *were* worth leaving the apartment for. I bundled up in my sheepskin coat and my old Soviet frontier officer fur hat. I pulled down the earflaps. When I stepped outside, I half expected to see penguins and polar bears parading across the Place Dauphine.

I had my head down against the wind on the way back from the grocery store, so I didn't see him coming over the bridge. I would have walked right past him if he hadn't stopped me. "Claire?" said a familiar voice.

I looked up, startled. "Jimmy?"

"Hi." We both stopped in the street. I was surprised by his hair. He had grown a shaggy shoulder-length mop. It gave him an unfamiliar sheepdog aspect.

"How are you?" I asked.

"I'm good." We looked at each other in the awkward way ex-lovers do when they accidentally run into each other after a long time has passed. His nose was red, and he looked absolutely freezing: He wasn't wearing a coat.

"What are you up to these days?" I asked.

A vile gust of wind blew over the Seine. He pulled his thin scarf tighter around his ears. "I'm moving out. Going back to Ireland."

"You are?"

"Yeah, some mates are going into real estate in Belfast. Gonna give them a hand."

If you had asked me five minutes before what Jimmy might have been into these days, real estate probably wouldn't have been on my short list, but I nodded and said, "That sounds good." Then, to fill the empty air between us, I said that I'd heard the Irish economy was really booming. We made a bit of small talk about the Irish economic miracle. Later it occurred to me that the conversation had nothing to do with what he'd just told me; Northern Ireland, unlike the mainland, is an economic basket case. I wasn't thinking it through, and I have to assume he wasn't either, then or in general. "I'm surprised to see you," he said. "I thought you'd moved to Italy."

"Italy? Why'd you think that?"

"I dropped by once, a while ago, to see if maybe I could pick up my coat. Some strange bugger answered the door and told me you'd moved there." He took a deep drag on his cigarette and shivered. His face looked more lined and worn than I remembered. His teeth were chattering.

"You know," I said, "I still have your coat in my storage room. Want to get it now?"

He looked surprised. "Yeah, I'd appreciate that." I looked at his chattering teeth; he noticed me looking. "It belonged to me da," he added, "so it's got sentimental value." As we walked he pulled a pouch of tobacco from his pocket and rolled himself another cigarette with one hand, then struggled to light it in the wind, trying over and over, failing, cursing, humping his hands and hunching his back in an effort to shelter the flame. The wind seemed to be coming at him from every direction at once. When he finally managed to get it lit, he mentioned that the man who had answered my door was "a right odd bastard." I asked what he meant. He shrugged. "He was just an odd bugger. There were two women there with him, these two big black skanks. They looked like pros to me. He invited me in, but I had a weird feeling about what he wanted. I just got out of there."

I rolled my eyes and said it came as no surprise.

When we got back to my building, I told him to wait in the lobby while I went down to the storage room. I found his coat under a pile of dust. I picked it up. It was threadbare and greasy. It sure didn't look anything like a treasured family heirloom. I suspected he hadn't been able to afford another one. I looked around and found an old Norwegian fisherman's sweater that looked a bit warmer than the one he was wearing and a pair of my old ski gloves.

"What are these?" he said when I brought them up.

"They were yours. Don't you remember?"

He looked puzzled. He tried to put the sweater on, but it was too small for him. He took off his own sweater to see if mine would fit over his T-shirt. When he did I noticed two little colored hooves on his muscular upper arm, poking out from under his sleeve. He noticed me trying to figure it out. "New tattoo," he said. "Got it last summer." He pushed up his sleeve to show me his bicep. The hooves belonged to a flute-playing Pan superimposed over a botched rendition of the Spanish flag.

He managed to fit the new sweater over the T-shirt. He wrapped the other one around his neck, put on that shabby hobo coat and the ski gloves—which were also too small for him—and thanked me.

"Well, I guess I'll see you around," he said as he headed for the door.

"Good luck in Ireland."

For a second our eyes met, and then I looked away.

• • •

Fighting a powerful sense of melancholy, I went upstairs and ran a hot bath to warm up. After sitting in it for quite some time, thinking about the strange way things turn out, I got up and dried off, then got into my warm flannel pajamas and slippers. I sat down at my computer to do some work. I checked my e-mail first.

There was a message from Imran. He was writing to tell me that marriage was a *splendid* institution. He and his bride wished to add to their family as soon as possible. "Soon there will be a little Imran running around the house!" He furnished a long update on Gulmira's progress—she had embroidered an eyeglass case for his spectacles; she had learned to use the microwave; she was reading *Totem and Taboo*. He signed his letter with love, then added a PS. "I saw this in the *Kyrgyzstan Daily Digest*. Isn't this that bloke?"

I had no idea what he was talking about. I clicked on the link he sent below the postscript. The headline read: "Afghanistan Expels Iranian Culture Consultant."

KABUL, Afghanistan—A UNESCO cultural consultant in Afghanistan has been ordered to leave the country within 48 hours, the Foreign Ministry has announced. The reason given for the expulsion was his "engagement in activities incompatible with his status."

The Iranian national, Dr. Arsalan Safavi, has been in Kabul for eight months as an advisor to the Special Afghan Conference on the Repatriation of Cultural Property.

According to the Ministry's official statement, "The Iranian ambassador was invited to the Foreign Affairs Ministry and informed that Dr. Safavi has been declared *persona non grata* in connection with activities causing damage to Afghan interests. The decision was taken after concluding the incompatibility of the activities of this person with the provisions of the Vienna Conventions."

In a tit-for-tat move, the Iranian government immediately arrested and expelled two unnamed Afghan aid workers in Sistan-Baluchistan province whom they accused of committing unspecified "hostile acts."

Above the article was a photograph. The caption identified the man in the photograph as the expelled UNESCO consultant. The man was—unquestionably—Arsalan.

I stared blankly at the photograph for a moment. What was he doing in Afghanistan, of all places? Why had he been expelled? At first I was excited to see a sign of life from him, but the more I looked at that article, the more queasy I felt.

I did a quick search on Google and found the same story reported in several outlets. An obscure online newspaper called *Asia Times* ran a longer article concerning the escalating espionage war between Iran and the new government of Afghanistan. It quoted unnamed "senior government sources" in Pakistan who claimed that Afghan intelligence agents on the American payroll had of late been attempting to infiltrate Iran's eastern border in a hunt for nuclear installations buried in Sistan-Baluchistan. It mentioned Arsalan only in passing, in the sixth paragraph: it described him as "a member of an Iranian spy ring in Afghanistan."

All at once I felt the way you do when you flip on the bathroom light in the middle of the night and see that the countertop is covered in roaches.

I looked for Charlene's phone number in Prague. She picked up the phone on the first ring, sounding brisk—she was at the office, even though it was a Saturday morning. I asked her if she was in front of her computer and told her to check out the *Kyrgyzstan Daily Digest*. "Whoa!" she said when she saw it.

"What?" I asked.

"Dude's a stone fox! Man, no *wonder* you were so hot for him!"

"Charlene—what does the *article* mean?"

"What do you mean what does it mean? Means just what it says—dude's one foxy-ass Iranian spy. Now you know why he never called you again."

· · ·

Charlene and I talked for about an hour. I'd never told her about Dave's book or his revelations about Sally. She snorted when I did.

" 'Textbook recruitment,' huh? Yeah, I'll bet. Another great moment in CIA history. What a bunch of asshats."

"What do you mean?"

"He was a double."

"What makes you so sure? I mean, maybe he was *our* spy over
there. Isn't that possible?"

"They would never tell an important Iranian asset to go to
Afghanistan and spy on a friendly regime. I mean, he could get
himself *exposed* that way. Which he did, as a matter of fact. Dumb-
ass. If that guy was out there spying on Afghanistan, he was *not* our
guy."

"But wait, Charlene; did they know all along? Was *that* why
they were after him?"

"You mean, they knew he was an Iranian spy, and they were
thinking they'd recruit him and run him back against his own
folks? Well, if they knew that, why would they have needed *you*?
Nope, I'd say this is a good old-fashioned fuck-up. Big time. Lots
of memos. Oh, can you hold on a second here? I've got another
call." She put me on hold.

While I waited, it began to sink in. Somehow, I had completely
misunderstood everything that had transpired—and evidently I
wasn't the only one. She returned to the line. "Charlene Pierce,"
she said professionally.

"Charlene, it's me."

"Oh, sorry. Hold on." Two minutes later she came back, complaining about the way her vendors just couldn't get their stupid
former-command-economy heads around the growth potential of
the energy-drink market. I tried to keep her focused.

"Oh yeah," she said. "Where were we?"

"You were saying why you were so sure they didn't know."

"Didn't know what?"

"That he was an Iranian spy."

"Yeah. Okay, it's like this. You want to recruit another spy, you
don't have to work too hard to meet him, as long as you know who
he is. He's got the same job as you, so he'll be going the same

places you go, right? He'll be at cocktail parties, working the room. He'll be traveling overseas. He's not hard to meet. If they knew he was some savvy-ass Iranian spy, they would have waited until he left Iran, then just walked up to him and said, 'Hey, bro! We're from the U.S. government and we're here to help!' But if they messed *you* up in it, they obviously didn't think he'd be so easy to meet. They must have really thought he was some archaeologist who'd be hard to approach. Generally speaking, you don't bring people who write books called *Loose Lips* into the loop if you can avoid it; you see what I'm saying?"

"But I don't understand—if the Iranians were trying to run a double against the CIA, why would they make him out to be someone who's so hard to approach? Why wouldn't he just walk into an embassy somewhere and say, 'I have information I want to share with the CIA'?"

Charlene spoke to me patiently, as if I were a child who was having trouble coming to grips with long division. "Because that would be *way* too suspicious. It would look too good to be true. CIA's like everyone else—they don't want to date anyone who's too into them. Turns 'em off. Makes them wonder, *What's wrong with this guy?* You play hard to get, and all of a sudden they get real excited."

"So what you're saying is, they create this guy, have him write to the not-very-renowned novelist Claire Berlinski about the finer points of Turkish grammar, and wait until the CIA shows up? That's nuts."

"I reckon he wrote to you about other things besides that. Didn't he tell you where he works?"

"Yeah, so?"

"They probably knew the CIA was looking for an archaeologist who worked at those sites."

"How would they know that?"

"Oh, lots of ways. Maybe some archaeologist over there told them the CIA tried to pick him up at a party. Maybe they heard it through the grapevine." She hummed a few bars of the Marvin

Gaye song. "Anyway, didn't he ever mention being just a little unhappy with the way things were being run in Iran?"

I remembered how furious he was about the dam-building
projects. "Sort of, I guess."

"Wrote to you in really good English, right? Mentioned how
he never really felt totally at home anywhere, seemed awfully
Westernized for an Iranian?"

I was doodling little cats on a notepad as I spoke to her. I
stopped in mid-doodle, my pen in the air. "Yes."

"Maybe drops a few hints that he's kind of a loner, a risk-taker,
thinks he's a little bit special?"

I got her point. That was not just the classic profile of a man
who would be attractive to women. It was the classic profile of a
man who would be tempted to commit espionage. "But still, why
would he think the CIA would be reading my mail?"

"He probably thought it was a reasonable bet, given the book
you wrote. But I'm sure the Iranians didn't just put all their eggs in
one basket. They were probably writing to everyone they thought
might get their mail read by the CIA."

"Wouldn't the CIA be suspicious of some guy who strikes up
conversations with everyone on the planet who's connected to the
CIA?"

"Well, of course they would be, if it was that same guy. But
that's why the Internet is so great. Use a different e-mail account,
different server, different story, change your name. Really good
value for money, marketing-wise."

"But why would they think there was the *remotest* chance that
the CIA was reading my mail? I'm a novelist. Do you mean to tell
me professional Iranian spies can't tell the difference between a
novel and reality? They can't be writing to every single spy novelist out there, hoping maybe her book was really true and the
CIA's so pissed at her that they've got her under surveillance."

"Sure they can. It's free to send spam. That's why your mailbox
is full of it every morning."

"Yeah, but it takes *time* to write personal letters like that. And why did he come up to Paris? That takes money."

"Good ops *do* take time and money. But Internet marketing's incredibly cost-effective compared to almost anything else. I just gave a presentation last Tuesday about the way Coke's shifting its marketing dollars to digital. Integrated Internet marketing strategy's where it's at."

I thought about it. *If* you decided spy novelists were worth a try, you'd probably have my name at the top of your list. Anyone who did a Google search under "CIA" would see my Google ad. At the top of my home page was a blurb for *Loose Lips*. It had been written by a real, well-known former CIA case officer named Bob Baer whose name was always in the news. I'd interviewed him while doing my research. "This looks like an insider's account," he had obligingly written when my editor asked him to provide a few words for the dust jacket. My editor was thrilled with that blurb; he thought the more it sounded as if I were a disgruntled former CIA employee, the better it was for publicity. I could see how someone might wonder if I had a connection to the place, the kind of connection that would make the CIA take a glance at my mail every now and again.

Finally I said, "Charlene, what was the point of all of this?"

"The point of all of what?"

I looked down at my notepad. I had put snouts and fangs on all the little cats, transforming them into wolves. "Why did they want to run a double against the CIA so badly that they'd go to all this trouble?"

"You run doubles in order to feed the other guy disinformation. He says he's an archaeologist; he knows where the underground bunkers are, right? He tells them they're beneath some priceless ruin he's been digging up. When it comes time to drop the bombs, the U.S. wipes out ancient whatever, the world goes nuts, and the Iranians still have their nukes, which are actually beneath his outhouse."

I wondered out loud if the CIA had realized its mistake yet. "Well sure," she said. "They read the papers, long as they're written in English. Someone there's having a real bad day right about now. Hey, look, I've got to go—I've got to finish this report before noon. And I gotta stop lookin' at this guy's picture! If I stare at it anymore I'm gonna have to take my hormones out back and separate 'em with a hose. Don't feel bad; I woulda done it with him too, even if I'd known. He's *too* fine."

. . .

I went over my conversation with Charlene in my head from every angle.

> ". . . *What do you say, boss, we gonna give this Arsalan character an adorable feline sidekick again?*"
>
> "*Yeah, that worked good the last time. And don't forget to croak his mom, the infidels always think that's so touching . . .*"

She had to be right, I concluded. I had been conned, and so had the CIA. But what I didn't understand was this: who was the man who had conned me? If not the man I thought I knew so well, then *who* had written to me about Isfahan's caravansaries and the shafts of bright light that punctured the dusty interior of the bazaar? *Who* had written about the arcades of copper workers banging loudly, the gold sellers and carpet merchants, the craftsmen who painted delicate designs on the copper plates and vases? Spam might be cheap to send, but I had not fallen in love with Obafemi Ogunleye, manager in foreign remittance to the Nigerian Electric Power Authority. He too dropped me notes every now and again to see if I might like to strike up a friendly correspondence. I had fallen in love with the Lion, instead, and not just because Nigerian lyric poetry hasn't much to commend it.

I had fallen in love with something real. The *letters* were real, if not the man who had written them, and I had fallen in love with what they evoked. I had fallen in love with a man who had explained to me the complex harmony and austere beauty of the Friday mosque, where the marble pool with festooned edges reflected every architectural age of Iran, from the simplicity of the Seljuk period through the baroque Safavid. I had fallen in love with a man who could tell me why Turks would rather buy satellite dishes than fix their streets. I had fallen in love with a man who understood why I would want to know.

Someone had written those letters, and that person had understood exactly what would interest me—and move me. Was the man who wrote those letters to me really an archaeologist? Had he truly dropped and broken a goblet displaying the world's earliest example of animation? Had he really grown up in a working-class neighborhood of London? The mother he had described so affectionately—were his descriptions of the woman based on his own mother? Or was it all entirely made up? There was some intersection between the author of those letters and the fictional narrator he had created. Of that I was sure. I write fiction—and trust me: there is *always* some intersection between what you write and the truth.

I suspected that most of the story he had told me about himself was true. Spies, after all, are taught to keep their lies simple and easy to remember, and the best way to do that is to lie as little as necessary. Somehow, after all, he had learned to speak and write English like that and had acquired a vast knowledge of the ancient world. The cat I had seen in his arms trusted him in the way only a much-pampered pet trusts his caretaker—that was no stray he'd snatched up in the street to use as a prop. But why would a man like him become a spy? *When* had he become a spy? Was he an ideologue? If he was an ideologue, was he a nationalist ideologue or a religious ideologue? Had he been visited in his youth with mystic visions, like the character in *The Mantle of the Prophet*? Had these persuaded him of the justice of the Islamic Revolution?

When I tried to answer this question to my own satisfaction, my mind returned over and over to two points: his family, he wrote, had gone back to Iran after the Revolution, and he had turned down a fellowship at the London School of Oriental and African Studies—because Iran, he said, was his home. I had no idea whether one single word he had written me was *literally* true, but perhaps those were clues—even if offered from an unconscious recess—about the true state of his psyche, about the depth of the nationalism of the person who had written to me.

Perhaps he had become a spy because he had never forgiven the English brats who bullied him as a child. Perhaps he had become a spy because he felt it would please his father. Or perhaps, like Sally, he just liked lying.

And the night he spent with me. I wondered about that, too. Was that business or pleasure? If it was business, I thought sourly, these martyrdom operations were getting to be a much better deal for the martyrs nowadays.

And for their victims, too. I had to give them that.

CHAPTER TEN

Dear Claire, I know who you really are and I know who all the people you
write about really are. In all reality I shouldn't be yappin' all my info to some
writer who works for THEM, but I guess after what I've been through I'm
fearless and you can't do worse to me than you've already done. . . .

—Strange e-mail
from a *Loose Lips* fan

When my book was published one month later, I no longer
had time to dwell on the Lion. My frighteningly keen publicist
sent me on a monthlong American publicity tour. She arranged
for me to sign books and give readings at every college function,
retirement home, veterans' association, Jewish Community Center, and Rotary Club from Grain Ball City to Leper's Depot. Every
toilet I used that month was sanitized for my protection.

In Los Angeles, I dropped in on Samantha and Lynne, who
had purchased a Spanish Colonial hacienda in Bel Air with the
proceeds of the endorsement deal they'd signed with Benetton. I

had never seen Samantha as Samantha before, and I was once again astonished. She had plucked her eyebrows on the way, shaved her legs, and he was a she—and she was every bit as convincing that way as she had been as a man. She was wearing a slim wool skirt, elegant high-heeled pumps, and a black Lycra bodysuit; her hair was in chin-length curls. Her strong features made her face handsome and interesting. I noticed that she had nice ankles. Like that, her low voice sounded really sexy, in a Marlene Dietrich way. Lynne too had blossomed. She told me she'd found a terrific allergist.

I flew back through London. Since I had a long layover, I dropped in on Imran for lunch. He had never looked happier. Gulmira's dowry of *shyrdaks*, *tush-kiyizes*, and *ala-kiyizes* were draped over his faux-chryselephantine Art Deco sculpture collection. His bride, he told me, had embroidered the shyrdaks herself. Her children were running about the living room, crawling under the table legs and over the Italian leather sofa, fencing with Imran's badger-bristle shaving brushes. "They've been playing with my loud-speakers all day," said Imran cheerfully, tousling Bogdan's hair. "This little rascal punched holes in the drivers with his fingers. All jammy, too. I fear the sonic characteristics may be changed forever." He said this as if it were the cleverest thing any child had ever done.

Gulmira, itty-bitty and kitten-faced, was a lioness of fashion in a Lurex minidress made out of the British flag and thigh-high white go-go boots. Imran fussed over her proudly, and she spent most of the meal gazing at him adoringly. "England must be a change for you," I said to her. "How are you liking the weather here?"

"Yes, too happy. Very love man. Father in Kyrgyzstan—no good! Too much controlling." Nodding sagely, Imran speared himself a largish hunk of *plov* and popped it into his mouth. We spent the meal chatting about her father—at least I think that was what we were chatting about.

When at last I returned to Paris, I was looking forward to

sleeping in my own bed. I set down my bags and washed my face, then, since it had been several days since I had last checked my e-mail, turned on my computer. Waiting for me were messages from my mother and my editor, about three hundred pieces of spam, and a missive from an e-mail address I didn't know— abs@ubirmingham.uk.edu. There was no subject line, but I opened it anyway.

From: abs@ubirmingham.uk.edu
Date: March 6, 2005 09:45 AM
To: Claire Berlinski claire@berlinski.com
Subject: (No subject)

Dear Claire,

How long it has been since I have permitted myself the luxury and the pleasure of writing your name!

My dear Claire, I hope you are not too angry with me. Your absence, far from making me forget you, has caused my affections to burn with greater vehemence, if that were possible. I know, I am certain, that this whole unfortunate business has had the most terrible repercussions for your career. For that, I know no apology from me will suffice, but perhaps you will take comfort in my certainty that you will land ever so nimbly on your feet, if you have not already? For your intellect is keener than a pointed sword; of this I am certain, and you have your youth and robust constitution. May I be permitted to suggest that I see the secret working of Providence in the retirement we have both been obliged prematurely to enter? For if you can forgive me my deceits, certainly I can forgive yours, and now, with no obstacle in place, we might resume our correspondence. A friendship such as ours is, after all, a delicious cake—and we do have so much in common.

And so I prostrate myself at your feet, my Claire, in the deepest humility and hope of your forgiveness. . . .

A.

PS: Perhaps you would wish to keep abreast of my recent research? I have made a most fascinating discovery.

Birmingham Journal of Antiquity *Vol 79:304, 2005 pp 257–268—Cloak . . .*

Blinking rapidly, I clicked on the link in the message. It took me to a page of abstracts in the online version of the *Birmingham Journal of Antiquity*. I scanned the page.

Arsalan Safavi

Institute of Archaeology and Antiquity
University of Birmingham

Cloak and Letters:
Rogue Espionage in the Persian Achaemenid Empire
Birmingham Journal of Antiquity 30 (2005) 163–180

Abstract: As detailed by Herodotus, Darius, the third of the great Persian kings, invaded Scythia in 514 BC. As the Persian army marched across the Danube to the Russian steppes, what should have been a casual victory resulted in chaos and confusion as Scythian nomads, retreating, devastated the countryside, forcing Darius to abandon the campaign for lack of supplies. The Scythian ability to anticipate and evade the Persians has until now been a mystery, but in the course of an emergency salvage operation to protect Persepolis from flood damage, an unusual and well-preserved baked-clay cuneiform cylinder, with a trilingual inscription in Elamite, Babylonian, and Persian, was uncovered. The cylinder seal depicts a lion trampling Darius's chariot horse—a most unusual image—and its contents afford us a rare insight into espionage techniques used to undermine the Persians' military efforts. The cylinder inscription suggests that the historic rout may be attributed to a deliberate, sophisticated disinformation campaign—one contrived not by the Scythians themselves but by a rogue Scythian counselor who subsequently confessed his activities to his Persian captors. Horrified by the prospect of an attack on ancestral Scythian sepulchers, and fearful that Scythian provocations would invite such an attack, the counselor launched a private counterespionage campaign to feed disinformation to Darius's army. Entering into a romantic correspondence with a vulnerable member of Darius's harem whose correspondence he believed—correctly—would be intercepted by Darius's spies, the counselor systematically misled Darius's army, drawing them repeatedly into fruitless military exercises while obscuring the real location of the sepulcher.

http://www.birmingham.edu/ja

I tried to find the article in its entirety, but every link on the page took me to an error message. *The page cannot be displayed. The page you are looking for is currently unavailable.* I searched Google, looking for another link to the article. I didn't find it, nor in fact did I find any further reference to the *Birmingham Journal of Antiquity,* but when I entered the term "Scythians" I did quickly learn something rather telling.

The Scythians were in no position to correspond with anyone. They were completely illiterate.

. . .

I supposed I could see why Arsalan had felt the need to encode his confession—if indeed it was a confession—given that every message we had ever sent each other had been intercepted. His point seemed clear enough: *He* was the Scythian who had run a rogue operation to protect his ancestral sepulchers from attack by feeding the enemy disinformation.

I read and reread his letter and the odd, phony abstract, trying to determine how it had transpired.

. . . It began two years ago, when Arsalan made a puzzling discovery at the Burnt City. While excavating at the bottom of the known ruins, he stumbled upon a second set of ruins—a small, subterranean complex of chambers and tunnels. Intrigued, he crawled through the largest tunnel. At the very end of the tunnel, he found something strange—was it some kind of lid? Perhaps, he thought, it was a well? When he gently pried it open, he discovered to his surprise that it was a shaft. He shined his flashlight down but couldn't see the bottom. It seemed to descend hundreds of meters.

He returned to his car for his rappelling gear.

As he descended, near the bottom of the shaft his flashlight glinted off a reflective surface. Odd, he thought. What could be reflective down here? But when he reached the bottom he saw exactly what it was.

He was in a massive cavern. In the middle was an object—a huge object. He did not know what it was, but one thing he did know: it had not been built 5000 years ago. Big as a small warehouse, the grotesque, gleaming thing was sitting on shock absorbers, surrounded by elaborate cooling and filtering ducts. He saw writing on the side—in Korean.

Terrified, he clambered back up. When he returned to the surface, he took a soil sample and later tested it in his laboratory. The concentration of uranium above the Burnt City was nearly twenty times greater than natural levels.

He was stunned—and he was furious. The United States

had recently invaded Iraq, ostensibly to neutralize its weapons of mass destruction. His beloved Lady of Warka had disappeared in the looting of the Iraqi National Museum. It was widely believed that Iran would be next. An invasion would be prefaced by air strikes against suspected underground bunkers. Artifacts could not be trusted to the care and competence of American military commanders!

If he could find this site, he thought, so could the CIA. So could American missiles. The Iranian government had put the whole Burnt City at risk. He imagined the ancient city obliterated, the remains of the ancient civilization vaporized. It was unacceptable, unthinkable. . . .

Several weeks later, he switched on the radio. He heard on the news that the United States had bombed a village wedding party in Afghanistan, killing many of the guests. The Americans blamed "mistaken targeting information." They had, they claimed, been given bad intelligence. Suddenly, it came to him: What if someone were to give the CIA bad intelligence about the location of the nuclear site? What if he told them it was half a mile to the south of the Burnt City? They would bomb the wrong place. They would realize their mistake sooner or later, of course, but it would buy him time. An extra year, an extra two years to excavate. . . .

". . . a vulnerable member of Darius's harem whose correspondence he believed—correctly—would be intercepted by Darius's spies. . . ."

But he is an archaeologist, not a spy. He has no idea how to contact the CIA. Is there a phone number? A website? He searches under the initials "CIA" on the Internet and sees a Google ad for Loose Lips. *He reads the reviews. He concludes that the author must be connected to the CIA. Perhaps she is an undercover officer. He writes to her.*

*She writes back. He hints, as best he can, that he has in-
formation that might be useful to her organization. Oddly, she
sends him a long letter about her personal life. It must be part
of her cover, he concludes. He admires her professionalism. He
proposes, opaquely, to pass her the information by means of an
unwitting intermediary in Istanbul, and she accepts. She flies
to Istanbul. He awaits her signal, but none is forthcoming.
She claims to be unable to find his contact, "the Baker." Perhaps she is telling him that it is unsafe—is she under surveillance?*

*At last, desperate, he proposes a meeting in Paris. He will fly
there personally. He hopes she will be able to evade her surveillance there. His hopes are not in vain. Within a day of his arrival, her colleague pitches him. He has rather a pleasant night
with "Claire," too. An unexpected bonus.*

*He readily agrees to work for the CIA. They ask for
reports—who is coming and going from the site? They ask for
soil samples. He provides everything they request in a series of
clandestine meetings in Berlin, Dubai, Caracas. They praise him
for his cooperation and deposit money in his Swiss bank account.
They do not realize that he is directing them away from the in-
stallation, not toward it, and that the soil samples he is spiriting
to them come straight from Wollef's litter box . . .*

The CIA must have intercepted my mail to him, terrified that I
would blow the whole operation.

*. . ."My government is deeply grateful for your cooperation,"
Sally said. "And I convey Claire's deep gratitude, too, as well as
her fondest wishes. Unfortunately, she must request that there be
no further contact between you. As you know, she is under very
deep cover, and it is her operational judgment that continued
contact would put you both at grave risk."*

"But—"

"I know, I know. But you'll always have Paris."

"No, that's not it. It's my cat! He is still in her apartment. I can't leave him behind!"

"Oh! Don't worry, Arsalan. We've got him right here." She waves to a man in a baggy suit and dark sunglasses who has been sitting at the table in the corner. He comes over with a large shopping bag. In it is a cat carrier.

He must have assumed, when he was arrested in Afghanistan, that my career had been ended in the scandal of his exposure. But what was he doing in Afghanistan, anyway? And if he thought I worked for the CIA, why would I need him to explain what had happened to me by means of some arcane phony journal abstract? Wouldn't I know already?

Then it struck me—he had read *Loose Lips*. Everything he knew about the CIA, he had learned from my book. And in my book, the heroine never knows how her cases turn out. That's key to the plot, in fact. The information is compartmentalized. She moves on to other assignments. She never knows who betrayed her, and she never knows the truth.

. . .

From: Claire Berlinski claire@berlinski.com
Date: March 6, 2005 01:36 PM
To: abs@ubirmingham.uk.edu
Subject: Re: (No subject)

Dear Arsalan,

I believe, if I've understood you correctly, that you're laboring under a grotesque misapprehension. I am not a spy and have never been a spy. You have predicated your entire operation on a ridiculous assumption. My career—*as a writer of fiction*—is just fine.

Yours, however, appears to be in some difficulty, if you're really in Birmingham.

Claire

From: abs@ubirmingham.uk.edu
Date: March 6, 2005 02:45 PM
To: Claire Berlinski claire@berlinski.com
Subject: Re: (No subject)

Oh, Claire, how wonderful to see your name arrive again in my mailbox! It has been such a long time, and I must own that I have so missed unbosoming myself to you. May I assume from your enthusiastic denials that things did not work out as badly for you as I had feared and you remain in the employ of the Persians, so to speak? That is very well; you did a most dedicated job, and it is certainly not your fault that I proved to be, as they say, a rotten apple. But best not to write of these things, I suspect! Alas, yes, I am really in Birmingham. I had no choice. My government is not taking my new celebrity well, I am afraid. They began asking rather probing questions of my friends and colleagues in Iran. I owe a great deal to Dr. Mostarshed, who at risk to himself contacted me and advised me not to return. And thus I have taken up residence in Britain—the obvious place, of course, since I hold a British passport. I cannot say I much care for Birmingham and its rain and its wretched fried fish, and it is with heavy affliction that I contemplate my future here. I would have much preferred to take the visiting fellowship I was offered at Stanford University, but obviously *your* government was not much inclined after all of this to offer me a visa. What a pity. But enough of me—I beg you to send me your news. Wollef is most well and sends his affectionate regards. I am so very delighted to hear from you. You must rest assured that in whatever part of the world I may be, you shall always have in me a most devoted friend and faithful correspondent!

I am as ever yours,

Arsalan

From: Claire Berlinski claire@berlinski.com
Date: March 6, 2005 04:55 PM
To: abs@ubirmingham.uk.edu
Subject: Re: Re: Re: (No subject)

Why were you arrested in Afghanistan?

From: abs@ubirmingham.uk.edu
Date: March 6, 2005 05:15 PM
To: Claire Berlinski claire@berlinski.com
Subject: Re: Re: Re: Re: (No subject)

They did not tell you? I told your colleagues everything when they debriefed me in London. I was correct, then, to think you might not know what had transpired! It is simple, Claire; I was trying to find the Sleeping Buddha. I had so hoped to find it *before* that wretched Afghan pimp Khozad. How I loathe him. That is all. An entirely innocent explanation. Do you see?

Below his message was another hyperlink. When I clicked on it, it took me to an old news item in the *Times of London*.

AFGHANISTAN DISCOVERY SPARKS SLEEPING BUDDHA RUMORS

BAMIYAN, Afghanistan—An archaeologist searching for the legendary Sleeping Buddha in Bamiyan province has raised hopes of a major discovery.

Since the Taliban destroyed Bamiyan's 1500-year-old Standing Buddhas in 2001, archaeologists around the world have dreamt of finding the so-called Sleeping Buddha, described in the travel diary of the seventh-century Chinese monk Xuan Zang and depicted in cave paintings in the Hindu Kush mountains west of Kabul.

Recently, a team led by the Afghan archaeologist Zemaryali Khozad began fresh excavations for the massive statue, said to represent the Buddha in a state of ultimate enlightenment.

On Tuesday, Khozad announced that the dig may have yielded fruit. "I have found a structure near the town of Daouti, in Bamiyan province, which may be part of the Sleeping Buddha," said Khozad.

The discovery has generated considerable excitement—and rivalry—among the foreign experts working in the Bamiyan Valley. "The statue would be a major archaeological treasure, and whoever discovered it would become a legend," said German archaeologist Uli Lindemann. "I am happy if it is discovered, but I would be much happier if I discovered it."

From: Claire Berlinski claire@berlinski.com
Date: March 6, 2005 06:07 PM
To: abs@ubirmingham.uk.edu
Subject: Re: Re: Re: Re: Re: (No subject)

No, I don't see. Why would you be accused of *spying* for doing that?

From: abs@ubirmingham.uk.edu
Date: March 6, 2005 06:15 PM
To: Claire Berlinski claire@berlinski.com
Subject: Re: Re: Re: Re: Re: Re: (No subject)

Oh, yes. Because I found this, instead, which they did not want me to see, and I wanted to see even less. Absolutely disgusting. So they contrived to run me out of the country. Do you see now?

There was another hyperlink beneath the message. I clicked on that, too. Again, it was a news item.

HUMAN RIGHTS GROUPS CALL FOR AFGHAN MASS GRAVE INQUIRY

KABUL, Afghanistan—Physicians for Human Rights (PHR) today condemned the refusal of the U.S. Government, the Afghan government, and the United Nations to secure and investigate the mass grave site at Dasht-e Leili, near Sheberghan in northern Afghanistan. The grave is believed to hold the bodies of hundreds of Taliban prisoners who died while captives of the Northern Alliance. Northern Alliance forces were U.S. allies in the war that defeated the Taliban. The Afghan government is now made up of many members of the alliance.

PHR investigators say witnesses told them that Northern Alliance soldiers dumped railway containers full of bodies into the area in late December and early January.

PHR also called for the investigation of another, apparently unrelated mass grave in the town of Daouti in Bamiyan province.

• • •

I was whipsawed by jet lag. My bags were unpacked; I had not yet bathed; my muscles ached. I got up from my desk and ran a tub. I lay in the hot soapy water for some time. At last, I emerged from the water and toweled off.

When I returned to the computer, he had written again.

From: abs@ubirmingham.uk.edu
Date: March 6, 2005 08:15 PM
To: Claire Berlinski claire@berlinski.com
Subject: (No subject)

Of course, Birmingham is not far from Paris; that is one redeeming matter in this whole business. I cannot recommend a trip here; there is nothing at all to see, but perhaps I might visit you? We might even travel together to Istanbul—this time for pleasure, not business! How very much I would enjoy that. What do you say? Come, my dear Claire, come away with me!

Come, fill the Cup, and in the fire of Spring
Your Winter garment of Repentance fling:
  The Bird of Time has but a little way
To flutter—and the Bird is on the Wing!

I am powerless to subdue my impatience for your answer, and I am as ever,

Your Lion

I sat quietly for some time before replying. I rubbed my aching neck and thought wistfully of time we had spent together. I remembered the cool blue tiles of the minarets in Isfahan, the pure air and the clear skies, the violet mountains on the horizon, the Zoroastrian fire temples on the hills. I thought of the pleasure gardens of the palaces of Isfahan, the bubbling water and birdsong, the stone fountains in the shape of lions, the horse-drawn carriages; I thought of the bridges of Isfahan, with their intersecting arches, and in those arches, the tiny teashops in which one could linger all afternoon, drinking sweet tea and watching the river slowly pass.

At last I answered.

From: Claire Berlinski claire@berlinski.com
Date: March 6, 2005 10:38 PM
To: abs@ubirmingham.uk.edu
Subject: Re:

Whoever you are, you are out of your mind. You lied to me, used me, betrayed me, and as far as I can tell brought the world another minute closer to midnight. Do you seriously believe I am going to start writing to you again as if nothing had happened? Out of the question. You are a madman. This correspondence is over.

Claire

I sat for a few minutes before my computer, looking at it as if seeing it for the first time. It was time to turn it off, I decided.

Start.

Shut Down?

OK.

The machine glowed and cogitated for a few moments, then flickered twice as if struggling for life. I pushed the small button at the base of the computer, and the screen went black.

I looked around the empty room. *Perhaps*, I thought idly, *I should get a puppy.*

I looked again at the dark screen. *Then again*, I thought, *I could always just turn it back on.*

EPILOGUE

When I tried to work out the plot of the novel this story so clearly begged to become, there was one thing I could never quite figure out. If in the end I did not work for the CIA—and certainly, I could not say *that* in the book—and if he did not work for Iranian intelligence, why had the CIA begun reading our mail?

It took me quite a while to solve the problem, and I would perhaps never have figured it out had I not ventured out, sometime later, to Mariage Frères. I was there to buy Sam and Lynne a Bhutanese tea set to celebrate their commitment ceremony.

It was a detail so insignificant that it had completely slipped my mind. Nor would it have ever returned to my mind without that unusual *aide-mémoire*. When I entered the tea room, I saw the same deathly pale man in a silk smoking jacket and slippers, with the same bizarre stuffed parrot on his shoulder. But even this provoked in me no instantaneous realization.

It was only when he began, for no obvious reason, flapping that fan wildly around his head that it came back to me.

"What did you say that place was again? Bird City?"

And if you think about it—that was the only possible explanation.

ACKNOWLEDGMENTS

To Jon Karp: Thank you for being there at the start. To Allison Dickens: Thank you for being there through the end. Allison, in addition to being a terrific editor—that goes without saying—is also a lovely, gentle, warm, tactful, patient, feminine, funny, and very wise woman. Thank you as well, Allison, for your Solomonic judgment in matters literary and personal. Thanks to Kathy Robbins for selling this book, and to Dan Greenberg for helping me figure out the best way to explain that it would be delivered, alas, very, very late.

As usual, my modest brother Mischa says he doesn't want his name on the cover, even though I think it deserves to be:

> Mischa: No, I didn't write one word of it. Not one. Not
>   even a comma. I did much more on *Loose Lips.*
> Claire: But all of the good ideas are yours.
> Mischa: Claire, you're wrong. I hardly did anything.

I disagree. But no point in us arguing! I have the evidence; you can judge for yourself.

Mischa: Now, how do you figure out who he really was?
Claire: Well, it has to somehow be through the news, I think.
Mischa: I was thinking that Dave tells you. In a roman à clef about being married to a CIA agent.
Claire: I *like* it!

See? I should mention as well that my brother has a particularly deft touch with moral support.

Claire: Istanbul is too noisy to work. The Internet has been down all morning. I just managed to log on. Now they've begun hammering again outside. I've gotten nothing done all morning, since I've been hassling with trying to get on the Internet.
Mischa: Claire, I'm sympathetic to your suffering, really I am, but I'm just not that interested, actually.

Not only did my father, David Berlinski, read every word of every draft of this book and provide simply invaluable editorial advice, he was and is the very model of paternal wisdom and affection, advising me at every stage, with infinite sagacity, on matters personal and financial. Consider, for example, his measured counsel in regards to my altercation with my noise-sensitive neighbor in Paris, who complained throughout the writing of this book that I was running my bathtub too loudly:

From: David Berlinski david@berlinski.com
Date: August 15, 2004 07:40 AM
To: Claire Berlinski claire@berlinski.com
Subject: Re: Re:

Claire Sweetie,

It will probably be worth your while to show up at your landlord's office in full combat gear. I'm sure you can get the stuff cheap at some Turkish bazaar. You can probably find one of those terrific-looking Army Ranger knives right here in Paris too. That and a couple of fake grenades (I know of a store that sells them just blocks from my apartment) should put you in a top negotiating position. You walk in, put your combat boots on the desk, and say, "All right fuckface, who's this piece-of-shit neighbor who's been hassling my war buddies." Maybe give the speech in Kurdish. Address your knife as little buddy, as in "Don't worry, little buddy, there's still work for you to do." Spit on the floor a lot.

Love,
Pop

And of course there is my mother, Toby Saks, who, bless her, has never given me one word of editorial advice. Thank God I have at least *one* relative who doesn't. Thank you so much, Mom, for just telling me that you liked the book and leaving it at that. Thanks also to my stepfather, Martin Greene, who was no doubt the one who advised her to follow this wise policy.

Moving right along, there's my e-mail friend Bill Walsh. I have never met him! But I do believe he's the smartest man alive. Bill read the manuscript and kindly pointed out the spelling errors not only in my Turkish, Persian, Arabic, Russian, German, Hungarian, Spanish, *and* my French, but in my English (that's right, my own native language), my Chinese and—I kid you not!—my Kyrgyz.

Mischa: He speaks Chinese and Kyrgyz, too?
Claire: Wild, huh?
Mischa: That's insane! Could he just be making it all up?
Claire: No. Every time I check the Internet, I see he's
　　　right. *Every* time. Not just most of the time, not just
　　　"you could argue it both ways," but *every* time.
Mischa: That's super amazing. Where did he learn so
　　　much?

Claire: Don't know. He's also an expert on lots of other
  things.
Mischa: Like what?
Claire: Military small arms. He was one of the many
  people who wrote to me about the recoil on an M16,
  or lack thereof, after *Loose Lips* came out.
Mischa: Wow.
Claire: So, if this were a novel, all the clues would be
  pointing in one and only one direction: Dude's a spy.
Mischa: You think he's trying to recruit you?
Claire: Why would he bother? I'm a novelist.
Mischa: Yes, but he *thinks* you're a spy! Claire! What a
  great idea for a novel!

Oh, Bill also caught innumerable embarrassing mistakes in my Ottoman history. And my Persian history. And my European history. If Bill's not a spy, he should be. Ladies and gentlemen: write to your congressmen today and tell them the CIA needs to *draft* this man. He's our only hope.

Norah Vincent, author of *Self-Made Man*, has been as good a friend to me as anyone I've ever really met. She has also been a *very* good sport. I took the idea for Sam and Samantha from her book, but of course she never did anything remotely so stupid as falling in love with Lynne. Norah, thank you—and this I truly do sign with sight-unseen love.

To all of my Iranian pen friends, thank you. (I've never met them, either!) To Jeff Jarvis (whom I've never met!) of buzzmachine.com: thank you for helping me find so many wonderful Iranian pen pals. A special thanks to Hossein Derakhshan and Rouzbeh Gerami, and, most especially, to Ali Azimi, who patiently answered about a million of my odd questions about, for example, the proper translation of the word "wanker" into Persian. I've never met *any* of you, but why would I need to when you come streaming into my apartment at 256k bits per second?

And last there is David Gross, who lives with me in real life and three dimensions and who has been *saintly* in his patience with *Lion Eyes*. He has never once complained that every single day for months on end I have left our bed each morning, gone upstairs to my computer, and betrayed him with some imaginary Persian archaeologist.

Reality, David, in the end, is better than anything I can imagine.

NOTE ON THE PERSIAN
POETRY IN *LION EYES*

This book's epigram is an adaptation of *The Leopard,* written by Sa'di and translated by John Charles Edward Bowen; I took the zoological and poetic liberty of changing the subject of the poem from a leopard to a lion. Also from Sa'di, translated by Edward Granville Browne, come these words:

> *No shield of parental protection his head*
> *Now shelters; be thou his protector instead.*

The words *She has escaped from the cage now, her wings spread in the air* are Arsalan's loose interpretation of Rumi, as translated by Annemarie Schimmel. Likewise from Rumi, translated by E. H. Whinfield:

> *Our wind whereby we are moved and our being are of thy gift;*
> *Your whole existence is from thy bringing into being.*

and, translated by Zara Houshmand:

> *Wrap my secrets within your soul, and hide*
> *even from myself, this state of mine.*

as well as this verse:

Everyone has someone, a friend to love,
And work, and skill to do it. All I have
Is a fantasy lover who hides
For safety in the dark of my heart's cave—

From Hafiz, translated by Gertrude Bell, come the words:

No tainted eye shall gaze upon her face,
No glass but that of an unsullied heart.

From Farid al-Din 'Attar, translated by A. J. Arberry:

When shall it come to pass, ah when,
That suddenly, beyond our ken,
We shall succeed to rend this veil
That hath our whole affair conceal?

All of the following verses are from Edward FitzGerald's *The Ruba'iyat of Omar Khayyam*:

Strange, is it not? that of the myriads who
Before us pass'd the door of Darkness through,
Not one returns to tell us of the Road,
Which to discover we must travel too.

and:

Think, in this batter'd Caravanserai
Whose Portals are alternate Night and Day,
How Sultan after Sultan with his Pomp
Abode his destined Hour, and went his way.

and:

Come, fill the Cup, and in the fire of Spring
Your Winter garment of Repentance fling:
    The Bird of Time has but a little way
To flutter—and the Bird is on the Wing!

I acknowledge my debt to these poets and translators with gratitude.

About the Author

CLAIRE BERLINSKI is the author of *Loose Lips* and the nonfiction journalistic exposé *Menace in Europe: Why the Continent's Crisis Is America's, Too*. Born in California, she received her undergraduate degree in modern history and her doctorate in international relations from Balliol College at Oxford University. Like the heroine of *Lion Eyes*, she divides her time between Paris and Istanbul, where she lives with photojournalist David Gross and a menagerie of adopted stray animals.

About the Type

The text of this book was set in Janson, a typeface designed in about 1690 by Nicholas Kis, a Hungarian living in Amsterdam, and for many years mistakenly attributed to the Dutch printer Anton Janson. In 1919 the matrices became the property of the Stempel Foundry in Frankfurt. It is an old-style book face of excellent clarity and sharpness. Janson serifs are concave and splayed; the contrast between thick and thin strokes is marked.